I'm in l

I waited for the wonder. I waited for the feeling that all is perfect in the world. Instead, I felt like a Monday morning. That Monday morning when you get out of bed and look at the bathroom mirror and lie to yourself by saying, "Damn, girl, you look good today."

Sean lay still in sleep. One arm hugged the pillow while the other lay crooked across my stomach. Lord, the man was gorgeous. His broad shoulders were relaxed in sleep and his dark blonde hair lay tousled on the pillow.

Last night, he'd caressed and kissed almost every inch of my body. He'd loved me in that curl-a-girl's-toes-come-back-for-more way. I'd had the cake and drunk the Kool-Aid. It was no wonder women lost their minds. I'd left every bit of my common sense on the floor with my nightgown. I looked at him and tears burned in the back of my throat. He was so damn handsome. Not the Hollywood stuff but the blue-gold of a summer sunrise over the Pacific, the intense warmth that turned cold sand into shimmering gold.

I wanted to bury my face in the nape of his neck and inhale but his eyes remained closed and his parted lips emitted a sigh. Just like a man: clueless.

FROST ON MY WINDOW

ANGELA WEAVER

Genesis Press, Inc.

INDIGO LOVE SPECTRUM

An imprint of Genesis Press, Inc.
Publishing Company

Genesis Press, Inc.
P.O. Box 101
Columbus, MS 39703

All characters in this book have no existence outside the imagination of the author and have no relation whatsoever to anyone bearing the same name or names. They are not even distantly inspired by any individual known or unknown to the author and all incidents are pure invention.

ISBN: 13 DIGIT : 978-1-58571-353-0
ISBN: 10 DIGIT : 1-58571-353-8
Manufactured in the United States of America

First Edition

Visit us at www.genesis-press.com
or call at 1-888-Indigo-1-4-0

DEDICATION

For J, who unknowingly inspired my creativity and gave me hope
I'm lucky to have someone like you in my life
(Quincy has totally blessed this dedication)

CHAPTER 1

Because you have shared in our lives by your friendship and love, we, Sherrie Mary Williams and Lance Clayton Phillips II, together with our parents, invite you, Leah Russell and a guest, to witness the joyous nuptials Sunday, the seventeenth of May, five o'clock in the evening at St. Paul's Enon Tabernacle Baptist Church, Philadelphia, Pennsylvania.

Reception to follow.

The rush of memories overwhelmed me when I pulled the invitation out of the half-unpacked cardboard box. My hands stilled.

Sitting down on the hardwood floor, I reached up to wipe away the perspiration on my brow and allowed myself to be pulled back in time to the biting cold of that Saturday afternoon, the heaviness of the ivory envelope I pulled from the mailbox. I remembered dusting off snowflakes clinging to my wool coat.

Even the scalding bitter blackberry sage tea I'd prepared once inside my apartment couldn't warm me. The snow continued to fall gently outside the window as I stared down at the thick gold embossed letters.

Joyous nuptials.

He was getting married to *her*. The person I had known all my life seemed like a stranger. Each elegantly curved letter seemed to twist around his image, drawing him further away.

My Lance.

"No matter what, Lee, we'll always have each other." His voice rose like steam in my mind.

In my memory of the last time we'd met before the wedding, black and white images began to pile up like the snow on Chestnut Street. Every other day the big trucks would come through and push it to one side, and the mound would grow until it rose to my hips and turned grey from exhaust and salt.

Closing my eyes, I went back to that night, back to one of the worst moments of my life.

Lance and I sat close over the small wooden café table clutching our glass mugs of Bailey's-laced coffee. I huddled more deeply into my jacket each time the door opened and the wind blew in small gusts of snow. I watched as snowflakes silently landed, then turned to shiny puddles on the marble floor. After getting the wedding invitation in the mail, I felt winter's coldness everywhere. Even Lance's smiles couldn't warm me. The hole in my stomach lingered, catching everything in its darkness.

"Come on, Leah, it'll be the whole crew, just like old times," he said excitedly.

Lance's voice was deep and beguiling. His lips curved into a smile and his head tilted as though he were listening to some invisible voice. His earth-colored eyes shadowed by curling lashes drifted closed as his long, brown piano player's fingers wrapped loosely around the mug.

I looked down into the creamy foam of my drink and struggled to push back the sound of denial in my head. Struggled to hold in that other person under my skin who wanted to cry, weep, gnash her teeth, and claw at this stranger sitting opposite me.

I took a cleansing breath and tried to drown myself in the thick smell of coffee beans, vanilla, and honey. I pushed back that other person within who stood on the edge of that black hole in my stomach, her screams lost in the jangling of spoons on glass and whispered conversations mixed with the whirr of the espresso machine.

"We've gone over this before, Lance. I'm moving out to California that week." My voice sounded hollow to my ears, but he didn't notice. Lance saw nothing but full, lush life, happy endings, and rainbows. His optimism was a magnet that drew people to him like bits of metal. You found it next to impossible to separate from him. If you could escape, some part of you would always long to come back. Like coming home.

"Don't you think you should reconsider? California's a long way from Philly."

I heard the echo of my parents' words and shivered. "It's a great opportunity. I can't just ignore it."

"You'll be alone out there," he pointed out.

I was alone here, in this café, sitting with a man I had loved all my life.

"No I won't. Rena's going to be moving out there in two or three months."

He sighed and sat back, placing his hands behind his head. "I'm not going to win this, am I?"

I shook my head negatively as I met his eyes, looking for the boy I'd grown up with. The man I'd spent half my life holding in my dreams. Just for a second, his eyes searched my face looking for something and I saw a glimpse of the boy I knew from around the corner. I saw him peek out from that stranger's eyes. The Lance I'd kissed on the cheek under Christmas mistletoe would have known I loved him. He would have understood; he would have chosen me.

"What's the problem between the two of you?" he asked.

The unexpectedness of his question unsettled me.

"Shouldn't you be asking your fiancée that question?" I responded.

"I did." He threw his hands up. "She just shrugged and kept telling me nothing."

"She told you the truth," I replied.

There was nothing between the two of us. The rage, jealousy, humiliation, and biting remarks had ended one night with the sharp sound of my palm striking her cheek.

I met his eyes steadily. "Look, Lance. I wish you the best. All I've ever wanted was for you to be happy, and you are."

"I really need you, Lee."

My throat closed and it was hard to swallow. Yet I smiled despite feeling bitter irony mixed with melancholy dreams.

"You'll be fine." I smiled sadly. "Just remember to look before you leap," I cautioned, reminding him of the time he'd jumped into a shallow ditch while showing off.

He laughed and the deep warm sound reverberated in the small café. Just for a brief moment, everything went still. A surprising richness swirled in the air. It filled me with memories of summers spent at the pool, soccer in the park, and popsicles on the front stairs.

We finished our drinks and headed out the narrow door into the small brightly lit lane. I stood on the sidewalk snuggled into Lance's side as he hugged me to him. I felt his reluctance to let go as I moved away. Smiling up at him, I turned my cheek for his kiss. His lips stung with cold. In the yellow haze, the falling snow looked like tarnished gold. The snowflakes caught in Lance's eyelashes as I wished him goodnight. I stood with my knees locked and grief stuck in my throat as he strolled in the opposite direction into the growing darkness, towards her.

CHAPTER 2

I shook my head and ran my finger over the reddish-brown smudge on the invitation, remembering the sting of the paper cut. Even after all this time, I remembered hearing the hiss of the radiator. Things changed after that night. Daylight seemed to always be shadowed. Cold. Everything I saw or touched was grey, as though filtered through dark glasses.

"Girl, what are you doing sitting in the middle of the floor when we've got so much work to do?"

Rena walked in with the cat right behind her. Simba padded over and delicately climbed into my lap, pausing before settling down. His warmth seeped into my skin. I handed over the wedding invitation. My cousin shook her head, sending her chocolate-colored dreadlocks tumbling around her shoulders.

"I still wonder if I should have told him I loved him," I murmured.

"You should have gone to the wedding." Rena stood there with her hand on her hip.

"Why?"

"To object."

"What?" I asked, thinking that I hadn't heard her correctly.

"The preacher always gotta ask if someone has any objections to the marriage," she clarified.

"Do you have a point?" I questioned.

"Yeah. You should have been there to stand up and object on the grounds that the bride was a gold digging, social climbing, cold hearted, Grade-A bitch." She laughed, tossing back her dreads with a disdainful twist of her neck.

Rena was always smiling. Her eyes were always filled with twinkling laughter. No matter what, Rena's lips curved when she saw me and I felt her joy. Only after wrestling with her own demons and too much alcohol would she let bitter remembrance chase away the laughter.

Those nights I would see Rena cry. She'd curl herself into a ball and rock back and forth, her lips frozen in a caricature of a smile. Her eyes would be puffy and face shiny with salty tears.

Rena never spoke of her parents' death. In her presence neither would anyone else in the family. The car accident had brought mortality to our door. For months after the funeral, it haunted my parents. Every scolding was followed by long, rocking hugs and kisses. The car accident was never mentioned but it hung like heavy drapes over the windows.

I hadn't known what grief was until Rena moved into our house. On the coldest day in January, Mom, Dad, Ralph and I gathered in the driveway to help move her stuff into the house.

I walked past her bedroom one night when the chill of the night wind leached through the old stones and crept on silent feet through the rooms. The sound of Rena's intermittent sniffles drew me in. She sat barefoot on the windowsill with her long, pink flannel nightgown tangled around her knees. The glass reflected her shadowed face. Joining her by the window, I noticed that her ragged breath had fogged the lower half of the windowpane.

"Where have they gone?" she whimpered, turning a tear-stained face towards mine.

We were both children, with children's understanding of the world. There was no blame or anger, acceptance, or recrimination. Death was a fable, a bedtime story imagined as a long, warm sleep until the next morning. But I saw grief that night, sorrow like silver icicles reaching towards the ground.

I took the long sleeve of my gown and wiped it across Rena's face, gently brushing her eyes. Standing on my tiptoes, I put an arm around her slender shoulders and led her towards the bed. Pulling back the covers, I tucked her in on one side and climbed into the other. The ice-cold sheets and the multi-layered blankets settled heavily at my neck. Reaching over I wrapped my arms around Rena's shaking frame. That night as I closed my eyes I hoped my warmth would wake us in the morning.

I scratched Simba's back, using the reality of his presence to focus on the present.

I shrugged before replying, "He'd have married her anyway."

"True. But you would have gotten a standing ovation for saying what we all thought," she laughed.

Shaking off sadness, I closed my eyes and chuckled. "Oh, yeah. They would have given me a standing ovation for what I *really* wanted to do."

"And what would that have been, sister-child?"

"I wanted to march into that chapel, pull out a gun and shoot that heifer in her perfect size six foot."

Rena laughed and waved a hand. "Whew. Evil. I would have thought something along the lines of cutting off her hair. But I like that."

I nodded. "And I would have gone to jail happy in the fact that there was no way Sherrie could walk down the aisle."

"I don't know, cuz," Rena began. "Now that I think about it that daddy of hers would have carried her down the aisle, bleeding foot and all. I'm sure he couldn't walk down the aisle fast enough to give her away."

"You're crazy, you know that?" I replied, smiling.

Rena's cheer dimmed for only a fraction of a second before she caught herself and chuckled. "Maybe, maybe not. I do know, however, that I'm the only one unpacking these boxes while you sit there staring at an old wedding invitation, still hung up on a foolish man."

I stood up, quickly displacing the cat. Taking a moment to dust off my pants, I rearranged my headscarf and snatched the invitation from Rena's outstretched hand. The burst of anger burnt away the heaviness of lingering regret. I took the card over to the oversized garbage bin and began to tear it into pieces. Only when the last of the scraps fluttered into the waiting garbage bag did I smile. Humming to myself, I returned to my box-filled bedroom to unpack.

"Okay, come out." Rena's voice traveled down the hallway.

"About time," I muttered.

I walked into a transformed living room. Open bookcases with recessed lighting stood between the windows. Each shelf was filled with books, pictures, and gifts. The soft glow of the halogen lamps reflected off the mahogany wood frame of the blues-inspired artwork. Soft oriental rugs lay arranged on the hardwood floor.

The entertainment center sat to the side, standing comfortably in its own niche. In the corner opposite the kitchen, the dining room table sat covered with two table settings and a vase filled with dried flowers. In the air hung the heavy scent of vanilla.

Two empty wine glasses sat next to a black bottle with a burgundy and gold label.

I strolled over to a grinning Rena and gave her a high five.

"Okay, let's have it," she chanted, hyped by her own creation.

"You're the woman. This place is fly. I never should have doubted."

"And you know this," she cheered, doing a little victory dance.

My girl had style. It practically leaked out of her pores. Only hours before the room had looked like a mini-warehouse. Now, as the sun fled towards the west, the place looked like a home. Not as big and airy as the townhouse in San Bernardino, but comfortable, intimate, quiet in the chaos of an ever-moving Brooklyn.

Later, after having gone though most of the bottle, we sat curled up on the deep cocoa-colored sofa eating pizza.

"Hey Leah?"

"Hmmm . . ."

"I know this is the last place you wanted to be right now, but thanks for coming with me."

"Hey, you did the same for me. Besides, it's not so bad," I assured her.

"Don't even try it," Rena chuckled. "You couldn't get off the East Coast fast enough. If I hadn't caught up with you, your butt would be some place in Asia right now."

"Seriously, Rena." I took a bite of the thin-crusted pepperoni pizza, savoring the light basil tomato sauce and fresh mozzarella. "Where else can I get real pizza? California might be heaven on earth for vegetarians and seafood nuts, but the pizza stinks."

"True. I would have moved back for the bagels alone," she replied.

"So when do you start work?"

"When I get there," Rena said in-between nibbles. "Michael did everything but propose to get me to move back here. He's got these guys on a tight leash and he knows it's just a matter of time before something comes along and cuts them loose."

Rena's "official" occupation was record executive. The truth is that Rena was a confidante to celebrities. She was their shrink, healer, guide, sista-girl, mother, and homie. She was their bottle to be filled. The gospel stars and

R&B singers drank of her humor and warmth as she dealt with their demons and fears.

If the celebrity reporters could pour stories from Rena's head, the *National Enquirer* would overflow. Rena rarely mentioned any names, keeping their secrets hidden behind her laughing eyes. But I knew them by the three a.m. phone calls and the heartfelt tokens of appreciation which would magically appear in the house.

"What about you?" she asked.

"What?" I swallowed another bite of pizza.

"Earth to Leah." She waved her wine glass. "When do you have to go to work?"

"I've got a couple of days to settle in. I'll go in on Thursday."

"Any plans in-between?" Her voice was laced with innuendo. From the first time Sean had come by to pick me up for dinner, Rena had been trying to make something out of nothing.

"Yeah, I'm going to drive down to Philly and spend a couple of days with Mom and Dad. Since you don't have anything to do you should come, too."

"Hmmm . . ."

"We could just chill out and grab some cheese steaks at that Italian place on South Street," I said, trying to tempt her.

"I'll have to think about that," she replied as her fingers toyed with a stray lock.

"Why? Afraid Mom's gonna nag you about your hair?"

"Nope." She finished off the last bite of her pizza crust and began to lick her fingers. "I'm not crazy about the idea of being in the car with you on the Jersey turnpike."

"Ha ha. Very funny, Ms. Lead Foot. At least I don't have any speeding tickets," I shot back.

"True, but I haven't had any accidents."

I glared at her over the rim of the wine glass. Rena was smiling like a Cheshire cat.

"None of those were my fault, and you know it."

"Please. You were driving slower than Miss Daisy. They couldn't help but hit you." She waved her wine glass.

"Fine. You drive."

"Which you hoped I'd do in the first place."

She had a point. "True. Now why don't we check out the bedrooms?" I suggested.

The wine lent a soft haze to the world, making everything look warm and welcoming. I stood leaning against my bedroom wall, proud of my creation. I'd decided that if I couldn't have California, I would bring the sunshine and sand back east. I hadn't grown up on the West Coast, but I'd been born to love it. I'd hung gold sheer drapes over the windows, and on the floor lay a room-size sand-colored, hand-woven Berber rug. Watercolor pictures of the coast lined the cream-colored walls. A small birch table sat in the corner. My laptop, along with the printer, sat surrounded by unsorted technology magazines.

The solid oak Shaker bed was covered with a matching duvet and pillows. Simba crouched at the bottom of the bed, staring aggressively at my two stuffed giraffes.

"Okay, Martha Stewart. All you need is the hand-made quilt," Rena laughed.

I poked her with my elbow. "Don't hate the home-maker, learn the game."

"Good Lord." Rena rolled her eyes and turned around, heading for her bedroom. "You might want to bring a notebook, because men don't get down with Martha. And no black man I know would sleep in those sheets."

"That's okay, I'm used to having the bed all to myself." I giggled. Rena's loud laughter echoed in the hallway. My cousin made being single sound like a felony, but in truth if not having a man in your bed was a crime, both of us would've been on death row.

I followed and stopped in the doorway, surveying Rena's oasis. Where my room was light, hers was rich. Rena's new dresser had a dark brown wood finish with crimson and cream candles scattered on top. An olive green cotton velvet armchair sat alongside the window, just outside the reach of the wine-red balloon shades. I turned my eyes towards a new bed that spoke of late mornings and early nights.

"Where did this come from?" I walked in and promptly collapsed on top of it. I looked over at Rena as she lay beside me gazing up at the ceiling with a whimsical expression.

"Guess I needed a little change," she replied.

"A little?" I laughed. "This place looks like something out of *Lawrence of Arabia.*"

Turning towards the headboard, I watched the fading sunlight play across the rich brown wood. Rena had mounted a wrought iron fixture over the bed and hung butternut-colored drapes from the crescent shaped bar. The cream-colored linen billowed across the front of the bed while curving around her printed pillows.

"Don't worry, cuz. We can switch rooms when Sean comes by."

I sat up and turned to look down at a smiling Rena. Her eyes were closed and her arms lay folded across her chest. My head swam at the quick movement and so I lay back down.

"It's not like that and you know it," I denied.

"What is it then?"

The truth was that I didn't know. The sound of the phone ringing came just in time. I watched as Rena hopped off the bed and unsteadily walked out of the room. In her place, a quiet Simba jumped on the bed and purposefully settled himself on my stomach.

"So everything's going well? Danny staying out of trouble? Great . . . yeah, she's right here. Just a minute." Rena walked back in waving the cordless phone like a fan.

"Who is it?" I whispered.

Rena's laugh was downright wicked. "Speak of the devil and he'll call you on the phone."

I frowned at her turn of phrase and sat up, slowly reaching for the cordless.

"Hello?" My voice came out husky and slightly slurred.

"Sleeping already?" came Sean's voice.

"No. Just taking a break from unpacking all these boxes."

"Wish I could be there to help you." Sean's pleasant baritone came through clear on the phone.

"So what city are you in tonight?" I asked.

"Dallas for one night and then Austin. Would you like to come see us play?"

"I've already promised to visit my parents tomorrow. Besides, aren't you going to be making your way through New York?" I cradled the phone to my ear.

"I'll be there in four weeks."

"I'll see you then."

Yes, I would see with my own eyes the rock star millions of women sought and men envied. I tried hard to think of him as if he were an older brother, but failed. The man had a way about him.

A way of looking at a woman out of those soulful, green eyes as if I were the only person in the world. A way of talking to me with that smoothly pitched, masculine voice as if he were the voice of my secret fantasies. A way of touching me with those long fingers so that even an innocent brush across my cheek sent a shiver of desire across my skin.

"I was hoping to see you before that. This tour . . . it's harder than I thought it would be."

I could feel the string tighten slightly. The slack built by absence gradually began to disappear as he pulled.

"Sean, you'll be fine. I promise."

"I believe you. Now, will you be at my concert?"

"Rena and I already bought tickets." I smiled.

"Why did you do that, Leah? You know I'll give you backstage passes."

I shook my head. "So Rena and I can be run over by a mob of screaming fans?" I laughed. "No, thanks. Plus, the press will be all over you guys."

"I want to see you. If you won't come backstage, will you at least sit in the front row?"

"I'll think about it," I answered evasively. He always asked that same question and I'd usually give him a flat-out 'not happening.'

"I'll tell Bob to send you the tickets. Now how's our boy?"

I looked at Simba, who lay stretched out on my stomach, his head pillowed in my tee shirt as his copper and black striped tummy slowly rose and fell. Sean and I had come across the stray one night. I'd ended up wrapping the injured cat in Sean's jacket and together we spent the night at the animal hospital.

"He's doing fine. Simba's already scared off the terrier next door."

"Good. I knew he'd do well."

I laughed and the cat opened his marble eyes and leveled me with an arrogant glare.

"What about the band? Is everything okay? Are you and the boys getting along?"

He answered in a high note of excitement. "We've got it back. Our sound, the style. The crowds are going crazy every night. It's incredible how well the new tracks have been welcomed."

I heard a knock in the background.

"I've gotta go back to the arena."

"Good luck," I said.

Sean's reply came after a short pause. "I miss you."

The rope suddenly got tauter with those three words. "I'll see you soon."

I hit the off switch and gently picked up Simba and laid him on the bed. Getting up, I walked out of the room carrying a chill and a longing. In that moment, I wanted the ocean back, the soothing feel of wet sand and rolling waves.

CHAPTER 3

Later that night as I lay in bed, I couldn't help but remember my first meeting with Sean. I'd met Rena at a star-studded shindig and I'd stood there amongst the navel-baring starlets, who seemed right at home wearing designer gowns. Taking a sip of champagne, I watched as male heads turned to observe the entrance of the newest Latin diva. Fina Caston moved like a cat through the crush. Her dark wavy hair captured men at a glance. But I just giggled, seeing myself in the black Paul Gaultier dress.

"What are you laughing about?" Rena stood beside me with a glass of some clear liquid.

"I was wondering if I could fit my leg in that dress."

Rena turned her eyes in the direction I was staring. "They probably had to either pour it on her or wax her down first."

"You've got to admit that she looks good," I observed.

"Hey, I'm not a hater. But if you paid as much as she does for plastic surgery, personal trainers, a live-in chef, and a dietician, you'd look damn good, too," she replied.

We laughed and clicked our glasses together in a mock toast. I left Rena and the group of media producers, superstars, and entertainers. In the middle of the party surrounded by people, I felt alone. But Rena, she was in her element as she moved from person to person working the crowd.

After telling my cousin not to look for me since I might leave early, I took a glass of wine and stepped out through the wide French doors leading to the pool. Further out, I could see the waters of the Pacific. Slipping off my sandals, I walked barefoot over the soft, manicured grass. The fresh scent of flowers and the hint of the ocean hung in the air like a fine mist of perfume. As with the inside of the Mediterranean-style villa, Jerrod Hughes had left no detail overlooked with the landscaping of his lawn.

As I drew up to the edge of the ocean drop-off, I saw a man standing next to the cliff with his arms outstretched. The moon above bathed everything in white and down below the ocean sparkled like diamonds. I guess I made some noise because I remember him slowly turning around.

I will never forget his eyes. Deep green rimmed with gold and filled with shadows. Before they closed and turned away, desolate sorrow stared at me. I was already nervous about being so close to the cliff, but the stranger stood less than a yard from an over hundred foot drop.

He broke the silence. "My mom would tell me such stories of the ocean when I was a lad."

I looked down the coast. The pale sand and jagged rocks were bathed in silver moonlight. His voice was but a whisper and I listened closely, trying to place his accent, guess his background.

"Early Saturday mornings, she would wake me up in the darkness and we'd sneak out of the house while Dad was asleep. She and I would walk barefoot along the empty beach, hunting for seashells as the sun rose." The stranger's words seemed to carry a lilt.

West Coast, I thought, turning my head to search his face. His wheat-colored hair fluttered in the breeze. Tall and lean with fair, sun-kissed skin, thick eyebrows, and a strong jaw, he conjured up magazine advertisements. *Classical looks*, my high school art teacher would have said. Whether or not he sensed my stare, he continued.

"Mom would tell me Scottish fairy tales." His clenched fists loosened. "The one I remember most was the 'Fisherman and the Mermaid,' " he said at last. "In this tale, the mermaids were humans who could wear the form of a seal. The story started with a fisherman's boat landing on the shore to hunt seals. After the men finished stripping the animals of their skins, they set sail into a storm. As the ship was on the verge of sinking, the mermaids offered the fisherman a bargain: if they returned the sealskins, their lives would be saved."

He paused. "Being desperate men, they threw the skins into the sea and waited for rescue. In one version of the story, the mermaids landed them safely on the nearest shore. In another version, the mermaids left the fisherman to drown."

Dropping my shoes on the soft grass, I took a step forward, and then another, until I stood beside the stranger as he stood staring straight ahead. "That was an interesting story," I said softly, hoping that he would take a step back from the edge. His breathing was fast and uneven, his hands quivering. My heart pounded in my ears as I tried to recall all the TV shows where the cop stepped out onto the ledge to talk the person down. I wasn't wild about the idea of standing on the edge of the cliffs, but I couldn't just leave him there alone.

"What's your name?" he asked without turning towards me.

"Leah." I looked up as he glanced my way.

"Leah, have you ever seen such a sight?" It was then that I smelled the sharp scent of alcohol.

"No." I thought of the only body of water at home and gave a slight laugh.

"You think this is funny?" His voice held a hint of irritation.

"No. It's just that where I come from the only water flowing is the river. Trust me, the California coast looks a lot different from the Schuylkill River."

"Where's that?"

"Philadelphia, Pennsylvania."

"You're from there, then?"

"Born and raised. What's your name?"

"Sean."

I put out my hand and watched as it was engulfed by his. An unexpected electric current set my fingers to tingling. The grip of his fingers was tight, but I didn't extract my hand until I'd managed to pull him further away from the edge. "So, Sean, where are you from?" I stained to keep my voice casual.

"You can't guess?" His accent became a little more pronounced.

"Los Angeles?" I guessed.

"Good God, no. My families from Scotland but I spent most of my time in Sonoma," his voice was filled with indignation.

"Sorry," I smiled. "You just fit my image of either an actor or a Calvin Klein underwear model."

His mouth opened and closed, and then he laughed and the sound echoed over the cliff, sending sleeping birds into the air. For a moment his face caught the moonlight and his eyes glowed burning green. I wondered later how I didn't recognize him. Then again, I was too wrapped up in mourning Lance's marriage, grappling with the loss of something I'd never had. It was Sean who spoke next.

"You did a very dangerous thing, Leah, coming out here alone."

I gestured towards the tall cliff. "And your standing right on the edge is safe?" The sarcasm in my voice could have cut through steel.

He seemed eager to change the subject. "So what is a beautiful woman like you doing all alone when the party of the year is taking place less than a hundred yards away?"

I shrugged my shoulders and then carefully sat down in the grass. "I'm not really in the party mood tonight."

"I find myself not wanting to attend these things either," Sean said.

"Is that what brought you out here?"

"No."

I watched as a shudder racked his body and his breathing became even more uneven and heavy. "Three years ago on this night," he said slowly, "my mother died of cancer."

We were quiet for a while and impulsively I reached over and took his hand. Sean's fingers clutched so tight I thought my fingers would break. And then the sobs came and I could barely hear his whispers. I'd only seen my father cry once, at a funeral. My mother had taken him aside and held him in her arms. Using that memory as an example, I did the same.

And so we sat next to the cliff and I talked steadily, with Sean quiet save a shudder, a laugh, or a muttered word. I talked all night about growing up happy, sassy, and loved in Philly. Sometime during the night, we stretched out on the grass, snuggled together for warmth. Much later, blinking to clear the sleep from my eyes, I sat up slowly.

The tide had rolled out, uncovering the rocks, and that place where the land ended abruptly and the ocean rolled in claiming the earth as its own was as close to perfect as I thought possible. I watched as the sea of silver tides gave way to waves of gold. With the sun peeking above skyline, I turned to look at the person at my side. His eyes were closed and lips slack with sleep.

In darkness, people unpeel the layers and reveal themselves. That night a stranger named Sean became a son missing his mother, a long-lost child remembering, and a human hurting. I reluctantly pulled my hand away from his as I continued to stare at his sleeping face and my heart felt lighter for the first time in months. I stood slowly and in the early light of day walked towards the house, not looking back. Having bared half my soul that night, I couldn't find the courage to stay and talk.

"Hey," came Rena's loud voice.

"Hmmm," I responded.

"Snap out of it, girlfriend, or we're about to take the scenic route through north Philly. Which exit do I take?"

I guided Rena towards home and felt my neck relax and breath ease as the car turned down each familiar street. Rena pulled up in the driveway and switched off the engine. Before I could open the car door, Mom and Pop walked out the front door. Their eyes held no reproach for my widely spaced visits and move to the West Coast. Ralph's transfer to Atlanta had broken their hearts. First born, first to leave. My older brother ran from Philly hoping to find the New York of the South more to his liking.

Mom started her fussing as soon as the hugs were over.

"You girls have gotten so thin. What have you been eating?" Her dark eyes scanned my frame. "I know you haven't been eating right. You need to get some more meat on your bones." Her fingers lightly pinched my arm. "I don't want to hear no mess about either of you picking up that white woman's disease. We won't have no . . ."

"Anorexia," Rena supplied.

Mom nodded her head. Lillie Russell looked fantastic. Mom walked two miles a day and her auburn-colored hair was pulled back in a stylish French twist.

"That's the one," she declared. "We won't have it in this family."

"Auntie . . . Mom," Rena and I said simultaneously.

Rena continued, "Neither of us is in any danger of becoming anorexic. Shoot, we have better chances at winning the lottery without buying a ticket."

I had to laugh at Rena's comeback. The women in our family are big boned. No matter how much time I spend at the gym, this backside of mine isn't going anywhere. It was a gift from someone on my mother's side of the family with a no money back, no return, no exchange policy attached.

"I almost can't believe the two of you made it," Mom exclaimed.

I looked over at Rena just in time to see her roll her eyes. The back of my throat tickled with mirth. This was going to be Rena at her best. She could wrap Mom around her little finger.

"How could we miss out on your red velvet cake? I've been dreaming about it since last week. Not to mention your pot roast. How could we pass that up?" Rena wrapped her arms around Mom's waist and started towards the door.

As if swept away by a sudden gust of wind, my mother's reprimands vanished. Cooking was her pride and joy, the kitchen her domain. Children and husband were allowed only to watch her work and to later offer proper praise for her delicious meals.

"She sure does know how to handle your mother," Pop leaned in close to whisper in my ear. I turned my head towards him and looked into a mirror. Father's daughter. I was Pop's spitting image, and he mine, visible Russell cheekbones and wide, almond-shaped eyes framed by clear, deep brown, maple skin.

"Maybe we should take lessons?" I whispered.

Rena, Mother's sister's child. To me Rena was a long-wished for sister and blood kin first cousin. Yet she was more to my mother. She was a chance to make the past right. Sister's child. She was my mother's best friend, accomplice, and little girl child. When younger, Rena would sit still for hours between her legs as Mom's hands braided and twisted, pulled and laced her hair.

My cousin would close her eyes and my mother's voice would always grow husky, as she wove stories of Aunt Mary into each strand of her hair. The gradual transformation would take place over hours as I watched. Mom's face would lose its firmness and her lips would soften as if she were asleep, napping with remembrance, and she would tell her childhood tales.

"Don't know about you, but I've been taking notes for some time. How you think I kept your Momma from leaving me?" Pop replied.

"By eating?" I joked.

We both burst into laughter. When I looked up with tears in my eyes, Mom and Rena had the two of us in their sights.

I watched Mom raise her eyebrows. "Anything the two of you'd like to share?" she asked.

"Nah," I responded.

· "Are you sure?" She looked from Pop's smiling face back to mine.

"Uh-huh."

"Positive," Pop answered, giving my hand a little squeeze.

I couldn't get the smile off my face. Later that night, as I was getting ready for bed, Rena walked into the bathroom and sat down on the cushioned toilet seat. I automatically handed her the toothpaste. Taking the facial soap and rubbing it on the washcloth, I began to scrub my face.

"So what were you and Pop laughing about?" Rena asked in between brushing her teeth. My eyes were closed but I could imagine her sitting there with her legs crossed holding the toothbrush like a scepter.

"Food," I replied before bending over the sink and cupping my hands underneath the lukewarm water. I took a breath and dunked my face in my hands, rinsing twice before reaching for the towel.

"Food?" Rena parroted.

I nodded my head and smiled. "Mom's cooking. That's the only reason Pop thinks she stays married to him. To fatten him up."

Rena let out a peal of laugher that bounced off the tiles of the bathroom and gladdened my heart. My father's weight was a mystery. The man I saw today looked exactly like the man in the old black and white photos. Maybe some extra lines about his mouth from laughing too hard, a little less hair on the top of his head and reading glasses, but no heavier.

"She asked me again," Rena said before spitting.

I paused from spreading the moisturizer over my face. "What?"

"She asked why you left after graduation."

"What did you tell her?" I asked.

"Same thing. More money, better opportunity, and all that jazz."

"She buy it?" I rubbed the night cream in. Rena shook her head and resumed brushing her teeth.

"Thought so," I muttered.

"Sooner or later, you're going to have to tell her."

"What am I going to say, Rena? I couldn't stand the cold? I grew up making snowmen in the middle of January."

"Gotta do better than that."

"How about I needed to keep your wild behind out of trouble?" I moved back, letting her rinse her toothbrush and mouth.

"That might work," Rena smiled.

"This shouldn't matter. We're back. Just two hours away."

"Close, but not too close. Ain't that right, cuz?"

I grinned. "Exactly."

CHAPTER 4

Accidentally waking up before the alarm went off, I lay motionless underneath the ivory-colored canopy of my bed. As a little girl, I'd never want to leave it on Saturday mornings. As an adult, I rolled over, wiped the crust out of my eyes, and gazed out the window to see the pale glow of sunrise reach through branches of an old oak tree.

Pulling away the light quilt, I sat up and put my feet on the cool hardwood floor. I stood and opened the closet door, then fit my feet into gray bunny slippers and went downstairs. The smell of chicory-laced coffee met me on the bottom stair.

I paused, wiping the cobwebs of sleep from my eyes as I entered the kitchen. Morning sunlight had begun to spread over the linoleum floor. Pop's aloe plants lined the windowsill. The automatic coffeemaker stood filled and Mom's yellow elephant clock still sat ticking away in the corner.

"What's got you up so early, pumpkin?" came Pop's voice.

I turned to see my father seated at the table with one hand gripping a coffee cup and the other paused in the act of turning the newspaper page. My heart contracted and I felt the threat of tears behind my eyes.

"Nothing. Just woke up early."

Warmth suffused every cell of my body as happiness I hadn't felt in a long time brought a smile to my face. It was being home, being here. It was the sound of my father's voice, memories of the mornings Pop would sneak and let me have a sip of his coffee. The past washed over me with every smell and object. Everything was a piece of me and Pop was the biggest piece of them all.

"Well, grab a cup of coffee and take a seat. You can help me make breakfast in a minute."

After reaching into the note-covered fridge, I stirred cream and sweetener into my cup before taking a seat across from my father.

"Anything interesting?" I asked, reaching for the comics section.

"Just more bad news," he replied.

"Ouch," I barked out, startled by the sharp rap on my hand.

"Leah, you know better than to go after that part of the paper until I finish. Did you lose your manners on the flight from California?" His eyes twinkled. "You gotta ask."

Some things never changed. I took a sip of coffee and waited. Soon Pop passed over the section, grinning as he continued to read.

A few newspaper articles and a political debate later, I used a glass to cut a perfect circle of dough for the best biscuits north of Virginia.

"Don't forget to grease the baking sheet."

"I won't, Pop."

"No, I don't mean that spray stuff your Mama uses. Get the Crisco."

"Okay."

I looked over at Pop as he laid the strips of turkey bacon on the broiler pan.

"You know, pumpkin, if you cook this stuff the right way it don't taste so bad," he admitted, shaking his head.

The corners of my mouth turned upwards. Mom's new found health kick seemed to be working. Little by little things had changed. Pork bacon to turkey. Salt to garlic salt and herbs, sugar to artificial sweetener.

"So do you miss California?" Pop's question ended my waiting. I had prepared for this since getting in the car yesterday afternoon.

I told a half-truth. "I miss my friends." I missed so many nameless things, treasured spaces. I missed the laid-back California lifestyle, the sunshine, the hills, and the scent of the ocean.

"Anybody in particular I should know about?"

I reached into the overhead cabinet and pulled out a small glass. "Not yet."

There had been friends, boyfriends, and dates. The problem was that none of them got past the second round with the ghost of Lance living in my heart.

Pop pulled down the oven door and placed the bacon on the top rack, then rinsed his hands in the sink.

"I had hoped . . ."

"I know." My smile was weak, tired.

"I worry about you, pumpkin. I won't be around forever, and your mama and me both want all you kids settled, happy."

Hot potato. My mind dropped the thought of my father's death faster than I could blink. My right hand automatically pressed the open end of the glass into the dough.

"I'm happy, Pop."

"You know what I mean. Married and giving me some grandkids to spoil. That son of mine ain't gonna be settling down anytime soon. Ralph's too busy running around to think about starting a family."

I picked up a buttermilk biscuit and laid it on the cookie sheet. A perfect white circle.

"I'd love to have that happen, but it's easier said than done."

Placing the glass to the side, I laid out all the biscuits in straight lines. I looked over to see Pop's back as he leaned over the stove. His soft, bushy salt and pepper hair stood unchanged since I was in high school. Right then, I wanted to crawl into his lap, be a little girl again, hear his voice as he fed Rena and me 'happily ever after' for dessert.

Putting on the orange-colored oven mitt, I walked behind him, placing the biscuits on the bottom rack of the oven. As I drew away, the smell of Cream of Wheat brought back memories of my grandmother making breakfast when I was a little girl. For the second time that morning, I felt like crying.

"Don't you cry when I'm gone 'cause I'll know about it." Momma's voice rose in my mind. I saw my grandmother standing by the kitchen sink with her black gold-rimmed Las Vegas cup. She was always the center of the kitchen in my mind. Her smooth, even-textured finger-tips often settled on my shoulder. When I buried my face in her robe, the familiar scent of Shalimar would rub off on my cheek.

"Oh, Momma, I wish you were here," I murmured as I put my hands in the soapy dishwater. Even after Pop installed a dishwasher, she would wash her dishes in the sink.

"Ain't no machine built that can clean my iron skillets. You just step aside and let me handle this," she'd order.

Ralph, Rena, and I would watch from our perches at the kitchen table. Our eyes widened to the size of saucers as we watched Mom and Pop's shoulders slump when grandmother would scold them for one thing or another. We would all take turns drying and putting up the pans. Then when it was all done and the table cleared, Momma would dry her hands on the flower-covered dishtowel, then reach into her pocket and pull out a small glass container. When she dipped her long fingers into the white cream and rubbed her hands together, the scent of roses filled the air.

"Why don't you go and get lazybones out of bed while I scramble some eggs," Pop said.

"Okay."

I heard Mama moving around in her bedroom as I passed by. Opening the door, I walked inside Rena's violet bedroom. The room was filled with sunlight, but Rena was asleep with her mouth slightly open and her locks spread out like vines over the pillow. I wondered if she felt it, too, the pull of the past, the warm safety of home. Maybe that was what kept her in bed. Maybe it was dreams. Dreams of yesterday. Dreams of parents long gone. I hated to wake her. It was as if my pulling her into morning would kill the peace I saw on her sleeping face.

I watched as Rena's eyes fluttered open as if she could hear my thoughts.

"Rise and shine, lazy. Breakfast is going to be on the table in about five minutes," I said cheerfully.

"Biscuits and gravy?" she yawned.

"And Cream of Wheat," I added.

"Freshly squeezed orange juice?" She smiled though half-closed eyes.

I put my hand on my hip. "Hey, this isn't the Ritz-Carlton. I did find apple juice in the fridge."

She sat up and rubbed the sleep out her eyes. "I'll be down in a minute."

I waved and skipped out of the room, running into Mom in the hallway. Mom leaned against the wall with her arms crossed, a brown satin headscarf tied tight around her head and a soft smile on her face. She reached out and hugged me tightly.

"I almost thought that I had dreamed that my two girls had come home."

I remembered opening my eyes last night as the door slowly swung open and the light from the hallway crept into my room. I saw the bottom of Mom's robe before my eyes drifted closed again. The warmth of her breath on my cheek and the smell of hand lotion had drifted over me as I fell asleep.

"Lee, long time no see."

Oh, hell!

I wanted to slam the door and run up to my room. Sometimes I felt unlucky, but this? Having the love of your life knock on the door was a curse. I stood holding onto the doorknob, half blinded by the glare of sunlight. My hand would not let go. I was squeezing the cold metal and inside I was shivering. The blast of summer's heated air had turned ice cold at the sound of my name on his lips.

"You, too, Lance. Come on in."

Maybe the coolness of my tone was lost in the humidity. It could have been one of the mornings when as children one of us would race through the other's door heading for the kitchen. He wrapped his arms around me as if I were twelve years old and just come back from camp. He hugged me like the boy I used to know, the best friend who missed me. That ache in my heart I thought long gone suddenly reappeared and I just wanted to be close to him.

"Man, it's quiet in here. Where's the folks?" he asked.

"Mom and Pop ran to the store to pick up some food for his poker game. Rena's taking a nap."

"What's Pistol Pete doing sleeping this time of day?" he asked, calling Rena by her nickname.

"She came down with a bad headache. You know how her sinuses used to act up during the summer. Want something to drink?"

"Sounds good," he replied.

Lance followed behind me as I turned and walked towards the kitchen.

"So what's been up with you? Where have you been?" I questioned as I walked over and took two glasses out of the cabinet. I turned briefly to watch him settle down at the kitchen table.

"Mom called me on Friday. She was telling me the neighborhood news when she mentioned that you and Rena had come for a visit."

I poured soda over the ice cubes and the sound of fizz seemed to fill my brain. "She told me that you were living in the Big Apple."

I picked up the glasses and walked over to place them on the table.

"Yeah," he responded. "I'm working on a consulting gig. Internet, e-commerce, and systems stuff. What about you?"

"Same industry, different field. I'm the content manager in the website design division of an advertising firm."

"Serious?" He sounded impressed.

"Uh-huh." I smiled. Lance's eyes had opened with surprise. I was an English and history girl while Lance got his first computer book from Pop.

"Silicon Alley?" he asked referring to New York's version of the California technology hub.

"You guessed it." I took a sip of the Coke and the liquid burned my throat, bringing tears to my eyes. For the first time, I looked at Lance outside the image of memory.

"You look great, Lee. California seems to have treated you well."

He gave me that look. The one a brother gives when he sees a woman lookin' fine with her hair done, black heels, and short red dress. I couldn't keep from feeling the warmth of his compliment.

"Thanks. You, too."

Time and experience had left their marks upon his face. Tiny lines around his eyes gave him a wiser look. The onee chubby cheeks were now defined. The generous mouth that had been quick to smile or crack a joke back in the day seemed still. But all that made the man look better.

"Hey, you remember Monica?" he asked unexpectedly.

"Yeah. What happened to her?" I smiled, remembering the petite girl who followed all of us around the neighborhood. We played basketball every day in the summer and then we'd walk Monica home. Lance would pick her up so she could dunk the ball.

"She got married three months ago."

"Is she still living in Philly?"

"Moved to Jersey. DJ got a job with Merrill Lynch."

My hand stilled as I reached for the glass. "DJ?" I repeated. "Monica married DJ?" I couldn't reconcile the idea with the image, the thought of Monica, the shy wallflower, with DJ.

"Couldn't believe it myself," Lance added.

Smart, soft-spoken, church-going Monica with DJ, the wannabe high school street thug. For a dollar a week, he'd promised to protect Ralph from the older schoolyard bullies.

"He's changed. I ran into him at the barbershop a couple of months back. He spent the entire time talking about 401Ks, home improvement, kids, Bible study, and buying a dog."

"Don't tell me. He wants a pit bull?"

"You guessed it," he laughed.

"Heard any more gossip?" I asked after taking another sip.

Lance's brow crinkled. "You remember Mr. DeRosa?"

"How could I forget him?" I chuckled with the remembrance of my social studies teacher. "Every time I see the fat guy with the small mustache on the Dunkin Doughnuts commercial, I think of Mr. DeRosa. What happened to him?" I asked.

"Guess we were too much for him. After we graduated he joined the Peace Corps, spent two years in Africa, and then became a Buddhist monk somewhere in Vietnam."

At that point my mouth dropped open. I felt a twinge of guilt. Of all the things I imagined Lance might say, that wasn't one of them.

"You have got to be kidding."

"You can't make this stuff up."

"True."

By chance, I looked towards Lance's left hand and couldn't stop the heady rush of satisfaction at the lack of a gold band on his ring finger. After church the other day, Mrs. Phillips had been downright gleeful telling Rena and me that Lance had divorced Sherrie. I had just sat there as Lance's Mom and Rena re-hashed all the drama and nodded their heads in mutual agreement.

"I guess you know Sherrie and I got divorced," Lance said, having caught my look at his left ring finger.

"Your Mom told me. I'm sorry."

Deep in the pit of my stomach, I felt a crack. Through the narrow fissure, the sound of wailing drifted up and filled my head. I looked up at the older, more hardened Lance sitting across from me staring into a half-empty glass.

"For a while I blamed you," he confessed.

"Me?" I echoed with surprise.

"You were my good luck charm. It seemed that all I had to do was hug you and everything would go my way." He looked up and I caught his glance before looking away. Naked pain. Whatever he had gone through was with him still. It hurt me to look at him.

"I wish . . ." My words trailed off. What should I say? I didn't know that day in the coffee house with the snow falling outside and I didn't know now.

Lance stared right past me, his eyes unfocused. "I was just being stupid. If it was anyone's fault, it was mine. I saw Sherrie as the person I wanted her to be, the woman I wanted to spend the rest of my days with, not the person she really was. Gotta tell you something, Lee. You can't hide your true nature when you're married."

"What did she do to you?" I leaned over and touched his hand.

"We said and did a lot of things to each other," he replied.

"Well, well. Look what the cat dragged in," Rena's voice called out.

"Have a nice nap, cuz?"

"You know it," she responded. "Hey, Lance."

Lance stood up and walked over and gave her a big hug. Rena's eyes never left mine for a moment.

"So Ms. Up and Coming Record Exec, can you hook an old friend up with one of those fine singers of yours? Nina maybe?"

Rena shook her head and moved towards the kitchen table. "Still haven't learned, have you? Always a sucker for a pretty face."

I had to bite my lip on that one. Rena rarely pulled her punches, and it looked like today wasn't going to Lance's lucky day.

"Come on now . . ." he replied.

"You might want to try checking for a pulse and a personality in the future, my friend," Rena added, giving Lance a thump on the back.

I was saved from hearing Lance's comeback by the sound of the kitchen door opening.

"We're back!"

I reached out to take the plastic grocery bag from Mom's hand. Lance was heading out the kitchen door to the open car trunk.

"Nice to see you, son." Pop patted Lance on the shoulder.

"Great to see you, too, Pop," Lance replied.

I turned from putting the groceries up to see my father give Lance a tight hug. Just like old times. Didn't matter whose kid you were in this house, we were all my father's children.

"You going to be joining us downstairs?"

"You sure about that, Pop?" Lance cracked his knuckles. "I don't want to take all your money."

"Boy, who you think you talking to? I was playing poker before you were a thought in your mama's mind. Take my money? By the time I get finished with you, you'll be walking home without those fancy shoes of yours."

The sound of Lance's laughter, which used to be loud and heavy, was muted. Rena and I shared a glance. She'd noticed, too. People change, some more than others. But it seemed that one thing hadn't changed: I still cared for him. I still wasn't over the boy I'd fallen in love with, even though he'd become a different man.

Saturday afternoons after they'd finished mowing the lawn, washing the car or shoveling the snow, my father's friends would leave their wives and kids to spend hours in our basement huddled over the card table drinking beer and eating grandmother's fried catfish with hot sauce.

During those loud hours, Mom would go to the salon and leave Pop in charge of the house. Ralph would pull up a chair next to the card table hoping to get a sip of beer or maybe a chance to take a puff of Pop's pipe. I sat next to Rena on the carpet-covered stairs and watched as my Pop transformed into a card shark named Deuce. The sweet smell of tobacco would waft upstairs and into the kitchen, mingling with the scent of catfish and chicken. Rena and I would run up and down the stairs taking messages and delivering food and drinks.

I watched Lance and Pop head towards the basement. For that one moment, I would have given anything to have that time back.

Only, time was supposed to heal. After we'd gotten home from the Sunday church service, I sat under the shade of the back porch and laid my head against the side banister. Forgiveness. The reverend's message played like an old song in my mind. The image of Rena's wet face and smile appeared in the darkness of my closed eyes. The sound of weeping as my mother fell to the floor, her chest heaving, and my father's whispers.

I felt the slight breeze on my skin and it hurt. Same wind, different day. The sun rose and set, the world turned, and God was there. The Lord was here, but he couldn't keep Rena's parents from dying. Couldn't keep my cousin and Mom from crying. I sighed and opened my eyes and looked up at a sky devoid of clouds. Just a sea of baby blue.

I missed my grandmama on days like this. All the memories I had of her shone like stained glass on a sunny day. All you could do was stare at the shimmering colors until the holy image hung on the back of your eyelids. I missed her but I'd always have a part of her with me. I carried Mama; her presence inside me was full and peaceful. I remembered everything about her.

"Hey, you okay?" came a soft voice.

I looked over to see Rena sitting next to me. She'd changed out of her church clothes into jeans and a knit top. I smiled and a wave of love washed over me.

"Yeah, just thinking," I answered.

"About the sermon?"

I nodded. The pastor's words were always thought provoking, but this morning's service hit close to home. "Yeah. You too?"

Forgive us our daily trespasses as we forgive those who trespass against us.

I looked down and saw a little ant carrying its prize across the stone steps. It could carry more than a hundred times its body weight. I wondered how much a woman could carry? How much sorrow could Rena bear? One day too soon, a letter would come. I'd have to watch Rena remember all the things she'd lost. The parents she'd only seen in photos and dreams. Wishful thinking never stopped the postman and wouldn't keep guilt from eating away at the man who'd killed Rena's parents. And I wanted him to hurt. I wanted him to suffer, and the intensity of that desire scared me.

"So what are Mom and Pop doing?" I asked.

"Mom's on the phone with Mrs. Barker."

I rolled my eyes skywards. "She didn't get enough of her gossip fix in church this morning?"

"Apparently not. When I left the kitchen she was trying to get the scoop on the newest members of the church."

"Rena?" I asked after a minute.

"Hmmm?"

"Isn't it nice being home again?"

She nodded. "I never realized how much I missed this place until this morning."

"It was the big breakfast, wasn't it?"

She kicked my shoe. "It's the people. We've known some of these people for years. Reverend Sanders actually poured water over your nappy little 'fro, and he directed all my Christmas plays."

"Not to mention Vacation Bible School," I added.

"True." Rena closed her eyes and angled her face towards the sun. Her locks flowed over the green sundress.

"I have to say, though, I'm ready to get back to New York." I sighed.

"Missing the bright lights already, huh?" Rena smiled.

"No. Just worried that Simba might have eaten all the plants by now."

"You and that cat," she muttered.

"Don't even try it. I've seen you sneak him pieces of tuna. That's why he's getting so fat. Pretty soon we'll have to put him on a diet."

Rena opened her mouth and closed it again. She shrugged and said, "Damn thing looked so pathetic I had to give him a little something."

"Pathetic? Simba's overweight," I pointed out. "You were with me when the vet told us to feed him that special cat food."

She wrinkled her nose. "The stuff smells nasty and looks worse. I wouldn't eat it, either."

"Yeah, well, it's either the special food or you're going to have to carry his lazy behind to the kitty litter."

"Point well taken. Now can we get back inside? It's hot out here and these steps are murder on my backside."

"Poor baby," I cooed. "Need a lift? Since you're getting on in years and all." I reached up to grab the railing.

"Shut up." Rena slapped at my leg and both of us walked through the back door laughing. Just like old times.

"It won't work," Rena repeated for about the fifteenth time.

"Rena . . ." I warned.

"Okay." She sat back and crossed her arms, frowning.

We'd been back from my parents for about two weeks when I got the itch to take the landlady's advice. The older Jamaican woman believed in the spirits. Since nothing else in my life seemed to be working, I thought I'd give the "other world" a try. Right now I had nothing left to lose. Having tried my luck on the West Coast and not found Price Charming, I wasn't overly optimistic that the brotha might be chilling out next door in Brooklyn. Then again, if he were, I probably wouldn't even recognize him.

I turned my attention back to the table and carefully laid out the burgundy blue cards. A frisson of excitement ran down my spine.

"Leah, I'm telling you this mess will get you into trouble."

"Girl, what's up with you?" I questioned. "I thought you always wanted to walk on the wild side."

"Wild side, cuz. Not the other side." She waved at the cards. "Why don't you call Ms. Cleo or some other psychic line? They got all the answers. Shoot, you could mess up and get stuck with Ike Turner for the rest of your life."

The remaining cards I held spilled out of my hand onto the table as I laughed. "Please. This is no kind of love spell. Mrs. Renard told me that they were just clarifying cards."

"Can you spell c-r-a-z-y?" Rena enunciated. "Clarifying cards? You ask the woman we both know can do some mystical stuff to help you clarify. Clarify what? That you've lost your mind? Lance isn't worth this," she announced while sweeping her hand over the table.

"You're right. Lance isn't worth this, but I'm worth it. Look at the cards, Rena."

I watched as she suspiciously turned one over.

STRENGTH.

"What is this?" she asked.

"Each card has a personality trait your soul mate should have."

Rena pulled her hand back as if she'd touched a hot flame.

"So you're going to let some random cards decide what your man's going to be like?" she questioned.

"No, I'm not."

"That's what it looks like to me. Girl, just because you've had one intense non-relationship with a man who couldn't see the swans through the chickenheads doesn't mean you should give up."

"This coming from the woman who has well-edu-cated, handsome, incredible men falling at her feet," I said sarcastically, while gathering my cards.

I sighed. "Look Rena, I know you don't mean to be critical, but you don't know where I'm coming from right now." I stood up.

"You're right about that. So why don't you tell me?" She leaned back.

"I want to have a plan. Get some direction in my life. When we were in Philly, I got a wake-up call. It's time I not only moved on but also put some effort into finding him."

"Him?"

"I know in my heart that although Lance is a Mr. Right, he was never Mr. Right for me. I want what Mom and Pop have and I've got to be able to recognize the man when I meet him."

"So you bought . . ." She pointed to the cards I held in my hands.

"Borrowed."

"The cards."

I nodded and eased back into the chair. "There's nothing random about this. I draw twenty cards and I turn over ten. The order that I turn them over is sequen-tial to their importance in what characteristics Mr. Right will need to have. That way I'll have a firm under-standing of what I need."

Though Rena smiled at me, her eyes still said, 'You're crazy.' But there was some understanding peeking out. She tapped her manicured finger on the table.

I pointed out my last important reason for trying out the cards. "Did you know I've taken more time to write my Christmas list than thinking about what I wanted in a man?"

Rena drew up in surprise. "Even in California, I always thought of Lance." I shook my head. "I didn't know it then but I compared every man I met to him, and who can compare with a dream? That's part of the reason I'm alone right now. I'm putting that ghost to bed tonight."

"Well, I'm happy you've finally gotten him out your system."

"Thanks, sister dear."

"Now why don't you do me a favor?" She held out her hand.

"What?"

"Hand over the cards and get us something to drink. If you can do it, so can I."

Lord, morning always came too soon. Especially after going through a half-gallon of Breyer's ice cream, a liter of Diet Coke, and staying up half the night. Through half-closed eyes, I poured a cup of hot coffee and inhaled. The warm, heavy scent of the mocha java gave me back the will to live. I hesitated before opening the refrigerator door. Hung between the magnets were our two lists.

CHAPTER 5

"This psych mess ain't working for me," Carol managed to get out during one of our twenty-second breaks. Carol and I had been friends since sophomore year Economics 101. I'd even been a bridesmaid at her wedding.

She had a point. We were supposed to be picturing an open road and blue skies. All I saw was the Energizer bunny. The spin class instructor was the size of a string bean and her high-pitched sugar-coated voice got on my last nerve. I didn't see daybreak from the comfort of my bed that morning. I saw the reflection of sun off another building while walking up the stairs to the second-floor gym.

"Stay with me, people. Almost done!" the instructor shouted.

"Don't she mean almost dead?" Carol huffed. Her slumped shoulders and sweat-laced forehead mimicked half the room.

I wiped a shaky hand across my neck. Membership. Monday at lunchtime the two of us had rushed out and signed our names to get our gym cards as if they were tickets through the heavenly gate. Except heaven turned out to be a hell called spinning class, weight machines, aerobics and skinny college kids that didn't weigh ninety pounds soaking wet.

I wasn't an ex-athlete trying to stay in shape or a woman desperate to lose weight. It was for clothes. I was sitting on this small hard seat with burning thighs for the current occupants of my closet. I wanted to wear them for another year. But all I could imagine as that loud techno music pounded into my brain was that if I pushed hard enough, pedaled long enough, the bike would break loose and I'd roll down Lexington Avenue towards the nearest bagel shop.

Carol and I watched as the class left the room. Most of the beginners were limping out the door.

"I . . . am . . . dying," Carol said as she lifted her feet off the pedals and stood up.

"Before you kick the bucket, we got to do some crunches," I said through gritted teeth as pain screamed up from my heels to my thighs.

"Do I get to lie down?" Her voice sounded hopeful.

"Oh, yeah." I sighed, grateful for little things.

"Leah, why are we doing this?" she questioned a little later.

I lay there staring at the ceiling, waiting for my breath to slow down. It was like being in the gynecologist's office except there were no pictures of the beach to distract you from the pain.

"Because we want to be healthy," I reminded her. "Not to mention you've got that anniversary trip coming up soon."

"No, why are we lying here doing these painful-ass crunches?"

I hadn't thought about that one. All I knew was that they were supposed to give me back my waistline. "So we'll eventually discover the abdominal muscles we're supposed to have."

"For you, maybe," she replied.

I looked over at Carol. She continued, "By the time I get an ab muscle, Charlie, Jr. will magically appear in my stomach."

"You're pregnant!" I pulled myself up and stared down at my friend. My eyes went immediately to her stomach.

She sat up and grimaced before turning to sit on the edge of the bench. "Not yet. But mark my words, it's gonna happen and all those abs I worked so hard for will turn to stretch marks. Shoot, I'll probably have railroad tracks across my stomach."

"Carol . . ."

She picked up her water bottle and took a drink. "I told you Charlie's been acting strange since we started working out, right?"

Strange? The man had come home before seven p.m. with two dozen roses, had cooked dinner three nights in a row, had taken her to a Broadway play and had invited her parents over for Sunday brunch. Damn it, I'd take her idea of strange any day of the week.

We got up and started walking towards the women's locker room. "My husband done got paranoid," Carol continued.

"Charlie?" I raised an eyebrow. "The man is about as laid back as a person can be without being six feet under."

"You know what he asked me this morning as I dragged myself out of bed to meet you?"

"What?"

"Am I gonna leave him for a personal trainer?" She mimicked her husband's slow Southern drawl perfectly.

I was laughing so hard I almost ran into the door. "Where did he get that idea?"

"One of his cronies," she huffed.

I pulled off my sneakers and chuckled, oblivious to the stares I was getting from the other silent occupants in the room.

"Shoot," Carol continued, "it's more like he'll leave me for one of those divorced trial attorneys."

That sent me into peals of laughter. I sat there clutching my sore stomach. There was a snowball's chance in hell of him ever leaving her. I'd seen the two of them together. That man would happily drink Carol's bathwater.

I shook my head and followed a still limping Carol towards the showers. Men. Even the ones with law degrees act stupid.

Eleven p.m. Thank God tomorrow's Friday. Unlocking the door to the apartment and quietly slipping inside, I set my gym bag down beside the closet and laid my keys alongside Rena's on the small side table. I walked into the living room to see my cousin curled up on the sofa holding her head. Lines of tension pulled tight across her brow. I pulled off my shoes and padded across the floor.

Gently, I sat down, maneuvering Rena's body over so that her head lay in my lap. In the dim light of the room, I could still see the tracks left by dried tears. Her pain-filled groan was a confirmation of my first thought. Migraine. Simba sat at my feet. Normally, the attention-hungry cat would meow and jump into my lap demanding to be petted. Instead he lay down with his tail switching back and forth, staring at Rena with his unblinking eyes.

I placed my fingertips lightly across her temples and kneaded, smoothing her brow. After a few minutes, Rena's breathing eased and her fingers unclenched.

"Bad day?" I whispered.

"They ambushed me. Told me they wanted my opinion on a new artist."

"What happened?"

"The fools wanted me to co-manage Nine. They forced me to listen to his entire solo album and read his bio. It read like a prison rap sheet. Then they brought him in."

Shudders ran through her body. This was bad.

"Leah, he stood in front of me looking like a mother's worst nightmare come to life and said, 'Ain't no tight-assed bitch gonna manage me.' " My cousin mimicked the rapper's voice.

I concentrated on keeping my hands from shaking with anger as I kept massaging her temples.

"What did Michael have to say?" I asked.

"Nothing. He just sat there like a puppet without strings," she sighed. Her eyes remained closed.

"Do you have to take him on?"

"No. I made sure to put that in my contract. I choose my artists."

"So what's got you so stressed out?"

"Michael."

"What does he have to do with you?" I asked. The senior executive had begged, cajoled, and bribed Rena to move back to NYC. The week after she started the job, Michael left to head the company's more lucrative hip-hop/rap artists.

"He came to my office an hour after the meeting. I took a good long look at him. What hair he ain't lost is turning gray. He offered me fifty thousand to help him, Leah. I swear he had tears in his eyes."

My hands stilled. Fifty thousand. Rena was bringing home a hefty salary, but that kind of money is hard to turn down. "Please tell me you said no."

Impossible causes were okay but this one was different. From what I'd heard and seen in the papers, Nine was for real. Rap music's newest poster boy was straight out of the Bronx ghetto, no suburban kid turned street thug. According to *XXL* and *Vibe*, the self-proclaimed leaders of street news, Nine had been in and out of juvenile and prison all his life.

Rena opened her eyes, and in the dimness I could see the pain. "I told him no and he left."

"Michael just got up and walked out?" I questioned.

"Didn't say a word," Rena added.

"Good." I didn't really like or trust the man. On more than one occasion he had tried to use me to get to Rena.

"Yeah, I had enough of that back west. I'm not going down that road again. Let someone else save him. Too tired." Her voice trailed off, heavy with sleep.

I sat in the darkness listening to the sounds of passing cars and the humming of the refrigerator. I'd been in the passenger seat as Rena struggled against her own demons while battling to help brothers who didn't want to save themselves. Ex-slanging, banging, badass brothers from the hood. All the support and money in the world couldn't help them. The Lord helps those who help themselves. My only regret was that Rena had found that out the hard way.

"Hey," she said all of a sudden.

I jumped. "Thought you were asleep."

"An overnight envelope came for you today. It's on the coffee table." She motioned with her hand.

I leaned over and turned on the lamp, then picked up the package. I ripped it open without looking at the return address. When I turned it upside down, two blue and white tickets fell into my right hand.

"What is it?" Rena asked.

"Front row tickets to Sean's concert at the Garden." My voice held a hint of disbelief. I hadn't remembered his promise. "What are we going to do with the ones you bought?"

"Don't worry," Rena chuckled weakly. "I already sold them for a tidy profit."

"But . . . ." I started.

"But what? Sean knows your phone number by heart. Even on a worldwide tour, he's calling at least three times a week."

"What does that have to do with you selling the tickets?"

"If you can't figure it out I'm not telling you. Now why are you home so late?"

Change of subject. I could tell Rena was starting to feel better already.

"Problem at the office. The web servers crashed as we were uploading this week's content."

"Isn't that why you're a vice-president? You're supposed to tell people what to do and then leave," she joked.

"All the articles got wiped out. I stayed to help recreate the pages from our backup documents."

"Did you eat?" Rena questioned.

"Yes, Mom. We ordered in. Chinese, on the company of course."

"Are you sure you're going to be able to make it to Nina's album release party tomorrow night?"

"I told you I would."

"Just checking, you being such an important woman and all."

"Yeah . . . yeah. Rub it in, Ms. Record Exec. Why don't we get to bed? I'm done for the night."

It started with Rena's phone call. I was flipping through the stations and paused on *Oprah* when the telephone rang.

"Hello?"

"You're home early," came Rena's voice over the line.

"It's Friday."

"And?"

"The director lets the division go home at four p.m.," I explained.

"I forgot. I need a favor."

"What's up?" I asked, sitting up.

"Can you go to Nina's party with Traxx?"

I almost dropped the phone as an image of the super handsome soul singer danced before my eyes. "What?" My voice cracked.

"Damon and I need to stay late. We have to finish up a project before Monday and I'm absolutely not coming into the office this weekend. Traxx is new to New York and doesn't have any real solid connections up here yet."

"Why me? The man has to beat women off with a stick." I listened to her laughter as it blended with another's. Damon, I assumed.

"Leave it to you to ask why. The truth is that you're the only woman I know that won't look at the man with either stars, dollar signs, a wedding ring, or a check from a tabloid magazine in her eyes."

"What's wrong with him?" I asked, trying to remember if I'd ever heard any gossip about the R&B singer.

"He's a good guy. Wouldn't be calling you if he wasn't. I was supposed to go with him but I won't be able to get out of here until eleven p.m. at the earliest."

"Oh." I chewed my lip. I tried to keep as far away from the entertainment business as possible. Being in the public eye was not one of my career goals.

"Aren't you the one who said 'Live life to the fullest?' "

Leave it to Rena to remember a drunken New Year's Eve resolution.

"True," I reluctantly admitted.

"And I have it on good authority that a certain someone from the UPenn, an ex-Mrs. Lance Phillips, will be making an appearance."

She knew me too well. "What time do I need to be there?"

"Traxx'll be driving back from a radio appearance in Philly. He'll pick you up at about nine-thirty p.m."

"Wait. How's he going to pick me up if he doesn't know the city?" I asked suspiciously.

"Please. My boy travels in style, plus he's got a navigation system."

"Good grief." The lifestyles of the rich and famous.

"Don't thank me," she sighed. "Anything for family. Now I gotta jet. See ya tonight."

I pressed the off button on the phone and sat back on the sofa. Simba took it as an invitation and jumped up into my lap. The semi-overweight cat stared up at me with narrowed eyes. I ran my hands over his fur and patted his back as he meowed before settling down.

"A date. I've got a date with the Best New Male Artist of the Year," I murmured out loud.

The sentence looped over and over in my mind like a refrain. Then I remembered Sherrie. The image conjured

by her name wiped away the giddy excitement. I closed
my eyes for a moment, trying to dredge up the nickname
everyone had given Lance's ex-wife. What was it? *The
Queen of Sheba.* And with the answer, I was thrust into
the memory of my sophomore year in college.

"You came. Come on in." Sherrie's smile was wide.

Any momentary feeling of ease I had vanished. I
wanted to wring Lance's neck for blackmailing me into
coming over to her apartment. She was smiling at me.
She wanted something. The woman was pretty. Her
unblemished brown sugar complexion, shoulder-length
black hair, and almond eyes attracted men like flies.

She waved me inside her apartment. She wore the
sweet expression that Lance saw when he looked at her.
Her warm, dulcet voice I'd heard before at the 'get to
know' you meetings and open sorority pledge events.

"Would you like something to eat or drink?"

"No, thank you." The Philly pizza steak I'd eaten for
lunch that afternoon threatened to rise up out of my
stomach.

The room was quiet. No loud music from freshman
neighbors or sounds of passing cars and ambulances
headed down Chestnut street towards University
Hospital. One of the advantages of living off-campus.

Sherrie walked to the far end of the room and gestured towards the sofa and chair. Against the beige walls
was a large mahogany bookcase, full of textbooks, strate-

gically placed knickknacks and picture frames. On the wall were two black and white photos of the Brooklyn Bridge and the Manhattan skyline. I knew that the photographer's initials were on the back. Lance had asked for my help in picking them out at the photography exhibit.

"Leah, have a seat." She gracefully seated herself in the side chair. I took a seat opposite her on the sofa. I sat on the edge and crossed my legs. My eyes focused on the arrangement of fresh flowers that graced the coffee table.

I reached out and touched the orchids. As a part of the sorority pledging process, one of us would have to deliver orchids to Sherrie once a week. I'd always wanted to keep the beautiful blossoms instead of handing them over into Sherrie's perfectly manicured fingers.

"You made us walk into Center City in the middle of winter to get these," I said.

"That's water under the bridge." She waved her manicured hand dismissively. Sherrie continued, "It was part of pledging. Besides we were reprimanded."

I leaned forward and inhaled the sweet perfume of the flowers before glancing over at her, meeting those wary eyes. She would never acknowledge that she'd gone too far those weeks we struggled through the sorority pledging process.

"I can't believe you're still holding a grudge," she said.

It had been two years since I'd had to watch her take a pair of scissors and hack off Allison's hair. I'd seen Sherrie's face that night. It was full of vengeful triumph as she held Allison's curly locks in her hand. I suppressed a shudder.

"I'm not holding a grudge, I'm holding a memory."

It could have been me, but it hadn't been. Sherrie had picked the weakest of my line sisters. Allison's mother had been an AKA. There was nothing she wouldn't do to join. That desire for acceptance and her long wavy hair had been all Sherrie had needed.

"Let he who is without sin cast the first stone," she said with a confident look on her face. Like she'd scored some huge point.

"Look, I called you over here tonight so that we can make a fresh start. I want us to be friends," she smiled.

Sherrie almost had me with that smooth line about forgiveness, but the look of triumph on her face killed any thought of being friendly with the woman.

I said, as evenly as I could, "You want to be friends?"

"Does that surprise you?"

The question was so ludicrous that I simply looked at her for a second or two. It took me two tries before I could find an answer. "Yeah, I'm surprised."

"We've never really taken the time to get to know one another. We're going to be graduating soon and I don't want to pass up the opportunity. You and I have so many things in common."

The light bulb went off. "I get it. This is about Lance."

Her face was an open book. The way her lips pressed together into a thin line showed her annoyance.

"Look, Leah," she sighed. "I'll admit that Lance would love it if we were cool and I'd like for us to be friends."

She sat back and crossed her legs expectantly, waiting for my reply. A queen on her throne. Somehow the woman made her statement sound more like an order than a request. The whole situation seemed unreal.

"You know what? I'm going to be honest with you. How about that?" I looked her in the eye. "You and I will never be friends. Since you're so holier than thou tonight, how about a new phrase: 'God don't like ugly.' You might have had to haze us a little while we were on line. That I understand. But cutting off a girl's hair, making us walk into Center City on the coldest day in winter and then sitting here still not willing to say you're sorry? Sherrie, I really don't need or want friends like you." I stood up. I'd had about enough.

"I should have known that you weren't woman enough to know when you're beat."

"Excuse me? What did you say?" My voice rose.

"Face it, girlfriend. Lance won't ever look at you." She pointedly made a show of looking me up and down and then tossing her hair. "This following him around like a lost puppy is really pathetic. You need to find someone else." She paused and laughed. Her laughter grated like a fingernails on a chalkboard.

She continued, "No one wants a stuck-up, tight-lipped, white girl wannabe like you."

I moved before I could think. My hand lashed out, striking her face. I wanted to scream as I stood trying to keep still when every nerve in my body wanted to beat her senseless. It took me a moment to realize I was shaking.

"You'll regret that," she threatened as she rubbed her cheek. Even under the glow of the halogen lamp, I could see the faint hint of redness in her skin. I couldn't tell if it was from my slap or her anger.

"No, I won't." I reached down to pick up my book bag.

"When Lance hears about this, he's going drop you like a bad habit," she screeched.

"And who's going to tell him?" I shot back.

Sherrie's smirk abruptly disappeared. In that moment, something alien welled up within me. Something dark and heavy under my skin. It lay there coiled and waiting. It felt as if I were bleeding and it hurt. I walked across the room and jerked open the door. I took two more steps before turning around to face her again.

"If you come against me, I promise that I won't stop until I've pulled down this house of cards that you've built."

As I stomped down the steps and walked through the streets towards my dorm, I heard her words echoing in my mind, *You'll regret this!*

In the end, she was right. I regretted not stomping her like a bug.

CHAPTER 6

"Come on in. I'm almost ready."

I waved Traxx through the door and hurried to my room. Part of me wanted to stand there with my mouth wide open like a star-stuck, hormone-crazed adolescent. The other part knew that Traxx was just a man with eyes the color of maple syrup on a Saturday morning. He was a tall, beautiful brother with a golden voice. I leaned against my dresser and drew an unsteady breath.

Just a man, I reminded myself. A gorgeous man that had me raiding Rena's closet for the low-cut black Armani dress I had on.

Just another highly paid multi-talented black man, I repeated to myself while putting on a dab of lipstick. He deals with the same daily drama just like everybody else and wipes his butt with two-ply toilet paper. He was the epitome of handsome. Traxx's midnight locks had given women across America a new reason to dream. When you saw him smile on video, your finger just itched to hit the pause button.

I came back to find Traxx looking at pictures on the mantle. As I took the chance to observe him, he was staring at one in particular. His hand reached out towards the picture of Rena sitting on the beach reading a book. His fingers seemed to caress her cheek through the glass.

The man had it bad. I sighed and took a step forward. Another one bites the dust.

"Ready to go?" I asked cheerfully.

"That was quick." He turned, surprised.

Closing and locking the door, I caught myself wondering what woman in her right mind had ever kept this man waiting. We settled into an awkward silence as we walked down the stairs. I was about to comment on the weather when Mrs. Renald stepped out the door with Jacques, her little chihuahua, trailing behind. Jacques immediately began barking. I bent down and gave him a pat on the head as he sniffed my shoes for Simba's scent.

"Sorry, ole boy, no treats this time," I whispered, giving the energetic dog a quick scratch behind the ear.

"Leah, you look *très belle.*"

I straightened up and smiled. "Thank you."

"Who is this young man with you?" She peered up at Traxx through her glasses.

"Let me introduce you to . . ." I opened and closed my mouth. I didn't know his real name.

He reached out and took her small delicate hand within his own. "Trey Matos. It's a pleasure to meet you."

My lips curved into a smile. The man was politeness itself.

The older woman shook his hand and then turned his large palm over in her small hands. She studied it closely. I watched as Traxx shifted uncomfortably and glanced at me in confusion. I gave him what I hoped was a reassuring smile.

Mrs. Renald patted Traxx's cheek with her other hand and smiled benignly.

"Oh, she gonna have her hands full with this one." The older woman adjusted her grip on Jacques's leash and opened the door leading out of the brownstone, leaving Traxx and me staring.

"What was that all about?" he asked.

I shrugged my shoulders and bit my lip to keep from laughing. He looked at me as if I was crazy anyway.

"Couldn't tell you." I had an idea, or maybe it was hope. Who knows? We walked out the building and he led me to the passenger side of his SUV, opened the door and helped me inside.

Traxx entered the Jeep as I looked out into the night through tinted windows.

"So you and Rena are sisters?" he asked later while merging onto the Brooklyn-Queens Expressway.

In my heart, we were sisters. "We grew up together." If Rena hadn't disclosed our connection, I wasn't about to.

"She told me you work with the Internet. That's cool."

I smiled. He thought my job was cool. I looked toward the roof to keep in a snort. Traxx's album had gone platinum and he had his own small money management firm. "It gets hectic sometimes but it's fun. What about you? Where'd you get the accent?"

"You noticed, huh?" He glanced at me. "Some of my relatives live in Arkansas. I love to listen to them tell their stories during our family reunions. I grew up in San Antonio, Texas. My family still lives there."

"How are you liking the East Coast?" I reached out to grab the door handle as he hit the brakes. He swore and honked his horn, just like a New Yorker.

"It's okay except for these crazy cab drivers."

I laughed, and the sound spread through the automobile. I knew exactly how he felt. "Next time try the subway. It'll save you the stress."

"Yeah, I'll think about that," he replied.

"So do you know . . ." I broke off at the sound of a woman's voice.

"Please exit at the next ramp."

" . . . Nina?"

"She and I went to Stanford together," he replied.

"Left turn onto Park Avenue."

"That's cool."

"I'm proud of my girl. She worked hard for this."

"She's got an amazing voice."

"Turn right at the next light."

We parked two blocks away from the club. Traxx put his arm around my back and we blended into the well-dressed club crowd headed towards Fifty-first Street. We turned the corner to see limousines slowly stopping to let out their glamorous passengers while photographers struggled to push past security and each other. Traxx somehow managed to walk us through security after nodding to the crew of muscular, black-clad guards.

Before I knew it we were walking up the stairs behind a trio of Versace-clad women. There were handsome men all over the place dressed in Brooks Brothers suits with nice shiny Kenneth Cole shoes. Every woman in the club was dressed to kill and the low lighting made everyone look nice.

We entered the room just as Nina stepped on stage. As soon as she got through the first verse, I knew I was going to have one of my 'I want a man to call my own for the rest of my life' moments. Her sultry voice enthralled everyone in the place.

Traxx urged me forward past the journalists and other guests towards the VIP area. I sank down into the small booth. A waiter magically appeared with a glass of champagne. I sipped the bubbly and then let out a sneeze.

"Bless you."

I turned towards Traxx and wanted to crawl under the table. I had been staring at the stage and forgotten he was there. I glanced around the room and felt better to see that 90 percent of the men in the place had forgotten to close their mouths.

Nina was one blessed sista. Not only was she beautiful, but girlfriend could sing like nobody's business. My eyes caught one man who seemed to be mesmerized by her performance. He hadn't even bothered to take a drink and his date had long since started tossing back martinis one after another.

Rena arrived about halfway through the performance. I glanced up in time to see her briefly greet Traxx, then slide in next to me. She'd changed into a chocolate-colored cocktail dress.

"How's my girl doing?" she whispered.

"Need you ask? Nina's going to have the critics eating out of the palm of her hand while everybody and their mother runs out to pick up a copy of her CD."

"Did you see her?" Rena asked a moment later.

"Who?" I questioned.

"At the bar on the left. Gold slinky dress, sitting next to the basketball player." Rena pointed before getting up and heading back towards the crowd that had gathered near the stage.

I turned and looked towards the bar. The sound of Nina's singing receded. My eyes locked on the face of a woman I'd never forget. Sherrie. Instead of facing the stage, she looked back towards our booth. Her eyes darted from Traxx to me and then back to Traxx. Recognition. I watched as she smiled and lifted her glass in a mock salute before turning back to the well-dressed man at her side.

"Want to dance?" came the deep voice at my side.

I turned to look at Traxx. He had gone silent since Rena left the table. Too many memories were whispering in my mind, taking me back.

"Sure." I stood and took his outstretched hand while checking the urge to turn and look into the faces of the people I knew were staring.

We joined the other couples on the dance floor. He put his arm politely around the small of my back and I placed my hand on his shoulder. *You're dancing with the choirboy.* I kept that image in my mind.

"Leah, can I ask you a question?"

I drew back to look at Traxx. "Sure."

I was happy for the distraction. I wanted to close my eyes. No matter where I looked I saw stares, measuring eyes and whispers. Maybe an actress, up and coming singer, artist, or family friend. The truth would have everyone laughing. Just a woman without stars in her eyes.

"How does someone get to know Rena better?"

Very smooth. The last man who tried date my cousin asked me how he could "get" Rena, as if she were something you could order off a MacDonald's menu.

"What have you tried?" I questioned.

Traxx looked over my shoulder. I saw his jaw tighten. I hurriedly explained, "I only ask because I can tell you what won't work better than what will."

He didn't say a word, just kept dancing. "I asked her out to dinner." The reluctant admission seemed to loosen him up.

"Okay."

"Three times," he sighed.

"Oh . . ."

"Is she playing hard to get or something?"

I shook my head. "Rena doesn't play games."

"If you say so." He sounded unconvinced.

I leaned over to look towards the backstage door. Rena was standing next to the well-known DJ. Then I glanced up at Traxx and caught a glimpse of longing in his eyes as he stared at my cousin. The polite Texan had half his heart sitting right under the sleeve I was holding. Damn, what can I say? I'm a sucker for a pretty face and a deep voice.

"Ask her to dance. But before she gives you an excuse mention the Children's Benefit Party. She's helping organize this year's charity event."

"Thanks, Leah."

"Just don't mess up."

"You're one mad cool sista."

"And you are a real gentleman. So just drop me off by the nearest empty seat and get to it."

❧

"If you're not careful you'll lose him."

I turned and looked at the owner of the voice. Sherrie. Her flawless face stared dispassionately at Rena and Traxx as they danced.

"No chance of that," I replied. Lose him? Like the man was a cell phone or an earring.

Sherrie strained her eyes. "Isn't that your cousin? I remember her from the wedding reception."

I turned back towards her, giving her my full attention. "Long time no see, Sherrie." Not long enough, I wanted to add.

"She might be your family, but I'd still put her in check if I were you."

My fingers tightened on the wine glass. The woman was giving me advice. I shook my head. Same old Sherrie. Never trust a woman. She was beautiful, educated, had a nice career and was still threatened by anything with breasts. Amazing.

"I'm fine, Sherrie. How are you?"

To underscore the statement, I gave Traxx a thumbs up sign before taking a sip. Hell. I was more than fine. To see Rena dancing and laughing with a man I knew could rock her world about made my night.

Sherrie looked at me as if trying to figure out what planet I had just stepped off. She raised a manicured eyebrow. "My . . . my . . . my. How people change."

"And some stay the same. What's up, Sherrie?"

"I thought I'd give you the opportunity to gloat. I bet you did a little victory dance when you heard about the divorce."

"What?" I only heard that last part of her speech.

"Lance divorced me. You can have him back." She looked at me like a queen granting a favor to a gracious subject.

I stared at her and blinked. Taking a deep breath I placed my hands flat on the cool table. I looked over at Sherrie's impassive face. "First, I have nothing to be happy about. Lance was my best friend. Unlike you, I don't delight in other people's misery. Second, I don't want Lance." I wanted to add I never had, but that was a lie and we both knew it.

She raised her glass in a mock salute. "Of course. Looks like you've stepped up your game. Bigger fish to filet?" I watched as she inclined her head in the direction of Rena and Traxx.

I was about to slap her back to slavery when her partner came by. Sherrie changed in an instant. She looked up at the man, the picture of warmth and innocence. The fool ate it up.

"Sorry I took so long, darling," he said, almost tripping over his own words.

"That's okay, Robert. I was just catching up with an old acquaintance."

She smiled at me and left. No introductions. No goodbyes. I took a drink and savored the sensation of the tiny bubbles of champagne slipping down my throat. The woman was a real piece of work.

We made it back to the car around two a.m. I was really tired from dancing and getting my boogie on. I took a seat up front with Traxx while my cousin stretched out in the back seat.

"Where did Nina disappear to, Rena? I wanted to tell her how awesome she was tonight."

"She had to run up to Jacobi Hospital."

"What's wrong?" I turned all the way around to look into the backseat.

Rena was smiling. "Her older sister went into labor. Nina's going to add 'aunt' as well as 'multi-platinum' to her credits."

"Girl or boy?" Traxx asked.

"Don't know. Her sister didn't want to know the sex of the baby. I know Nina's brother-in-law wanted a girl. Nina was rooting for a boy."

Traxx drove confidently towards Brooklyn. I looked towards the dashboard and tracked the progress of the little car-shaped object as it moved along the series of lines. Impressive. I sat back and turned my attention to the conversation between Rena and Traxx.

"Damien didn't tell me how long you were going to be in New York, Traxx," Rena said.

"Yeah. We decided to leave that open." Traxx began to chuckle. "Sorry, private joke. Damien wasn't sure how this Texas boy would take to big city life."

I could hear the frown in Rena's voice. "But you went to Stanford."

"Yeah. I guess that doesn't count." He smiled.

"Doing damn good so far," I commented as he smoothly exited off the expressway and pulled to a stop at the light.

"Amen," Rena echoed.

"Thank you, ladies. Now if you'd like to continue singing my praises, I could use the backup on Monday."

"Monday?" Rena questioned.

"I'm gonna be in the studio with Quentin Marks. Wants me to lay out a track on his new blues album. Some really old school, sweet rhythm and blues sound."

"Nice," I commented.

"Yeah. It's just you don't work with artists like him but once in a lifetime. My Dad would listen to his records all day while working in the garage." His voice was filled with muted awe.

Quentin Marks, the blues man dubbed America's Beethoven of Jazz, could make a piano cry. Pop had all his records lined up on the shelves in the den. Sunday afternoons when Rena and I would help in the kitchen, the sound of a piano, the smooth deep rasp of the singer's voice, and the wail of a saxophone would fill the house. Rena and I would mimic Mom's slow swinging hips. Our houseshoe-clad feet would tap to the beat of the low-sounding bass. All the while the piano man would play.

"Your dad is a mechanic?" Rena asked.

"Naw," Traxx replied. "He just likes to fix up old cars. Says it's the only vice my Mom will let him have. Dad's a doctor and my Mom's a child psychologist."

Rena and Traxx continued the conversation as we entered the apartment. Taking a moment to turn up the air conditioner, I watched, amused, as Simba stared at Traxx before strolling over to the tall man and rubbing up against his legs.

"So have I passed the test?" Traxx asked, looking down towards the cat.

"Looks like it," I heard Rena answer as I entered the kitchen.

"So what happens to those who don't pass?" he asked.

I laughed after handing glasses of iced tea them. "Well, there was this one guy that Rena . . ."

"Ahh, don't want to hear it," Rena interjected. I closed my mouth and took a seat as Traxx looked back and forth between Rena and me.

"I'll save that story for later. So Traxx, how did you get into the music business?" I asked curiously.

"I was discovered three years back at a church choir competition in Dallas."

"How did that happen?" Rena questioned.

"I was home for a minute and my mom's choir director needed another alto, so I volunteered. Damon, the talent scout who was checking out the competition for a back-up singer for a new group his label had just signed, found me."

"Talk about luck," I commented.

Traxx nodded his head before leaning back on the sofa. "Yeah, it just kinda happened. Damon gave me his card and asked me to call him. I figured I had nothing to lose. Everything just fell into place after that."

"So what do you do when you're not working, Traxx?" Rena asked.

"Please, call me Trey." He smiled at my cousin. "I help run a YMCA in our community. I like hanging out with the kids and shooting hoops."

My eyes drifted closed as he and Rena talked about giving back to the community and being involved. When I woke from my light doze, I was careful to keep my eyes closed.

"You've got to be kidding. You actually liked Vanilla Ice?" Rena exclaimed.

"Come on now," Traxx challenged. "You've got to admit you thought his beats were pretty good."

"No way," Rena denied.

"So you're telling me that you didn't get your little groove on to a few of his songs?"

"Okay, I'm busted, I'll admit I liked it. But it was only that one track."

"Your secret's safe with me," Traxx promised.

I heard Rena let out a yawn. "Sorry," she said.

"No. It's late and I'd better leave. Thanks for a great evening, Rena."

"You're welcome . . . Trey."

"Could you let Leah know I had a good time?"

"Of course, that is, if that sleepyhead cousin of mine ever wakes up."

I strained to listen as they moved towards the door.

"So will I see you this week?" he asked.

"I'll be around the office," Rena replied. "Drop by and say hello."

"Are you on the same floor as Damon? I've never seen you in the hallway."

"One floor up. I'm on twenty-eight," she said.

"Twenty-eight, huh?"

"Yes."

"Okay, so can I take you to lunch sometime?"

"We'll see," Rena answered evasively.

"All right, then. Good night, Rena."

"Night, Trey. Take care."

I opened my eyes as soon as the door closed. "Night, Trey," I mimicked in a deep, sultry voice.

"I knew your behind was faking," Rena laughed.

I stood up and stretched. "My work here is done."

"Don't be getting any ideas, cuz."

"Of course not," I lied and bent to pick up Simba. Winking at the cat, I beamed at a frowning Rena just before turning and heading to my room.

I woke to the sound of the phone ringing. Reaching over I picked up the receiver and opened my eyes to look at the clock. Eleven a.m. So much for getting up early.

Rolling over, I put the phone to my ear and closed my eyes, expecting to hear my mother's voice.

"Hello?" I grumbled sleepily.

"Leah . . ."

My eyes shot open and I sat up. "Sean, how are you?"

"I'm okay. Getting some rest before the next show."

"So where are you?" I had a flyer he had given me before leaving. It was probably nestled in a purse somewhere in my closet.

"Miami."

"Ahh . . ." I smiled and closed my eyes.

"Now what's that supposed to mean?" he asked.

I knew at that moment he was smiling. Lounging alone on some plush white leather coach in some ultra-trendy resort hotel, Sean was guaranteed to be watching Saturday morning cartoons.

"Nothing. I don't think that you could have picked a better place to rest. So have you checked out South Beach?"

Sean fit right in with the beautiful people. Only he wouldn't hang out amongst the rich, famous, and party addicted. The charming bad boy of alternative rock always went his own way. The jet set world had never interested him, but the dark hidden places in the human heart would always send him to some quiet place to write.

"It's beautiful near the water, but right now I wouldn't mind being in Arizona. Anyway, how are you?"

"Hot. The city's battling another heat wave," I explained.

"How long?" His concern came through the phone line. My heart jumped a little. This was my little secret, the small treasured thing held close. Singer Sean Andrews of Exile cared. I switched the phone to my right ear and sat up.

"It's been two days. The weatherman says we'll get some relief tomorrow night."

"Good. So are you liking the big city?"

I leaned against the headboard, resting my head against the wall. "It's wonderful. This place is exciting, lots of different people, hundreds of things to do. I really want to give New York a chance."

"But there's something missing?"

Damn, the man was perceptive.

"I miss the quiet sometimes. The open spaces and the sky. There's nothing like the Los Angeles skyline after a long, hard rain. I don't miss the traffic, though. I think everybody should have a chance to take a break from driving."

"I know how you feel. I won't miss being on the road day after day."

"How much longer are you going to be on tour?" I asked.

"Just one more month."

"Any plans for afterwards?"

"I'll take a few weeks and go out west. Spend some time at the ranch. Then I think I'll head to New York."

I almost dropped the phone in surprise. Somewhere in the back of my mind, I had thought the connection between the two of us would be severed by time and distance.

"I didn't know you liked New York. Thought you were a California boy."

He laughed. "Don't be fooled by the blond hair. I've already leased an apartment in Hell's Kitchen."

"Oh."

"I'll be staying there when I'm in town next week."

The tickets. "That's right, your concert's next week. I heard you sold out the Garden. Nervous?"

"Some. But not for the reasons you think."

"Oh? So what's got Mr. Confident nervous?"

I couldn't think of anything more intimidating than playing to a packed house in Madison Square Garden. Although a newcomer, I'd already heard that all the greats had played on that stage and if you weren't good, New Yorkers didn't hesitate to let you know it. But I'd also heard that if they loved you, they would keep you in their hearts forever.

"You've never been at one of my concerts before."

My heart stilled and then beat slowly as my mind struggled to come up with a response. I wanted Rena's advice more than I wanted anything at this moment, but the girl never got out of bed before noon on Saturdays. This was her world, the friendship, the caring. I'd never get used to the switch. One minute Sean was a regular guy off the street and then he was *the man*, the one whose singing spoke to people all over the world and captured women's hearts.

"If my being there will make you nervous . . ." I started.

"No. I want you and Rena to be there. Did you get the tickets?"

"Yes, thank you. I've never been so close to the stage before. It'll be wild."

"Just make sure you stay out of trouble," he teased.

"Ha. You mean don't get trampled by teenagers with runaway hormones?"

He laughed. "Tom promised me that security will be pretty tight."

"That's good to hear."

"I'm going to be in the city for the week giving interviews. Would you mind being my dinner companion one night?"

Would I mind? Hell no. "Any place in particular you want to eat? For some of the good spots you need to make early reservations."

As soon as the words left my mouth I wanted to pull them back. Sean was a celebrity and in New York that meant something, including immediate access to the top restaurants.

"How about we play it by ear?"

"Sounds good to me," I replied and got out of bed. Stretching, I walked over to the windows and opened the blinds, squinting as my eyes adjusted to the sudden deluge of bright light.

"So you can fit me into your schedule?" he asked.

"For you, my friend, I'll even skip my gym class."

"You've joined a gym?" His voice was incredulous.

I laughed as I walked down the hallway towards the kitchen with Simba trailing behind. I remembered telling

Sean about how much I hated being inside LA gyms. The emphasis on gym fashion and looks far outweighed the supposedly friendly atmosphere.

"Not all of us have world-class personal trainers," I teased.

"So you're actually going to the gym?" Disbelief was evident in his tone.

"One of my college friends and I work out in the morning before going to work. I've actually taken a couple of spin classes."

"Uh-huh," he murmured.

"What's that supposed to mean?" I asked while scooping cat food into Simba's bowl.

"Maybe this is something I have to see to believe. You're getting up at six in the morning?"

"Five-thirty," I automatically corrected.

"To go to the gym?"

I could still hear the skepticism in Sean's voice. "Miracles do happen once in a while," I laughed.

"Good for you. I'm proud of you."

"Now that you've had your laughs for the day, why don't you go and do something useful, like lie on the beach?"

"Ouch. That hurt."

"Really? Good."

"You are one tough lady, Leah Russell."

"Yeah, just because you can't wrap me around your finger doesn't mean I'm tough. Just means I'm immune."

"Immune? You make me sound like a disease."

"As in immune to your charms. Now, some of us have work to do. So I'll leave you to rest."

"It's Saturday," he protested.

"For those of us without bodyguards, personal assistants, room service and maids, Saturday's not a holiday. I've got a ton of laundry and some grocery shopping to do."

"Oh."

My lips twitched. "Oh."

"Well, I'll call you Tuesday."

"Okay."

"Take care, Leah."

"You too, Sean."

I pressed the off button on the phone and laid it on the countertop. Simba rubbed his tail against my leg, purring. Absentmindedly, I leaned down and patted him on the back before putting his food bowl on the floor. Switching on the coffeemaker, I sauntered towards the bathroom with a smile on my face and giddiness in my heart. Sean Andrews had invited me, Leah Russell, to dinner. Although there was nothing romantic about it and we'd had dinner together many times before, I still sang in the shower.

CHAPTER 7

When I went out in public with Sean, we met for drinks at a bar or for dinner at a small, family-owned Mexican restaurant where our faces never raised eyebrows or startled whispers.

He'd order an assortment of dishes while I laughed at him over the rim of my Corona. Sometimes I'd just pretend, always imagining things were more than what they were. After leaving Sean sleeping by the cliff that morning after the party, I hadn't expected to hear from him.

I had chalked the night up to doing a good deed, just helping a stranger. Then the flowers arrived. Rena was always getting flowers, but two days after the party, a bouquet of orange-red orchids and pale violet lavender nestled with white lilies arrived. The card had my name. I'd opened the small beige-colored envelope with shaking hands.

He remembered, I had thought. Lance remembered my birthday. Instead, I found a note from Sean written in bold blue letters.

You left before I could say thank you. Have dinner with me. Friday, eight p.m.

The first time Sean and I had dinner it was in an exclusive restaurant in Beverly Hills. We sat in the back near bay windows hidden by bamboo screens. I sat amazed as waiters fell all over themselves to serve us and almost dissolved into laughter when the restaurant chef with his French accent and tall white hat came to ask about the meal.

I spent most of the dinner trying to convince him that he owed me nothing. Sean, on the other hand, sat back and smiled. The man just asked questions, so many questions. Like he wanted to crawl inside my skin and wallow in my mind. At first, I thought he was just an eccentric white boy. He wore a black curly wig like the spoiled rich kid who refused to grow up. But after witnessing the attention and all the special treatment, I came to realize that the man not only had money and connections, he was famous.

I didn't know what game he was playing, but I went along with it. And the flowers kept coming, dozens of roses, daises, iris, tiger lilies — until I agreed to have dinner with him again. When I told my cousin Sean's name, her face squelched up a little with puzzlement as though chasing a lost memory and then she shrugged her shoulders. Actors, musicians, entertainers, and celebrities flocked to Los Angeles. There was no telling which group Sean fell into.

Soon Rena started to worry, and so did I. Somewhere after the tenth delivery of flowers, Sean had crossed the line from being a sad suicidal rich boy to a would-be stalker. The night of the second dinner, after I spent the day pleading, Rena agreed to get me out of the mess I'd somehow gotten myself into.

Rena opened the front door and burst into laughter. I stood with my fingers ready to dial 911 when Sean walked into the room. My cousin with tears in her eyes took the cordless phone from my nerveless fingers and sat down on the couch.

"Cuz, let me introduce you to Sean Patrick Andrews. Your would-be stalker just happens to be the lead singer, guitarist, and songwriter of Grammy-winning alternative rock band, Exile."

She wagged her finger at me. "See what happens when you talk to strangers."

I just stood there looking back and forth between Sean and Rena. He broke into laughter and I followed soon after.

Sean threw himself into my life like a man drowning. His sorrow and rage about his mother's death sometimes threatened to overwhelm me. Nights on the beach I'd try to pour my warm happy memories of home into him. Then he would fly like a kite in the wind. His joy was so strong and so deep that I couldn't breathe.

He saw many things and felt them with an intensity that showed in his green eyes. In those moments, dressed like a teenager and walking on the sidewalk, I knew what it was to feel like a true actress. I was a lead character and Sean was the tragic hero, my chance to correct past mistakes. I'd save him from himself.

We would sit in the corner of a small restaurant and I'd place my elbows on the table and put my face between my hands and he would talk. I was captivated by the way he saw life around him. He saw into the marrow, the quick. He heard music in everything. Sean savored music's richness, the feel of words lapped together and poured out on the strings of his guitar.

I found myself not remembering when Sean wasn't a friend, when I didn't pick up the phone and listen as he put the receiver up close to his six-string guitar and strummed some melody that had come floating up in his ear. Rena would laugh and click her tongue against the roof of her mouth. Some nights he would call while I was sitting on the sofa watching a basketball game. After we finished talking trash about which team was going to win, he would talk about the band and his self-doubts and I'd talk about work and bad dates and serious regrets.

Only on the nights when both of us were full of life and good food would he mention his mother. She floated like a ghost between us. Clad in oversized cargo pants and a black shirt, Sean would sit on the floor of his million-dollar bungalow in Beverly Hills, a lost look on his face as his fingers swept over the guitar strings. The recessed lighting softened the deepening shadows under his eyes and I would sit quiet, his audience of one.

He would sing and I could close my eyes and my mother's face would come swimming up in my thoughts. His deep raspy voice never cracked as memories overflowed into the music. To me it was as if he were singing lullabies.

One night I crawled towards him on the soft carpet and placed my hand on his head as though soothing a small child. His eyes glowed with unshed tears, yet his fingers kept strumming. His grief seemed to fill up the large living room.

The night I met him standing next to the cliff had been the third anniversary of his mother's death from cancer. Each time he left me at my front door after hanging out in the obscure sections of Los Angeles, I'd unsteadily rushed to the phone only to catch myself before dialing home just to hear my parents' voices. And as sleep came washing over me, all I could do was pray that the Lord would keep me and mine safe.

"You have got to be kidding," Rena said, barely glancing at the video I held in my hand.

"What's wrong with it?" I asked.

"Can we say 'white chick flick'?" she replied.

"Hey!" I put my hand on my hip.

"Cuz, tonight is not the night to watch blonde women with no intelligence, breast implants, and clothing issues lament over the wrong man, but end up marrying Mr. Wonderful and living in the five-bedroom Colonial house by the end of the film."

"Good point." I put the movie back on the shelf. "So what did you pick?"

I took a look at the video she held in her hands and shook my head. The first clue was the chalk outline of a body. "Nope."

"Why?" Rena asked.

"No chick flick, no murder movies."

"So what are we going to get?" she asked, exasperated.

After twenty minutes of looking and fifteen minutes of arguing, we stood in line with a mystery and an action comedy.

"Hey Rena?" I whispered, looking towards the new release section.

"Hmmm?" she replied absentmindedly, her gaze focused on the overhead video screen.

"Cute man at four o'clock," I whispered.

Rena languidly turned to look in the direction I was subtly pointing.

"No good." She shook her head.

"Why? What's wrong with him? The man is fine." Just to make sure I gave him another glance.

"Take a good, long, hard look and pay attention to the shoes."

I examined the pressed khaki pants and the nice indigo polo shirt that wasn't tight but managed to accentuate the brother's milk chocolate complexion and flat stomach.

"I don't get it."

Rena tisked. "Girl, didn't I teach you anything? He's matched and he's pressed."

"And . . ."

"That means he's either married, gay, shacking up, or living with his mama. There's no way he dressed himself that nice and checked for the matching socks and shoes."

I started to protest but the object of our speculation took that exact moment to walk by on his way to the other side of the store. I very carefully followed his movements, checking for the gold band. As I looked up it turned out that I didn't need to. I watched as a smile lit his face and he embraced a petite black woman who'd just entered the store.

"Another one bites the dust," I sighed.

"No kidding," Rena agreed. "At least we've got some movies."

"At least you've got Trey coming over," I added. The singer was back in town from a quick trip home to Texas.

"What?" Rena's neck should have snapped from the speed at which she turned back towards me.

"He's coming over to hang out, don't you remember?" I tried to play it off.

"Remembering implies that I was told."

"Oops, guess I let the cat out of the bag."

"Trey is not coming over," she said, giving me a warning look.

"I invited him."

"Without telling me?" Her voice rose.

I shrugged. "Chill, it's just a movie. You don't even have to speak to the man." I watched as she rolled her eyes.

"Look, Rena. Trey just wants to hang out, eat some pizza, and watch a movie."

My cousin stared at me with a suspicious frown. "I'm going to remember this."

"Yeah, I know," I laughed before reaching over to take the videos out of her hand. "Just to make it up to you, I'll pay for the movies."

"And the pizza," Rena added.

"No need. Trey's got the food and drink covered."

Twenty minutes later, after we'd gotten home, Rena was still protesting. "Leah, he can't come over," she repeated as we both sat on the sofa.

Just at that moment, the doorbell rang. I smiled as she let out an exasperated sigh.

"Too late," I announced, standing up and walking towards the door.

Four days later and two hours before Sean's sold-out concert at Madison Square Garden, I was the one on pins and needles.

"Are you ready to go?" Rena's head peeked through the doorway. I ignored her and continued tracing the edge of my lips with the brown liner. My hand shook with excitement. Tonight I'd see Sean in concert.

"We're going to a rock concert. Why are you looking like we're going uptown to the ballet?"

"What's wrong with what I'm wearing?" I asked.

Rena leaned against the doorway and smiled. "Nothing if we were going to Carnegie Hall to see Mary J. Blige. But we're going to a rock concert, sweetie."

"And?" I replied before replacing the cap on my lipstick.

She rolled her eyes toward the ceiling. "That means the music going to be loud, the crowd wild, and the teenagers crazy."

"I'm waiting for you to make your point."

"Trust me, Leah. Just go back to your closet and put on some jeans and sneakers. We may have front row seats, but I doubt that either one of us is going to be doing any sitting and those heels you've got on are going to hurt like hell after an hour of standing."

I looked at her standing there in jeans and a short-sleeved top and I nodded my head. Rena was in the music business and I'd rather be safe than sorry.

"You win. What color top should I wear? Green or blue?"

"Red," she replied without hesitating.

"Why red?"

"The better for Sean to see you with," she teased.

"You're about to get on my last nerve," I tossed out over my shoulder as I walked into my room. I heard Rena's laughter coming from close behind me.

"My . . . my . . . my, aren't we sensitive." She rolled her eyes at me.

"Gee, does Trey know you can be such a brat?" I answered back.

I turned to see the smile slip from Rena's face as she took a seat on the foot of my bed.

"What does Trey have to do with this? We were talking about your personal life, cuz."

"Funny," I said while pushing aside some clothes to reach into the back of the closet for a nice pair of jeans. "I could have sworn it was you talking about my personal life. Since we're on the topic, when are you going to cut the brotha a break?" I asked.

Rena was still smarting from my inviting the singer over for dinner and a movie. Even though those two got along like a house afire, my cousin was determined to ignore the fact that the man was hell-bent on getting her to like him.

"I don't date people in the entertainment industry." It was the same standard line I'd heard her give a million times before. I pulled down the long skirt I'd been wearing, but paused before pulling up my soft, fitted blue jeans. I looked at my cousin as she unconsciously played with one of her dreads.

"Oh, so they're good enough to work with, but you can't date them?"

"That's not it," she shot back.

"Really? So there's some other reason you won't put the man out of his misery and agree to a real date?" Trey and I had exchanged numerous emails about Rena's different excuses.

"Why are you so pro-Trey?"

"Because the man hasn't given up on you yet." I pulled the lightweight cotton floral tee shirt over my head. "He seems like a decent guy. Plus, I like him."

"You and every other woman on earth."

"So that's the reason you won't go out with him." I crossed my arms and took a seat on the edge of my bed.

"What?"

"Afraid of the competition? I'm shocked. My superfly cousin admitting that she's insecure just like the rest of us mere women," I taunted.

"Wrong." Her chin shot up a notch. "I just . . ." She was interrupted when the phone rang. I reached towards the nightstand and picked it up.

"Hello?"

"May I speak to Rena Mason?" came a loud, unfamiliar voice against a noisy background.

I frowned while handing the phone over to Rena.

"It's for you."

I sat back down on the bed and put on my shoes. I had just finished putting some things in my pocket book when Rena came back into the room. I turned around to see her pale face. "What's wrong?" A chill swept up my spine.

"I can't go with you to the concert."

"What happened?"

Her eyes went from sorrow-filled to a deep, dark anger. I looked down at her shaking hands and took them in my own.

"You're scaring me, Rena."

"Nina's in the hospital," she whispered.

"What happened? Was she in an accident? I'm coming with you."

"No." Rena replied and then seemed to shake herself. She took a deep breath and hugged me.

"I can't tell you what happened, but I can tell you that Nina's going to be okay."

"Rena . . ." I warned.

"Listen to me, Leah. She doesn't want people to know, okay? You've got to go to this concert."

I waved off her concern. "Sean will understand if I'm not there."

"There's nothing you can do. She's at Lennox Hill Hospital, which isn't far away from the Garden. I'll drop you off on my way over."

"I want to come with you," I said, trying again.

"I know, and I'll tell Nina that you wanted to be there."

"Are you sure?" I asked.

"Positive. You just have fun, and I'll expect the inside scoop on how it all went down, okay? Now let's roll," she said, turning and heading out of the room.

"Are you sure?" I asked Rena for the fiftieth time.

"Yes," she answered, pulling up behind a line of stopped cars. I watched as wave after wave of people crowded the sidewalk heading towards the entrance to Madison Square Garden. Their loud voices and rushed movements began to rub off on me and my heart sped up.

I opened the car door and moved to get out; I stopped at the touch of Rena's hand on my arm. I turned to see her smile.

"Tell Sean I'll catch him on the next go-round."

Before I could tell her that I wouldn't be able to tell him anything, a police siren sounded somewhere down the street.

"See you later, cuz." I stepped onto the sidewalk and watched as Rena maneuvered the sporty BMW into the slow-moving traffic headed uptown.

I was swept towards the open doors of the auditorium with the crowd. The very air seemed to be alive with excitement; vendors lined the corridors selling CDs, videos, shirts, pictures and calendars of the band. Exile was playing to a sold-out crowd tonight. I was sure that Sean would be pleased. I slowly maneuvered my way through the crowd of teenagers to the front. By the time I passed through all the checkpoints and settled into my seat, I couldn't wait for the show to start. The front row section was filled with young and old professionals who could afford to spend $500 a ticket.

By the time Exile took the stage, the crowd was on its feet. I looked up into the outer stands, seeing blurred faces chanting the band's name. As Sean walked towards the center of the raised stage, I was standing and clapping, along with everyone else. The mood of the crowd was electric, filled with anticipation and energy.

The light show began and three enormous video screens glowed. Sean stepped up to the standing microphone and strummed his opening note. The huge arena was so silent you could hear a pin drop. I'd heard Sean sing before, but nothing had prepared me for this. His voice rode the guitar and edged over the sounds of the drum and keyboard. I turned to look at the faces of those surrounding me and found them captivated by Sean.

When he closed his eyes and sang, my throat tightened with remembrance, the memory of cradling his head on my shoulder as his tears stained my shirt. It was the song for his mother that would haunt me for all my days. Sean sang each note straight from his soul. I saw his mother the way he saw her.

The song cast a shadow over the audience. Everyone in the arena felt the touch of a mother's love and a son's mourning. When I tore my eyes away from Sean I saw that his song had brought tears to the eyes of many of the audience.

Tonight the critics would pick up their pens noting that a major part of Sean's life emerged in verses about love and loss, happiness and pain. Sean took the wide breadth of the human condition and narrowed it down into three or four syllables coupled with an unforgettable melody.

Then the music changed and I could only watch as Sean seemed to transform before my eyes. Like the wind, he blew hot and cold. His music swung, a combination of two different people: one angry and tortured, the other haunted by grief. That mixture showed in his every move, every song, and made people want him more. The band seemed to push forward and their body language which moments before was laid back and slow turned edgy.

The music was loud, quick, high energy with its angst-ridden riffs and chords. Sean moved into a low crouch and swung the guitar back and forth, writhing, as his voice grew more forceful and fiery. It frightened me a little; I had only seen the gentle side of Sean. As I watched him play to the rage and anger, the high emotions running rampant through the crowd, I shivered.

As he neared the end of the concert, Sean slowed the pace of the music and the tender side of his music took the lead. The music that poured from his guitar strings was honey mixed with bitter ale. From his lips came words of memory gathered from an old grief and a deep love.

He sang songs that spoke to the solitary person inside. His words conjured images of faraway places. I felt tears start behind my eyes as he sang of wars and loves come and gone, mothers looking up at snow-covered mountains waiting for the return of sons and husbands, lonely abbeys without words of peace, silent gray-red stones, and crumbling arches.

When the applause came, Sean bowed and joined the rest of Exile at the front of the stage. It was deafening. I looked up at him and saw him give me one of his big grins as he waved to the crowd before he turned to leave the stage. I turned to follow the crowd towards the exit, only to stop short at the approach of a tall, well-built, black-clad concert security guard.

"Miss, may I see your ticket please?"

"Okay." I pulled the ticket stub slowly from my bag while giving the man a confused stare.

"If you would come with me," he said, placing a hand on my left arm.

"Excuse me," I said. As he led me further away from the exiting crowd, I dug in my heels. "Excuse me. Is there a problem?"

He looked down at me, a curious expression on his big face.

"No problem at all. Your ticket was selected to go backstage and meet the members of Exile."

I shook my head with disbelief as he smiled benignly and led me through the thong of screaming people and line of security. Damn the man. Give him an inch and he'll take a mile. Before I knew it, I was ushered through the doorway of Sean's dressing room. He sat sprawled out on the only sofa in the room. I leaned back against the door and cleared my throat, causing him to spill some of his bottled water.

A slow smile spread across his face. He looked both handsome and charmingly boyish as he hesitated there, one hand holding the water and the other hanging by his side. I tried to keep my lips from curving upward, but couldn't do it for long. Instead, I started laughing. The famous singer was sitting with half a bottle of water on his already sweat-soaked shirt.

"I impressed you that much, huh?" he joked.

"I'm still speechless." ·

"What'd you think of it?" His lips were grinning but I could see the seriousness peeking out from his eyes.

"You were wonderful and you know it. If New York didn't love you before they are head over heels now."

"Really?" He looked almost disbelieving.

I gave him the thumbs up. "Trust me. The critics will be raving."

"Where's Rena?"

"She had an emergency she had to take care of. She wanted me to tell you that she'll catch you on the next one."

"Hmmm . . ."

I watched as he stood, placed his guitar in its hard black case and snapped the locks closed. I opened my mouth to speak and let out a yawn.

"Stop that," he warned. "You know yawns are contagious."

I watched as he let out a large one. "Tired?" I teased.

"Hungry," he responded. "Would you join me for a late night meal?"

"Sure, why not? I don't have work tomorrow."

"Let's go then."

"Okay." I turned to open the door.

"Not that way." Sean gestured to the door on the opposite side of the room.

He opened the door to reveal two guards standing in an empty hallway. He waved then goodnight and pulled on a baseball cap.

"Where are we headed?" I asked.

"This tunnel leads from Madison Square Garden to the office tower. Once we go through that door, we can just hop in the car without having to go through the crowd."

I nodded. "Good idea."

"Do you mind if we go back to my place first?" He seemed a little embarrassed. "I need to take a shower."

I squinched up my nose, pretending to smell something rotten. "Yeah, you do need to hit the water."

He opened the door to the black Lincoln Continental and gently pushed me inside.

CHAPTER 8

Ten blocks, forty minutes, and a bag of Chinese take-out later, I leaned back in Sean's dining room chair.

"Nice setup you've got here," I commented after Sean and I sat down at the mahogany dining table. He spread the boxes of Chinese take-out over the table. The man had ordered enough for an army.

"Surprised?"

"I didn't think you were serious about spending time in New York."

Not only was the real estate nice, but the apartment was gorgeous. The prewar two-bedroom had an open living room and dining area. I'd taken a peek into one of the bathrooms and had almost succeeded in killing myself on the slick marble floor. The large kitchen with new appliances and bright lighting would have made even my mother smile.

"Why do you think that?" His green eyes twinkled as he plopped a shrimp dumpling into his mouth.

After having to choose between going out and finding an empty restaurant where he wouldn't be recognized or ordering in, we'd settled on getting food brought in. The shower he'd taken had done a lot to rid him of the adrenaline rush of playing to a packed arena. Sean reveled in the faded jeans and shirt he'd changed into. The man could wear some pants. He was blessed with the kind of body most men would envy. Broad shoulders, strong muscled arms, powerful chest and tight stomach.

"Like it or not, my friend, you're a California boy."

"But that doesn't mean I can't appreciate the beauty of the city."

The look he gave me made me almost made me lose my grip on the chopsticks. I'd have had to be deaf, dumb, and blind to miss the implication in his response. But even though I was fairly immune to Sean's unconscious need to flirt, my heart still gave a quick squeeze. I concentrated on maneuvering my chopsticks and let the compliment fly way over my head.

"So how did the visit go with your family?" he asked.

I placed the chopsticks on the rim of the delicate porcelain dinner plate and picked up my wine glass. Taking a sip, I looked at Sean.

"It was great to be home again. Rena and I walked around South Street, gorged ourselves on Italian ice, cheese steaks, and French fries. Mom made all our favorite foods and Pop arranged for a surprise visit to Franklin Mills."

"Oh? What's that?"

"A large shopping outlet just outside of Philly."

"And your friend Lance?" Sean asked.

"Lance . . ." I almost choked on a bite of chicken.

There was a name that threw me. Sean and I had shared many secrets that night by the cliffs. Telling him about Lance was one of my biggest regrets. Yet speaking of past or present loves was something that we both shied away from, until now. Even as close friends we didn't talk about the other's relationships. For me there was no need since Sean's latest love interests always appeared in the celebrity section of magazines.

"Rena mentioned that he stopped by for a visit." He gave me a searching look.

I narrowed my eyes at the protective glint in his. "You and Rena must have done a lot of talking." The mention of Lance's name had brought with it the unwelcome ghost of Sherrie.

"She's just concerned about you," Sean replied.

"Concerned?" I barked. "That's just a nice way of saying she's stressed." Sean's serious expression didn't change.

"Look, for the thirtieth time, and please feel free to share this with my overprotective cousin, I'm over the man. Lance has been and will continue to be a friend. Anything more is just Rena's overactive imagination, *comprende?*"

I picked up my chopsticks and grabbed a broccoli floret. "How's your dad doing, by the way?"

I wanted to change the subject. The thought of my cousin and Sean discussing me was unsettling.

He leaned back and put his hand behind his head. "I just found out that he's getting remarried. I'm to be the best man."

"Oh. Do you know the future bride?"

"Her name is Brigit. She was one of my mother's friends."

Open mouth and insert foot. Damn, apparently white women operated differently from sistas. You never dated your friend's man and you sure as hell didn't marry a friend's widower. So much for loyalty.

"Are you okay?" I asked, not knowing what else to say and really sorry I asked.

"It seems natural. Her husband died of a heart attack three years ago. I guess it brought the two of them together."

"I can't imagine Pop without Momma." The comment slipped out before I could stop it. Open mouth, insert other foot.

"He needs someone in his life to care for and vice-versa. My mother understood that about him."

"She sounds like a wonderful woman."

He nodded. "Finished?" he asked, standing up and beginning to clean the table.

"Stuffed," I honestly admitted, smiling faintly. I felt a wave of contentment wash over me at having a full stomach.

"You'll be hungry in about . . ." He looked at his watch. "Three hours. Are you sure you don't want to finish off the last of this sesame chicken?"

"Positive."

He looked at me with that puppy dog look in his eyes and I just leaned back and smiled. "So do you think you can make room for your fortune cookie?" he asked.

He reached into the plastic bag and set two plastic wrapped Chinese cookies on the table.

"Okay, you pick first," I said.

Sean tore open the wrapper, broke the cookie in half and pulled out the small white strip of paper.

"Mine reads, 'Two things to aim for in life—to get what you want and to enjoy it.' Now that's pretty good advice."

He put his down on the table. "Now you."

I carefully tore open the wrapper and gingerly pulled out the fortune without cracking the cookie shell. Grinning, I waved the strip triumphantly.

"Okay, Ms. Perfectionist. What does it say?" Sean questioned.

I turned it over and read the words out loud, "'Trust your intuition. The universe is guiding your life.'"

I placed the scrap of paper in my pocket. "Could you get a little more vague than that?"

"Sounds pretty straightforward to me."

"It would. You're one of the most 'go with the flow' guys I know."

"Yeah? Well, I'm going to go put the rest of these leftovers in the fridge. Why don't you relax on the couch? I'll fix us some tea."

I was reading the foreword in a book of Scottish history when he returned from the kitchen. His shadow fell over the page and I looked up to see his serious expression.

"Do you mind if we watch TV in the bedroom?" he smiled. "I just want to stretch out."

If it had been anyone other than Sean who asked that question, I would have laughed the man out of the room. I stood up with an amused smile. "No surprise pillow fights?"

"Promise," he replied.

I grabbed the tall glass mug he held out in his hand and then bent over to retrieve the book from the sofa before following Sean down the hallway. Quiet Japanese woodblock paintings lined the walls, while recessed ceiling lights led the way past what I guessed was the guest room.

I entered the master bedroom behind Sean and found it different from the one I'd seen briefly in his house in L.A. The person who had designed it must have known him well, judging from the sage green walls, frosted, curtainless windows, and the Japanese-style soft tatami rug. I admired the decorated fireplace with a screen of wrought iron leafy vines and log holder, which held what looked like old books instead of wood. A large, light-colored wooden bed sat in the middle of the room.

"So when did you become such a history buff?" I questioned, setting my cup on the nightstand before taking off my shoes and sitting on the bed.

"When I realized one night on a late flight over the Atlantic that we all carry the past with us," he responded, picking up the remote control and turning on the large flat-screen television that hung on the opposite wall.

"Interested in learning more about your proud Scottish roots?"

"No, not in that way. I'm not wanting to change who I am by grabbing hold of my parents' roots. I just wanted to know a little more." He stretched out on the bed and leaned against the headboard. "I think about the highland lords who rode over the valleys and into war against the British. I wonder what it felt like for them to go to fight for a cause. I pretend that I can hear the sound of a thousand hooves beating against the earth, smell the smoke in the air, taste the bitter fear and feel the icy winds on my face," he said.

"That sounds more like a nightmare than a daydream," I commented after picking up my tea.

"No way, Leah. You'd love it in Scotland. Think about it." He spread his arms wide. "We could go walking along the banks of shimmering mountain lakes and picnic in fields of wild heather."

"Careful, your sentimental side is coming out," I warned.

"I'm not kidding."

"I believe you," I replied, taking a sip of the herbal tea. The fruity taste of peaches and the tartness of ginseng slid down my throat. "I mean, one minute you're happily settled in a new bungalow in L.A., the next you're flying to Arizona to build a ranch in the middle of nowhere, then you pull a disappearing act and call me from Glasgow. So how'd you find this place?" I asked, referring to the condominium.

"Pete has an old college buddy who's in the Manhattan real estate market. I saw a couple of places in Greenwich and Chelsea, but I liked the unexpected quietness of the area. Then again, with the name Hell's Kitchen, I couldn't pass it up."

"Nice neighbors?"

He shrugged. "Don't know. I haven't had a chance to meet them. Pete's barely given me time to eat and sleep on the tour."

"Speaking of the tour, when's the last concert?"

He leaned back against the headboard and took a sip of his tea. "Two more weeks. It's been a lot of fun, but all of us agree that Seattle can't come soon enough. I've got too many things that I've put on hold for too long."

"You guys have earned some time out of the spotlight. So what do you plan on doing besides taking in some much needed R & R?"

"For one, I've shamefully neglected our son." He shifted to sit cross-legged facing me. "I'll understand if you're a might bit angry with me." His half-hearted attempt to wipe the smile off his face didn't work.

Simba. "I'd almost forgotten that you promised to take joint responsibility. You're right, *your son*. He could definitely use some discipline. The oversized fleabag is bullying my next door neighbor's chihuahua."

"Did you say chihuahua?" he managed to get out between chuckles.

"Yes."

"Then it's not so bad then. Does he really have fleas?"

"No." I paused. "What do you mean, it's not so bad?"

"Can't blame the cat for not liking the hairless over-grown rat, now can you?" His grin was devastating. I felt it roll over me from head to toe.

"You're insane," I laughed.

"No. I'm just a feline lover."

I rolled my eyes upwards and laughed at his off-the-wall reply. Glancing down at my watch, I started to move off the bed, but stopped as Sean caught my wrist.

"Stay and watch cartoons with me." He moved to stand up. "I'm just running to the bathroom. Promise not to disappear?"

"I'll be right here."

I moved to put down my glass mug of tea and found it next to a notebook. Curious, I opened it and looked at the date. The note was written last year, the day after he and I met on the cliffs. Fascinated, I read Sean's words.

Memory. An image, a feeling, a smell, and sound. The past is like a cup filled with what could have been. It's the sweetest mead to drink. The more you take, the more you want as the present moves back to past. Nothing but the honeyed nectar of childhood days seems to fill the craving. The addiction of memories. Wanting only the stuff of remembrance and dreams.

I turned to see Sean standing on the side of the bed. I hadn't heard him enter the room. Embarrassment fought with guilt as I realized that I was invading the man's privacy. "I'm sorry, I shouldn't have opened this."

"I've shared far more intimidate details of my life with you than the scribbles in that book."

"Still," I persisted. "I had no right."

"Apology accepted." Sean grinned and jumped on the bed. He looked over and glanced at the open page. "I've been thinking about turning that into a song," he explained.

"It's beautiful."

"It's been a while since I felt that way. I hadn't realized how much I still held onto the past."

I nodded. "As you said before, we all carry the past with us, it seems." I wore mine like a jacket, keeping out possibilities.

"True. But I couldn't let go of Mom," he replied, sitting down on the bed.

"Have things gotten better?"

"Thanks to you and my music."

"I can't take credit for that. You took the first step to get your life back," I reminded him.

"You helped, Leah." He took my hand in his and kissed it gently.

"What am I going to do with you?" I shook my head, smiling.

"Stay up all night and watch cartoons with me," he answered.

"It was a rhetorical question," I replied, settling back down on the bed.

"And I was giving you a rhetorical answer. Now where's that remote control?" he asked.

"Over there." I pointed to the nightstand and rolled my eyes. Sean, a thirty-five-year-old man, was transformed into a ten-year-old kid at the touch of a button. I had gotten used to his changing moodiness. There were times when he was a little kid again and other times when he seemed to withdraw into himself just to hold the pain and turmoil of life away.

A couple of months into our friendship, I knew when to push and when to walk away. Everyone needed time to be alone, and Sean needed more than most. I respected it. I didn't envy his life-style, the people, the money, and the fame. Its price was too high.

Soon after we'd settled into friendship, Sean had tried to give me presents and convince me to take on a job as his publicist, something I had no experience or interest in doing. I'd politely said no to both the job and the diamond/emerald bracelet he'd bought as a token of friendship. Spoiling for a fight, Sean had turned the whole thing into a battle. I didn't call for two days, thinking to give him space. The following Saturday morning I opened the door to find Sean standing on the front steps holding a quart of chocolate chip ice cream and offering an apology.

"You're such a spoiled brat," I teased, wanting to make him smile.

"Hey. I don't get much time for the fun stuff."

"You'll have plenty in two weeks."

"No, I won't. Jon doesn't believe in vacation. The man is a machine."

Jon was one of Sean's publicists and he happened to be one of the best in the business. "What do you mean?"

"He agreed for me to go on *The View* and he didn't tell me until yesterday. I can't back out of the damn thing."

"You've done lots of interviews before," I pointed out.

"True. It's just . . ." His voice trailed off as his eyes refocused on the television screen.

"Just?" I leaned closer.

"It's four women, not to mention *the* Barbara Walters." He shuddered.

I leaned forward and buried my head in the pillow to keep from laughing. This six-foot mega star was afraid of four women. Priceless.

"I'm sure you'll do a good job," I encouraged. "Once you give them that smile of yours and throw in a couple of witty answers in that Scottish-American brogue, they'll be eating out of your hands."

"Umm," was Sean's only reply. I looked down to see his closed eyes.

"I used to be a brat," he murmured. "Everything I ever wanted, but the cancer didn't listen to my prayers."

"I can believe that you were the world's worst brat," I teased.

"You would. You know me too well. I feel so comfortable around you. You're nice to be with . . ."

"Sean, you make me sound like a favorite pair of jeans."

"Not a bad idea." He smiled with his eyes closed, then cracked open an eye. "You know what that means, don't you?"

"No." I shook my head.

"It means we fit, darling." His voice slurred with the beginnings of sleep. "Quite comfortably, if I say so myself." Before closing his eyes, he gave me a smile that could charm the girdle off a sixty-year-old nun.

I ended up cradling Sean's head in my lap. Sliding my palms under his head I used my fingertips to massage his temples with small circular motions. I watched *Tom and Jerry* until Sean's breath came evenly and the arm resting against my stomach went limp. Rubbing my fingers along the nape of his neck, I savored the feel of soft, baby-fine hair.

Looking down at Sean's sleeping face, I could barely keep from sighing. Whenever his arms wrapped around me, I was reminded of putting on a just-pressed shirt in the middle of winter. I would bury my face in the sleeve and savor the smell of lemon starch as the warm fabric settled over my bare skin.

I managed to move his head from my lap without waking him. I paused in the doorway to look back at him sprawled out on the bed asleep. Turning out the light, I quietly returned to the living room, gathered up my purse, put on my sneakers, and left the apartment like a thief in the night.

As I rode down in the empty elevator, I thought about what Mom would say if she could see me now. I laughed out loud. Truly unbelievable. The doorman didn't look all that surprised to see me leaving. Then again, I didn't think there was anything a New York City doorman hadn't seen or heard before.

Just as I'd expected, I saw Will, Sean's body-guard/driver, leaning against the back door of the black Lincoln as soon as I walked through the glass doors. I paused and then let him open the door, take my hand and lower me into the car. I'd never get used to the life Sean led, people who adored him, assistants at his beck and call.

The car pulled away and drove through the still-buzzing Times Square while I stared blankly out the window at the taxis darting through the streets. As the soothing sounds of piano music drifted through the car, I couldn't get the words I'd read in last month's entertainment magazine out of my mind.

The gossip reporter had hinted that Sean's days as a sought-after bachelor might be over. According to friends of model-turned-actress Dalia Deburgh, she hoped so.

Thirty minutes later, I walked into my dark, stuffy apartment and hit the button on the answering machine.

Saturday, 9:15 p.m.

"Lee, it's Lance. I just got back in town and wanted to hook up for dinner. Buzz me on my cell when you get this message."

Beep.

Sunday 1:32 a.m.

"Leah, Hope the concert went well. I'm going to spend the night at Nina's place. I'll see you tomorrow. Love you, Rena."

Every feeling of annoyance I felt disappeared at the sound of Rena's voice on the answering machine. That Nina could leave the hospital was good news, but the heavy weariness I heard in Rena's voice tied a knot in my stomach. All thought of sleep left to be replaced with worried anger.

Buzz me on my cell.

Like I was some dog brought to heel. Like Lance was so important. I kicked off my shoes and sat on the coach. Picking up the remote control, I flipped through channels and stopped on the Cartoon Network. Wrapping my arms around the paisley pillow, I lay down and stared at the screen. Sleep washed over me as Wile E. Coyote took yet another fall.

CHAPTER 9

When Sean left for the West Coast Sunday night, I still hadn't seen Rena since she'd left to look after Nina. I missed my cousin's solid presence, and, as much as I liked Nina, I wanted the beautiful singer to pick someone else to lean on. I was just finishing the last set of changes to a proposal when the phone buzzed.

"Leah Russell."

"I'm eighth in line for take-off and can't wait to see the last of Seattle's infamous clouds and rain," came Sean's voice over the static-filled phone line.

"You loved Seattle that much, huh?"

"Love the people, hate the godawful weather. I don't think my clothes will ever dry out."

"So where are you headed this time? Some secluded beach in the Florida Keys?" I teased.

"I'm coming your way."

"Oh. You're flying to New York?" I suppressed the small quiver of glee his announcement brought.

"With a little stopover in Chicago. I'll be landing on Friday morning. How about we hang out and have dinner?"

I played with my pen and stared blankly at the flashing appointment reminder message that scrolled across the computer screen.

"What time?"

"How about two o'clock?"

"I've got work. How about later?"

"Play hooky," he encouraged.

"You're going to get me into trouble," I responded, but my mind was automatically rescheduling my regular Friday afternoon meetings to Thursday.

"You, Ms. Leah Russell, are trouble."

I could hear the revving sound of the jet engine in the background.

"Two o'clock Friday," I agreed.

"I'll pick you up at the office."

That was all I heard before the line went dead. I hung up the phone and turned the chair around to stare out the window, down through the haze to the city below. Reaching over I switched on the headset and dialed Carol's phone number. I needed the humor and pep talk that only a sista-friend could provide. Anything to push back the memories of Sean's face as he slept.

"Saunders and Goddard, may I help you?"

"Carol Rogers, please."

"One moment while I transfer you."

"Carol speaking." Her calm voice came though the line.

"Cece. What are you doing?" I asked.

"Trying to keep from taking a gun to this laptop. The damn thing just gave me the blue screen of death and then shut off."

"Sounds bad."

"Yeah, and the tech support guy just left after thirty minutes of standing here and scratching his head like a dumbass."

"Ouch." Laugher bubbled out of my throat.

"What's up, girlfriend?" Carol asked.

"I've been robbed, girl." I put all my heart into sounding serious.

"What?" came the loud screech on the other end of the phone. I pulled the headset away from my ear.

"I've been robbed," I repeated, trying my best not to laugh.

"Where?" she asked.

"At the office."

"Did you call the police?"

"Forget the police. I need to call Johnny Cochran."

"Huh?"

"I'm suing the IRS, New York State, and New York City."

"Have you lost your mind? Why in the world are you going to sue the New York government?"

"The IRS took half my relocation bonus, New York State and City took the rest."

Carol's laugh came through the phone and set me to giggling.

"Girl, this ain't funny." I waved my pencil towards the window. "I've been robbed, hoodwinked, bamboozled, tricked."

"Hold up, Malcolm X. Do you have enough for a pair of shoes?" she asked.

"Yes," I reluctantly admitted.

"Well, that's all you need. Look on the bright side. It's more than what you had."

"I still feel like I'm working to pay the IRS."

"We all gotta pay Uncle Sam, girl . . ."

"Please," I rolled my eyes. "No uncle of mine steals."

"That is so true. Hey, love to take longer but the tech man just came back. We still on for Wednesday?"

"Yeah."

"Houston's?"

"Sounds good to me." I leaned back.

"See you."

"Bye."

I clicked off the phone and looked out the window. Back to my thoughts about Sean, back to images of a gorgeous man, images of a friend and feelings that had nothing to do with friendship and more to do with late nights.

Later that evening, I walked in the door of the apartment and started venting. "Rena, you won't believe what happened at work today. I swear the IRS is out to get me . . ." My voice trailed off into the silence of the apartment.

"Anybody home?" I shouted. The only response was the familiar thud of Simba jumping down off the windowsill.

Unstrapping my sandals, I turned to check the answering machine and saw a white envelope perched on top with my name on it.

I pulled the paper from the envelope and turned on the halogen lamp to read Rena's hastily scrawled handwriting.

Leah,

I'm taking Nina home to her parents in Bermuda. I should be back in a couple of days. I left a message for Mom and Dad telling them I was going on a quick vacation. Don't worry, everything's okay and I'll call you when I get her settled.

Love,

Rena

PS. Please don't tell anyone where I've gone. (That includes Trey!)

Sighing, I went into the kitchen and fixed a sandwich. Waiting for the microwave to finish up, I stared out the window, uneasy. Mom and Dad were leaving for their anniversary cruise in two days and Leah was missing-in-action for reasons I couldn't guess.

Don't worry, I told myself. That's about all I could seem to do.

"I am so tired of that mess," I growled, losing my smile.

Here I was after having gotten out of the office while the sun was still shining and I was mad at a talk show. Rena had gone with Nina to the Bahamas and I was missing my cousin.

"Girl, what are you talking about?" Carol asked as she took another bite of the artichoke spinach dip. The margarita had done its job and washed away all my desire to think about work. I was with my girl at Houston's and the only thing on my mind stood ten feet away.

I raised my salt-crusted glass towards the television screen. " 'Marry me or else! Baby mommas speak out.' "

"I can't believe you watch that garbage," she commented.

I raised my eyebrow as Carol took another bite. "Don't even try it. You were the one telling me about seeing your former classmate on an episode of Ricki Lake."

She patted her mouth and let out a loud laugh. "Too true. The girl used to be Ms. Thing at our school. I know it's evil, but seeing her sitting up on stage begging this no-good man to give her a ring made me feel good for a moment."

"And then . . ." I waved my hand.

Carol sighed. "Then the embarrassment sets in. I'm just tired of seeing black women degrading themselves on national television. It's gotten to the point where I'm afraid to watch anything but *Oprah*. Harold likes to watch *People's Court* sometimes."

I snorted. A couple of days after moving back to New York had been long enough to let me know that airing dirty laundry on national television had become the new African-American pastime.

Carol shook her head, sending her razor-cut bob bouncing. "I wonder about that man I married. He'll sit there and watch that stuff like it's better than the Super Bowl. I have to leave the room sometimes 'cause I get so disgusted."

I dipped the fresh-baked chip in the thick artichoke and spinach dip. "I know it must be close to impossible for these shows to find black women who aren't unmarried with three kids, on welfare, fighting with their baby's father, and sleeping with their best friend's man," I sarcastically added.

"Something you want to talk about?" Carol really looked at me. Like I'd grown a new head or something.

No, I wanted to do something. I wished I had a giant eraser and I could wipe out the image of the bitter, angry, young black woman screaming expletives at a just as messed up black man.

I finished off another chip. "Maybe being back on the East Coast is starting to mess with me."

"Girl, you haven't been here a hot minute. What's really on your mind?"

"I'm just irritated. One of the assistants broke down today. I thought it had something to do with her family. I pulled her into my office and shut the door and gave her some tissues." I sat back on the soft leather bench and crossed my legs.

"What happened?"

"She had an argument with her boyfriend. The man hadn't paid a dime of rent in the past three months. He told her last night that he was leaving her and wanted her to contribute to the cost of renting a moving truck."

"You have got to be kidding."

I took another sip of the margarita, savoring the bittersweet taste of lime on my tongue. "That's not all of it. She asked me what she should do."

"Go out have a drink and thank God his sorry ass is gone," Carol suggested.

"No, she wanted me to give her advice on how to get him back."

Carol's mouth dropped to the table and then she rolled her eyes toward the ceiling. "So that's what's got you in such a funk."

"She's about five years older than me. Lives in a nice section of Queens and is the best assistant in the whole office. This woman sat there looking into my eyes and expecting me to understand. I don't understand. The last thing I hope I'll ever do is to beg a man to stay," I proclaimed.

I shook my head and picked up my fork and knife to dig in to the entrées the waiter placed on the table.

"That's because the only man you've gone out with recently happens to be stuck on your cousin."

"True."

"By the way, what's up with Rena?"

"She had to go out of town. She should be back this Sunday."

Rena was going to have her hands full with Trey when she got back. He had called every day that she'd been gone, hoping to hear something about Rena or Nina. I smiled, thinking it was about time my cousin met someone that she couldn't wrap around her little finger.

"Leah, there's no shortage of eligible black men in New York."

"I know this . . ."

"So why haven't you taken advantage?"

My lips curled. "What makes you think I haven't?"

She raised her eyebrows. "Oh, it's like that? Do tell."

"Sorry, girlfriend. Nothing to tell . . . yet. But I'll definitely let you know if I find him."

"I just read another article asking where all the good Black men had gone. Makes me glad I got married when I did," she responded.

"I don't think there's a problem," I said after taking a bite of chicken.

"You know you're in the minority, don't you? My hairdresser almost broke her neck agreeing with the writer."

"Seriously, Carol, where have all the good black men gone? Nowhere." I waved my hand towards the bar where men milled around watching the NCAA. "I've dated them and liked them. They just weren't *him*. The one that my grandmother told me about, the one Billie Holiday raised hell about. That's why you see articles like that one. I want more, and so does everybody else. So when we black women can't find that one man to turn our world upside down and inside out, we think all the good black men have dropped off the face of the earth."

Carol nodded her head in agreement. "On to more important things. How's the food?"

The roasted chicken dripping with honey and wine was so tender I could eat it with a fork. I sampled the mashed potatoes and let out a groan. The flavor of garlic and butter made me wanna holler. One of the things I liked about New York, besides its fascinating mixture of people, was that it had the best food outside my mama's kitchen.

"All I can say is that these dishes put my cooking to shame," I confessed.

"Not to mention your cholesterol level," Carol added.

"And the waistline."

We both took large bites out of our respective mounds of mashed potatoes.

"A girl has to live a little," I chuckled.

"Shoot. With this," she waved at the food on the table, "we're living a lot."

"Remind me of how good this was when we have to do ten extra minutes on the treadmill," I laughed.

"All right. You just remember to bring that CD you bought."

"Which one?"

"The one you picked up on the corner in Chinatown."

"The studio mix?"

"Yeah . . . I don't understand a word they're saying, but the beat keeps me from thinking about the pains shooting up my legs or the fool that walked into my office this morning."

"What happened?"

"This sawed-off, baldheaded, big-lipped black man came into my office thirty minutes late for his first appointment."

"Carol . . ." I laughed, trying to sound like I was shocked.

"Leah," she waved her fork, "he strolled in with his about-to-be wife number three and she wasn't bigger than a fried fart. The girl had watermelon-sized breast implants and unbelievable blonde hair extensions."

"Your Southern roots are showing, girlfriend. Now what did he want?"

"Fool had finally picked up a clue and decided to get a prenuptial agreement."

"You are crazy," I laughed.

"No, I'm not." She shook her head while taking a sip of her drink. "That big-gold-ring-wearing man was sporting a cowboy hat. This ain't the Wild West and he sure as hell wasn't the Lone Ranger. Negro thought he was Big Pimping."

I laughed so hard tears came to my eyes and my stomach started to hurt. I laid my head down on the cool wood table and just tried to breathe.

"Miss, are you okay?" came the voice of our waitress.

"She's fine," Carol replied. "Just needs to catch her breath. Poor girl's getting old."

I fell into laughter again and almost choked. I had finished off my drink earlier so instead I sipped on the ice water.

☙

On my way home, I sat gazing out the subway car window, watching the blue tunnel lights streak by. Single, medium maintenance, independent, successful professional, well-rounded, non-money hungry, heterosexual black woman with a bachelor's degree, fluent in two languages, no kids, no debt, no obsessions, no diseases, no self-destructive behavioral patterns.

Where did I fit in? Sometimes I felt like a rare exotic animal prowling the streets of Manhattan and Brooklyn. Where was the guide to dealing with my loneliness? I opened the door to an empty apartment wondering when I would get to read *Being Black, Female, Single, and Happy for Dummies?*

CHAPTER 10

"I envy you sometimes, Leah. You're young, successful, and free."

Putting down my sandwich, I looked at Bahni in puzzlement. The last time I checked the young Indian woman was still single. She caught my puzzled look.

"I don't mean single," she explained. "You can go where you want, date who you want. You get to call all your own shots."

"You can't?" I tried to keep my surprise from showing.

Bahni smiled and pushed back her long black hair, revealing gold hoop earrings.

"My parents are in the process of looking for a husband for me. They're afraid that if I don't marry soon I'll be too old."

My appetite took a nosedive even as Bahni reached for another French fry. I took a sip of lemonade. Some things you just don't want to know. When you think you've got it bad, someone else has got it worse.

"Do you at least get to choose amongst the potential candidates?" I tried to keep my tone light. I couldn't condemn the idea of arranged marriages. Growing up in Philly had taught me to keep an open mind.

She nodded her head. "Yeah. My little sister says they're nice looking, but if I've got to spend the rest of my life with someone, good looks take a backseat to personality."

I nodded my head. "No kidding. So when is all this going to take place?" What can I say? I just had to be nosey.

"Not for another year. One of the potentials is in medical school and the other works at General Electric's Mumbai office."

"Will you stay in New York?" I was selfishly hoping she'd say yes. Bahni wasn't only a great member of the team, she brought her unique kind of cheer and graphic artistry to every project.

"I'm not sure. I want to stay. I'll be finished with my degree in May, and I'm already thinking about starting my masters. But if the one I pick doesn't want to leave India . . ." She shrugged.

I studied her face and saw the yearning in her eyes. I remembered when I spoke so indecisively about returning home, torn between complete freedom and the seductive call of home with its familiar people and places.

"I don't envy your decision."

Bahni shook her head and polished off the chicken sandwich. "I have a favor to ask."

I wiped my mouth with the napkin. "What can I do for you?"

"I know it's last minute, but the women's group I belong to is having a round table discussion tonight. We're discussing successful women in the twentieth century. I'd really love it if you could participate."

"Wow." I sat back. I'd paid my dues. I really enjoyed my job. But was I what you'd call a success? "Are you sure I'm the right person for this?"

"Of course." Bahni leaned forward. "Leah, you're one of my role models and a kick-ass mentor. You've given me excellent advice and senior management loves you. You're so together. I think that makes you the perfect person to talk with us."

"All right, enough of the snow job, I'm sold. What time and where?"

What time and where? I shook my head. I'd expected to walk into a small windowless room in the basement of an old building like the meeting rooms we had at school before I graduated and the million dollar donations started pouring in. Instead, I entered into an auditorium of sorts. Shorts-clad and suit-wearing women of all ages mingled over a table of refreshments.

"Hey, Leah. Glad you could make it." I turned to see Bahni.

"Sorry I'm late. Got pulled into a conference call."

"That's okay. Want something to drink? We're about to get started."

"Thanks. I'll just have a bottled water," I said, following her down the sloping aisle.

"So where are you sitting?"

"We," she pointed towards the students, "are sitting down here. You get to sit up there."

She pointed to the row of chairs on the raised dais. I looked back at her.

"You're kidding."

Bahni flashed me what I think she thought was a reassuring smile. "No."

"You realize I'm going to remember this when bonus discussions come up," I said, trying to keep a serious face. Her grin only got wider.

"Just think of this as an early wedding gift. My professor's giving me extra credit." She patted my shoulder.

She ushered me to the stage and I had no choice but to turn and greet the other participants before taking my seat.

After the introductions and speeches, the meeting really got started. The questions came hard and fast. What had begun as a low-key networking how-to turned into an all out bashing session against the glass ceiling, old boys networks, and white corporate America. From time to time I put in my two cents. After going at it for over an hour, the session seemed to be winding down when a young black student sporting dreadlocks Rena would have drooled over approached the microphone.

"I have a question for Ms. Russell."

I sat up straighter and waited for the question I had dreaded to hear.

"In comparison to white women, is it harder being a black woman in the workplace?"

I had paused, considering if I really wanted to answer her question, when I caught the glance of another young black woman sitting forward in her chair.

The truth came out before I could stop it. "Hell yes."

I waited for a moment until the murmurs died down. "It's subtle. Just being a woman takes all of your focus, but my mentor, a very senior black executive at a software company, opened my eyes. I could tell you about the racial discrimination black women face, but that's something that is very obvious and gets a lot of press. What doesn't, however, are the hidden time bombs.

"Let me explain. Although slavery ended well over two hundred years ago, some of its vestiges remain embedded in the corporate world. The mammy figure still follows black women. On Southern plantations, black women were expected to raise the kids, cook, and be the one person that anyone in the white household could lean on. This still holds true throughout most of corporate America. Even in leadership positions a black woman is expected to do more, be more, often on a more informal personal level.

"For example, my mentor, a woman whose academic and professional credentials are very impressive, was frequently put into situations to act as a counselor between subordinates and managers of her own and other divisions instead of being able to concentrate on the more formal tasks that she had been hired for. Her senior management expected her to take control of emotional situations rather than the business situations.

"On a more personal note, I've got to admit that balancing my formal and informal roles as a manager when senior management comes calling gets tough. I can't say for certain I'm pushed more towards the Human Resources role because of the influence of race or sex. I'm inclined to see it as a combination of both. The key is that as a black woman you have to be aware that these issues are out there. If you're not watching out you may wake up and find that the glass ceiling has enclosed you in a cage."

"Excuse me!"

Hearing the man's words, I kept right on walking. I was becoming more and more of a New Yorker every day. Loud voices no longer bothered me; the beeping of horns didn't make me want to cuss. I had more on my mind than ever after that impromptu discussion about sexism and racism in the corporate arena. I sighed. Even in the nice section of Brooklyn where I lived you still get the men who think that they have license to talk to any woman they meet.

"Excuse me? Lady." The voice and the touch of someone's hand on my shoulder stopped me.

"Get your hands off me!" I shouted as my heart jumped with fear. I clutched my purse and took two steps back as the big hand released my elbow.

"My bad. Is your name Leah Russell?"

"Why?" I asked guardedly, prepared to run at the first sign of him moving closer.

"I'm looking for Rena Mason, and I was told that you might know where she is."

"Who are you? Who gave you my name and why are you looking for Rena?" I looked up at the large black man with the Caesar haircut and thick roped gold chain.

He looked astonished at my questions and I couldn't fathom why.

"The name is Nine and everything else don't matter. All you need to do is tell me where Rena's at and I'll get outta ya way."

If he'd moved, I would have turned and run down the street, but he just stood there on the sidewalk watching me with a strange sort of pleading look on his face. I glanced at the black Lincoln Navigator double-parked on the street. The vehicle held two occupants who seemed to be studying me as intently as I looked at them.

"Rena is out of town." I looked Nine in the eye.

He sighed. "I know that. Can you tell me where she and Nina went?"

I shook my head and lied. "I don't know."

"You trying to tell me your own cousin up and left without telling you where she went?"

"She left in a hurry."

I watched as all his earlier confidence seemed to vanish, replaced by fear. "Look, Ms. Russell. I don't mean to cause you any trouble. I just need to talk to Nina. Tell her I'm sorry. I was just drinkin'. I didn't know," he said hurriedly.

"I'm sorry but I really can't help you." I'd given my word to Rena and nothing could make me break it.

His shoulders slumped and he turned away. I watched as Nine got into the passenger side of the

Navigator and the car drove away. The fear I'd seen in the boy's eyes stayed with me as I entered the apartment. Shaking off the incident, I closed the door, making sure to turn the deadbolt. Simba lay on the windowsill, and, as I bent down to take off my shoes, I heard a thump and the pitter-patter of feet on the floor.

The cat brushed himself across my legs and unthinking I scooped him up into my arms and carried him over to the sofa. I needed to hold something, feel something. The fear in Nine's eyes as I mentioned Rena's quick departure bothered me. Not even the thought of Rena's coming home would erase the blue/black bruise I knew I'd see on my arm in the morning.

Even after I'd showered and changed into my pajamas that night, I still had knots in my stomach. All I could think about were the challenges I'd faced getting through school and paying my dues as the only black woman in a division of two hundred. As I looked into the mirror while brushing my teeth, I couldn't see my own reflection. Instead, I saw the room filled with students. I saw their eyes as they watched me. I could see the effect of my answers wash over their faces and I wanted to take that picture they had of me, the one where I stood alone at the top of the world with my legs wide planted across the North Pole. I wanted to take that image, that Strong Black Woman image, and light a match under it. See that old lie, the black woman's honorary title, burn.

I curled up in the bed with their awed faces in my mind. The truth swirled like bitter wine in my stomach.

It was all a lie. Just another mask I wore during the day and took off the moment I set foot in the apartment. I didn't want to be strong. I didn't want to be admired by those women sitting and drinking their bottles of Evian while dreaming of conquering the business world.

The truth was that I wanted to be loved. To hell with fighting for a place in corporate America. I'd rather have a wedding ring on my left hand. SBW: Successful Black Woman. More like Selfish Black Woman. I wanted it all. The great husband, the good kids, the nice house, and Disney World vacations. I wanted all the love, care, comfort, companionship, security, and happiness I could get out of life. I wanted that special someone to take care of me, love me, protect me, fight for me. I wondered how much of my soul I'd have to sacrifice to get it.

I looked at Sean in puzzlement as the car came to a stop in front of the Metropolitan Museum of Art. I was playing hooky for this? Although I loved the idea of spending time wandering through art-filled corridors with Sean, the last place I wanted to be on a beautiful Friday afternoon was a building packed full of tourists, teenagers, and elementary school kids.

"The museum?" I asked. We'd been to such places before, but I'd never seen Sean so excited.

"Trust me." He held out his hand and I let him assist me out of the car. The smell of popcorn rose on the breeze from the stand on the sidewalk. The warmth of the sun on my skin was a pleasant shock after the artificial air conditioning of the car.

Sean held my hand as we entered the building and I watched as he flashed a card at the entrance attendant. As we headed towards the back of the museum through the Egyptian collection, I heard the first note of music. The echo of drums filled the space. I blindly followed Sean as we entered the Sackler Wing. The large, open courtyard with a glass wall looking out over Central Park was a beautiful room, but today it was breathtaking.

I was entranced. All I could do was gaze around the open space and windowed courtyard. Sunlight poured through tall windows, cascading over the Temple of Dendur. The small Egyptian temple had been donated to the Metropolitan Museum back in the 1960s. Through high arched windows I saw trees and people strolling through the park. I took a deep breath and the lush sweet smell of orchids filled my nostrils. I shook my head and looked over at the front of the temple. All I could see was the blur of moving dancers. Around me people had begun to take their seats.

"The show just started. Why don't we take a seat?" Sean suggested.

I settled down beside him on the cool metal chairs and watched the white-clothed dancers weave amongst the flower arrangements. The men and women moved with such a light grace that they seemed to skate across the floor. Intricate islands of orchids and vines had been set up around the tall palm trees. I leaned against Sean and settled in with his arm resting behind my chair. I was so into the dancing that it wasn't until near the end I noticed the rhythmic movement of Sean's fingers on my shoulders.

"Did you like it?" Sean's voice startled me from my reverie. I had been so caught up in the music and the dance I didn't realize that it was over. We stood up and joined the rest of the audience in clapping. As people milled out, Sean and I stood near the side. I stretched, hoping to wake up my numb behind as he adjusted his baseball cap.

"Can we go up to the temple and look at the flowers?" I asked.

He smiled and grabbed my hand. "I don't see why not."

"How did you find out about this event?"

"My banker's with Merrill Lynch. I was talking to Jim this morning and he mentioned that they were sponsoring this little event and I thought you'd be interested."

"You're right. This was great."

"It's not over yet."

I looked at him in surprise, wondering what he meant by that comment. Before I could ask I lost my train of thought to the aroma and sight of the flower displays.

We walked past flowers of every color and size. The beautiful multi-colored orchids were displayed in a wonderful array of pink, green, raspberry, yellow and orange petals nestled in green oval leaves. Each of the different orchids seemed to complement the other in color and fragrance. We paused and stared at exotic rich purple, maroon and blue blooms with banded or speckled green leaves.

We ended up finishing our walk outside in the park. Sean stopped and leaned against a tree. I stood next to him enjoying the breeze. The moment reminded me of Los Angeles.

In the fall when Exile was taking a break from playing, Sean and I drove to California parks and sat out under trees and watched the kids playing. He'd urge me to join in the fun and play Frisbee. Sometimes we would spend the afternoon playing soccer.

"Did I tell you I bought a new car?"

"No, what'd you get?" I inquired, not surprised one bit.

"It's going to be a charcoal gray BMW, four-door, but it looks sporty."

"Going to be?" I asked, puzzled. Sean was one for instant gratification, and with his bank account he could afford it.

"I haven't really seen it yet. I ordered it off the Internet last night."

"You ordered your car online? Let me guess, the dealership was closed?"

"Well, yes, but I was looking at the BMW website and they have this service so that I could have the car custom built. I picked out the insides and everything," he said with a child-like glee.

I sighed, but couldn't help smiling. "You have got to be kidding."

"No, I'm not. I can go online and check on the status. They even emailed me a picture."

"Along with a fat bill, of course."

"Would you believe me if I said I got a discount?" He grinned.

"Hmmm . . . No," I teased.

"Would it make you feel better to know that 10 percent of the proceeds from Exile's tour is going to be donated to the Cancer Society?"

"You're a wonderful guy, Sean." I turned and gave him a big hug. He'd managed to take my mind completely off my problems.

I watched his nose wrinkle as though he smelled something fishy and then a light blush spread to his cheeks. "I'm not a saint, Leah," he said, holding me close.

"I know." I smiled up at him, winking devilishly through my sunglasses. "You're selfish and you're a bully."

"Who told you that?" he asked.

"Fox." Fox was Exile's lead bassist. The six-foot-five musician had the build of an ex-bodybuilder and a heart of gold.

"And you believed him?" Sean rested his hands on my shoulders and looked into my eyes. I could see his lips twitching, trying to resist the urge to laugh.

"I believe that you took the man's last pint of Guinness."

"So he told you about that, huh? I like getting what I want. You can't blame a man for taking the last can of beer."

"Yes, I can."

"I'm wounded."

"No, you're not."

He laughed and grabbed my hand, pulling me behind him as a teenager on roller blades whizzed by.

"That was close," I commented.

"Yes, it was. I don't know about you but I'm kinda hungry."

"I could use a bite to eat. Got any ideas?"

"As a matter of fact, I do." He looked at his watch.

"You're wearing it," I exclaimed excitedly.

He glanced up at me, surprised, and then held the watch up to show me. "I always wear it."

"I'm just surprised you haven't lost it yet."

"Not a chance. You know me so well that it's hard to remember a time when you weren't in my life."

I'd given the G-Shock watch to Sean as a joke. He'd somehow managed to lose or misplace two Rolexes in the space of two months. I'd seen the black rubber digital watch in the mall while I was shopping one afternoon and impulsively bought it, thinking that there was no way Sean could misplace something that large.

I blushed slightly and shook my head. "You must have one short memory then," I joked.

"Hmmm, I remember the look on your face when I dropped by your place six months ago. The mud masks you and Rena were wearing were unforgettable." His eyes widened in a look of pure terror. "I don't think I've ever seen you so surprised," he said, smirking.

"Well, I don't think I've ever seen you laugh so hard," I commented.

"I almost choked to death."

"Serves you right for just dropping in." I pinched him on the arm and he shook his head. I couldn't do anything but laugh as Sean put his arm around my shoulders and turned to walk back towards the waiting car.

"I almost walked by the place the first time I was meeting some co-workers for dinner and drinks last month." I stepped in front of Sean as he held the door open.

The host, who was dressed in a trademark indigo blue button-down dress shirt, greeted us warmly at the front door of the upscale restaurant. The after-work crowd had yet to settle into the high cushioned burgundy chairs around the bar. The smell of roasting meat drifted through the brick-lined room, circulated by black and gold ceiling fans.

"You told me once that this was one of your favorite restaurants," Sean said as he placed his hand on my lower back and politely guided me towards the back of the restaurant.

I smiled, more than a little surprised he remembered. The Shark Bar, a hideaway nestled between the busy streets of Amsterdam and Broadway, was a place that Broadway actors, sports stars and media-weary entertainers stopped in for a quiet meal. I saw recognition and curiosity on the faces of some of the patrons as Sean and I walked up the stairs and entered the dining area. Its yellow walls and low lighting provided an intimate setting.

"Come here often?" Sean asked as we settled down into the back booth.

"This is my third time,"

"It's nice. I like it."

"Not too down-to-earth for you?" I teased.

"You know me better than that," he chided while flipping a lock of hair out of his eyes.

I picked up my water glass as my mouth suddenly went dry. Sean was staring at me. I looked into his eyes and they were the same dark green, but different. The warm affection reflected there made my breath catch in my throat. Picking up the leather-bound menu, I stared blankly at the menu choices, feeling somehow saddened. Sean's look wasn't for me.

I concentrated on other things after the waiter came to take our order, and a mutual silence fell over our table. That was the thing between us. Sometimes we didn't need words. The silence seemed to hold all our thoughts and reflections. There had been many evenings when we sat for hours by Sean's pool without saying a word. We would both just gaze at the rippling water and breathe. Some Sundays Sean would just sit with a pen and pad furiously writing while I sat in a reclining chair sipping lemonade and typing away on my laptop.

I never felt as though I had to say something witty or fill the time we spent together with my problems or lack thereof. So I sat back and took in the ambiance of the moment. The smooth rhythms of jazz seemed to delicately cover the clatter and tinkling of glasses and silverware, the murmur of voices. The corner booth we sat in was shaded by pulled back plum velvet curtains.

When we left the crowded restaurant after dinner, a light summer rain had just begun to fall. Sean and I paused, looking at one another, before we jumped into the waiting car. I could tell that he was remembering one of our nights out in L.A.

I'd never thought of rain as something beautiful until I met Sean. One night after too many memories, laughter, and food, we walked down a small avenue in L.A. huddled together under my umbrella looking for his car.

"Do you see it, Leah?"

I looked towards Sean. The childlike wonder in his voice caught and held my attention. He was referring to the rain. I rolled my eyes, thinking that only a white person could think that the rain was a beautiful thing. Rain was rain, and, to this sista who had just got her hair done two days before, it was the ultimate enemy. I thought of unexpected showers as Mother Nature's way of reminding black women who was really in charge.

I turned and followed his gaze, looking towards the florescent streetlight. My sarcastic comments died in my throat before they could pass through my lips. The winds were light that night and the warm rain came down straight like a curtain of stringed teardrops. The beeping of a car horn broke the spell, but just for a second I had seen it: a glimpse into Sean's soul. The memory would live on every time I saw a streetlight in the rain.

CHAPTER 11

When the phone rang the next morning, I picked it up knowing I'd hear Rena's voice on the other line.

"Leah, it's Lance."

"What's up?" My half-drowsy disappointed tone wasn't anywhere near welcoming. I wanted some answers only my absentee cousin could provide, not aggravation from the previous love of my life.

His voice was hurried. "I got a situation."

"Okay," I said, slowly falling back into the habit of caring about his well being. "What is it?"

"Lee, I know this is last minute, but I need you to come over to my place."

I heard the sounds of someone screaming in the background and sat up in the bed. "What was that, Lance?"

"That would be the situation," he said hurriedly. "Look Lee, you have more than enough cause to hang up, but I really need your help. Can you come over to my place?"

I let out a sigh, then sat up in the bed. "What's the address?"

I pulled a sheet of paper and a pen out of the night-stand drawer. It took me twenty minutes to shower and get dressed. The drive into the city would have normally taken over an hour, but this rainy morning the streets were empty of the usual lines of taxicabs driving over the Brooklyn Bridge.

I was at Lance's high-rise apartment in under an hour and a half. I had to drive around the area for a good fifteen minutes before finding a parking space. I strolled though the glass doors that were held open by the white-gloved doorman and made my way towards the front desk.

"I'm here to see Lance Phillips."

"Your name, please?" he asked.

"Leah Russell."

"One moment, Ms. Russell."

The gray-haired security officer picked up the phone, and I glanced around the entry foyer while I waited. The place reeked of new money and Wall Street arrogance. The marble floors covered with dark colored rugs softened the otherwise overwhelming lobby. Freshly cut flowers spilled out of delicate Ming vases, while crystal chandeliers graced the high ceiling.

"You may go up, Ms. Russell. Please take the elevator to your left. Mr. Phillips resides on the twenty-fifth floor, apartment 2502."

I nervously waited as the elevator shot up to Lance's floor. When the doors opened onto the wide carpet-lined hallway of the twenty-fifth floor, I heard the sound of a baby wailing. My finger had barely pressed the doorbell to apartment 2502 when the door opened. Lance looked like hell. His bloodshot eyes, ashy complexion and overall disheveled appearance shocked me.

"Come in," he said eagerly, stepping aside and practically pulling me inside.

I stepped into the condo and scanned the room as Lance closed the door behind me. The place could have been declared a national disaster. The luxury condominium that I knew he had to be paying at least a couple of grand a month for was a mess. I couldn't see the floor through the litter of Chinese take-out boxes and it stunk to high heaven. The burgundy-colored leather sofa was covered with clothes, papers, books, and dry cleaner bags.

"Lance, what's that smell?" I fought the urge to cover my nose.

"I haven't been able to take out the garbage." If Lance hadn't taken that moment to look as though he wanted to sink though the floor with shame, I would have turned around and walked out.

Just then the sound of a baby crying filled the apartment. I turned and looked at him. His hand was over his eyes as he impatiently rubbed his temples.

"He's been like that since I found him last night," he said.

"Found him?" I repeated.

I followed Lance back into the bedroom. It looked like the rest of the apartment except that in the middle of the bed, on top of the *New York Times* front page, a little baby lay flailing his arms. I fought the urge to throw up as the smell of baby poop permeated the room. I took a step closer to the bed and stared down at the little baby boy. Lance's spitting image lay looking back up at me.

"Congratulations. What's his name?"

"Michael."

"Where's Michael's mother?" I knew that there wasn't a woman in her right mind that would be crazy enough to leave her baby with this man. Lance was the last person in the world that I'd trust to baby sit.

He twisted his face into a grimace. "I don't know where she is. We hooked up for the weekend at the end of last summer and she just disappeared. All I know is that when I opened the door this morning, he was there in a stroller. By the time I got downstairs, she was long gone. All I had was this baby, a suitcase, birth certificate, and a damn note."

I moved towards the bed and gingerly began pulling back the elastic straps that held the soiled diaper around his tiny waist. Concentrate on the problem, I kept telling myself. "Where are the diapers?"

"In the bag."

I rolled my eyes. "Make yourself useful. Get me a diaper and come over here."

Lance handed me the Pamper as if holding a bomb. "Bring over the wipes, too."

He dropped the carton by my side and then turned to move away. I grabbed his shirtsleeve and held it tight in my fist. "Don't you dare move!" I ordered. "This is your mess and you're going to help me clean it up."

"Men in my family don't change diapers," he said.

"Well, the men in my family don't have babies out of wedlock," I snapped back.

I was holding on to my sanity by the skin of my teeth. Of all the things I'd expected of my friend, this was the last. His marriage to Sherrie: big mistake. But who can hold a grudge when a man gets suckered in by a pretty face? But a one-night stand with a woman who abandoned her son in a hallway? My respect for him all but disappeared.

"What do you need me to do?"

"Take responsibility," I answered sarcastically. I paused, took the baby's legs, and gently lifted his rear end out of the soiled diaper. "Now wipe it all off."

"I think I'm going to be sick," he groaned.

"No, you're not. Just start wiping. Hold your breath if you have to."

It took us ten minutes to get Michael clean, dry, dusted and Pampered. After we were finished, he just lay there, his little round face wrinkled with smiles, gurgling and kicking his tiny feet. I reached down and picked up the tiny bundle and inhaled the sweet scent of baby powder, only to grimace as his hands grabbed hold of my hair. I turned to see Lance bagging up the diaper and the newspapers that had been strewn across the bed.

"Here." I leaned towards Lance, ready to transfer little Michael into his arms.

"That's okay. He looks really comfortable right where he is," he responded.

"Lance, this is your son. It's about time you got used to holding him."

He sighed and reached out. Little Michael seemed to recognize the other half of his genes, because his chubby arms reached for his father.

"What am I gonna do?" he complained.

"Be a father?" I joked. "Call your Mom?" I could imagine what Mrs. Phillips would have to say about this mess.

"Did that this morning. Do you know how hard it is to get into contact with someone on a cruise ship? I offered to buy her and Dad round-trip tickets home from the next port, and an outside cabin with balcony on any cruise they wanted if they helped me out. Mom blessed the hell out me and hung up."

"You really planned to drop your own child on your parents' doorstep?" I stared at him as if he had crawled out from under a slimy rock.

"Don't look at me like that, Lee. You've seen my place and you know a consultant's life is either on the road or on a plane. There's no way I can make it as a single parent."

"You're telling me this why?"

"I have to be in San Francisco on Monday for a company meeting."

"Yes and . . ." I waited for the shoe to drop.

"Can you keep Michael for me?"

I shook my head and took a deep breath as I watched the baby move his little neck to get a closer look at Lance's watch. I almost wanted to say 'yes' just because I couldn't condemn anyone, much less a baby, to the living conditions in the place. Lance's look of serene confidence stopped me cold.

"No."

The expression of complete shock on his face had the little girl in my head cackling with glee. His expression looked like mine the day I found out that he was marrying Sherrie.

"Lee, come on now," he began. "You can't leave a brotha hanging. I don't know anything about taking care of a kid."

"Then you might want to do what all consultants do: learn. And I suggest you start taking notes, because I can't help you with this one, Lance."

"Can't or won't?" he shot back.

"Both."

Letting the obsessive-compulsive side of me out, I turned and automatically started picking up the clothes lying on the floor. I balled them up and put them in the white laundry bag that had been tossed over the chair.

"Lee, it'll only be until I find Christine."

"At least you remember her name," I snorted. I walked out of the bedroom and began to pick up things in the living room. I put myself on autopilot. Moving distracted me from letting go of the anger that I had buried inside. It was the same anger that had eaten at me since that night in Sherrie's apartment.

"I was still hurting from the divorce, Lee. I met her the day the divorce was finalized. I was drinking, and she and I just connected. I was lonely and she was there and open and honest. I thought—"

"Lance, stop right there." I shook my head. "You didn't think. If you had we wouldn't be having this conversation and little Michael wouldn't be trying to eat your fingers. Have you fed the baby?"

"I tried this morning and he didn't want it."

"What time this morning?"

"About nine o'clock."

I looked at my watch and sighed: one o'clock.

"He's hungry. Come with me to the kitchen and I'll show you how to make his formula."

"Look at that, Michael," he cooed. "Auntie Leah's such a natural. She won't let anything bad happen to you, like leaving you alone with Daddy."

"Don't try it, Lance. No games, no manipulation, or I walk out that door." It was an empty threat, but the anger I injected into my voice made it believable.

"Okay."

I dug though the baby bag and pulled out a can of formula. It only took me three minutes to mix it properly and pour it into the small pot.

"You're going to need more of his formula," I pointed out after pulling out three extra cans.

"Can I order it online?" he asked.

I gritted my teeth at his dumb question. Can I order it online? What world was he living in? Not mine.

"No. I'll write you out a list of things to buy. The supermarket down the street should be stocked with baby supplies. You're going to need more Pampers, wipes, bottles, disposable inserts and some snacks."

I paused, giving Lance time to enter the grocery list into his PDA. I just shook my head and turned back to pouring water into the pot and setting it on the stove. "You have to make sure that everything's clean. Michael's immune system isn't as developed as ours. He'll pick up colds and viruses more easily. Put his bottles in boiling water to sterilize them before filling them with formula. If you pick up the disposable inserts, you won't have to sterilize the bottles every time you prepare one."

By the time I finished giving Lance notes on preparing a bottle and formula, Michael was ready to eat. His whimpers had turned to cries before the bottle cooled enough for him to drink. I sat Lance down on the coach and showed him how to hold Michael slightly elevated so that he wouldn't choke.

"Now give him the bottle."

"Wow," Lance said as the baby started sucking hard on the plastic nipple. "Guess he was kind of hungry."

I smiled. "When he starts to slow down, take away the bottle, place him over your shoulder and gently pat his back so he can burp."

I went to the hallway closet and pulled out a monogrammed Polo hand towel. I walked behind the coach and placed the towel over Lance's shoulder.

"Babies have a tendency to spit up after they eat, so I suggest you keep a towel with you at all times. If you forget to burp him he'll get gas, and you don't want a baby with gas. Trust me when I say that he'll be miserable and he'll make you miserable, too."

"Where did you learn all this stuff, Lee?"

"From the Discovery Channel," I said sarcastically. "I learned from helping out in Vacation Bible School while you were too busy trying to hide from Mrs. Rigley."

His lips turned in a tired smile and I looked at him closely. A sob welled up in my chest at the sight of him holding the small squirming bundle. We'd played house in the middle of his parents' den. I'd fix him dinner, hold my little Raggedy Anne doll, and pretend we were married and living in a big house with a white picket fence.

In my imagination, Lance would come home from a long hard day in the office and Max, the poodle I'd always wanted, would greet him at the door with slippers while I stood next to the kitchen table looking cute in my designer apron and sexy high-heeled shoes.

"I'm sorry, Lee. God, I've made such a mess of my life. I guess I haven't been thinking. I wish . . ."

All I needed was another shoulda, woulda, coulda session. The sight of Lance holding the little boy in his arms was one more nail in the coffin of my dreams. I had to cut this off quickly, so I lifted my hand and gestured for him stop.

"Lance, before you start crying a river . . ." Like the Mississippi I felt welling up behind my eyes. "You've been given a precious gift. Don't mess it up by blaming yourself."

He hugged Michael closer to his chest and looked down at the little bundle whose eyes were already half-closed in slumber. "What am I going to tell my boss?"

"The truth."

He rubbed his head and sighed. "Man, they'll never believe it."

"Give it a try."

"How am I going to keep him? He's too young for pre-school, right?"

I just stared at the fool and kept my mouth shut.

"Right," he sighed. "I guess I could request a leave of absence."

"Let me help you out. There's this wonderful thing called paternity leave, and I think that you can qualify for it given your extenuating circumstances." My voice was laced with sarcasm.

"How much time do I get?" he asked, beginning to look a little more alert.

"A month, I think."

"One month. That's a lot of time."

"Trust me, it'll pass quickly. Now, raise him up a little and gently pat him on the back."

Lance gave me a look filled with uncertainty, and I couldn't help smiling. "You can do it. He won't break, but he will cry."

When Michael let out a loud burp, the grin that spread across Lance's face stretched from the Bronx to Staten Island. You would have thought the man had just scored the winning touchdown in the Super Bowl.

"Now why don't you lay Michael down on the bed and put some pillows around him in case he rolls over."

"Do I lay him on his back or on his stomach?"

"Put him on his stomach so he won't choke in case he spits up again."

"Then what do I do?" he asked.

I groaned. "First, take out the garbage and get a maid."

"I've already got one. She comes on Monday."

"Then you need to extend the contract to three days a week. Before all that, you need to go down the street, get baby supplies and food. There's nothing but beer, mold and frozen French fries in your refrigerator, Lance.

You're a father now. I think it's time you started living like one."

After he'd gone I started cleaning the apartment. I thought about how easily those earlier words had rolled off my tongue. *You're a father now.* I wanted more than anything to just watch little Michael sleep, but I walked out of that bedroom and started cleaning. I'd finished with the living room by the time Lance unlocked the front door. I watched as he came in followed by two delivery boys with bags of groceries.

"Did you buy the whole store?" I asked while helping him put the groceries away.

"Nope, but I got enough bonus points to pick up an eight-person gourmet meal for Thanksgiving," Lance boasted.

I just looked around the bag-littered kitchen floor and fought to keep the hysterical laugh in my throat.

We took our time in the quiet kitchen. I threw away the expired boxes of Frosted Flakes and filled the empty shelves with canned goods. After I finished putting the last cans of spinach and green peas in the cabinet, I felt Lance's hand on my shoulder. I allowed him to pull me into his arms and I was enveloped with his scent of talcum powder and cologne.

I finally saw Lance not as the boy he had been but the man he'd become and I could have slapped myself. All that time spent waiting, hoping, dreaming for a person who only existed in my memories. I'd thought I'd always want to be in his arms, but at that moment it wasn't

Lance's arms I wanted wrapped around me. I wanted Sean, and that knowledge washed over me like a bucket of ice-cold water. History just kept repeating itself. Here I was again wishing for a man I could only have in daydreams and fantasies, wanting to have somebody else's arms to catch me instead of my own.

CHAPTER 12

I woke up Sunday morning with a runny nose, red eyes, and a headache. The wonderful day I'd spent with Sean seemed a decade ago. I could barely remember the smell of the orchids and the perfect day Sean and I had shared. Turning over and getting out of bed was the hardest thing in the world.

I'd have lain there all day with the blinds closed and the sheet pulled up to my neck if Simba hadn't started his meowing. Damned cat sounded like he hadn't had a meal in weeks. I knew that if I didn't get up and pour him a bowl of his veterinarian-prescribed kitty food, the Himalayan next door would join in the yowling and then there'd be hell to pay for disturbing the Sunday morning peace.

I wanted to pick up the phone and talk to my mother even though I knew what she'd say. "You need to have your behind in church and not in the bed. Your father and I didn't raise no heathens."

But she and Pop were lying on lounge chairs in the Caribbean. I knew they'd be partying all night and playing shuffleboard in the morning before hopping off the cruise ship for a day filled with shopping and guided tours.

"Got a problem. Talk to the Lord." Mom's words echoed in my head. I'd talked to the Lord all last night.

My tears and sobs sent out a plea for guidance or a little peace from the haunting specter of being alone for the rest of my life. Everybody except me seemed to have someone.

One of the things I loved best about my job was the ability to work from home. I'd just finished sketching out a new web page design when the clock struck five. The muted sound of children playing drifted through the open windows. The hard rain last night had washed away the humidity and pollen. Looking down at the smooth interface and well-positioned web bar, I smiled. All it needed now was content and color. By the time the web designers finished with it, the homepage would practically jump off the screen.

I was just clearing the table when the doorbell rang. Sighing, I pushed the chair back and stood up. The last thing I needed was company. Rounding the table, I walked through the living room, undid the bolt, and opened the door. Sean stood there wearing an old pair of jeans and a white tee shirt.

"I come bearing gifts," he announced, holding up two plastic bags.

"What kind of gifts?" I asked, trying not to smile.

"I bring you Singapore noodles and white chocolate raspberry ice cream."

"Okay, you can come in." I stepped aside, waving him into the room. I followed Sean into the kitchen and watched as he put the ice cream into the freezer.

I pulled out two glasses and filled them with ice cubes and sweet tea. "So what's the occasion?" I asked after we both sat down at the table and started eating.

"Rena called me."

My grasp loosened on the chopsticks and I dropped a baby shrimp.

"She told me you sounded a little down on the phone when she talked to you earlier this morning."

"I'm fine," I denied.

"Really?" he questioned.

"No," I replied honestly.

"What's wrong?"

"Nothing, now that you're here," I answered, not really wanting to get into to it.

"Don't want to talk about it, Leah?"

"Not really. Maybe later," I suggested, taking a sip of tea and hoping that later would never come.

An hour later, after filling myself with noodles and ice cream, I almost felt like myself again.

"What's that?" Sean asked as he came back into my bedroom. I stopped in the process of putting my latest reading club selection back on the bookshelf.

"Nothing." I turned, holding the book behind my back.

"Okay." He smiled and took three steps closer to me.

"Everything all right with the group?" I asked about the phone call he'd just taken from Mike, his manager.

"Yep," he replied in an offhand manner. Before I could ask another question, his arm snaked behind mine and grabbed my book.

"Give it back." I tried to keep the humiliated panic out of my voice.

I cringed as he opened the book to where my bookmark lay and started to read. *"Women are like undiscovered countries to a man. Men want to be explorers. A woman must always be a mystery on the horizon, an idea unknown that whispers to him of places unseen and treasures not yet unearthed. He must take care to travel in her world for he knows not where the journey leads, forest or desert, hostile or welcoming. As he attempts to draw her, put ink to paper and map her hills, rivers and valleys, she must always remember to keep a part of herself distant. Give no aid for he must be a man, strong and independent so that he might continue on his journey, ever thoughtful and intrigued no matter what trials and tribulations might fall upon his path . . ."*

My cheeks burned. "Great. You can read. Now may I have my book back?"

Grinning, Sean shook his head. "You don't need this. You're a beautiful, self-assured, intelligent, overall wonderful woman."

He held on to the book and I just gave up and headed for the door. "I'm thirsty." I tossed over my shoulder. "Would you like some more iced tea?"

"That would be good. Thanks."

I watched as he made himself comfortable in my chair and fought the urge to smack him as he continued reading.

I walked back into my bedroom with the glasses just as he was finishing a conversation on his cell phone.

I handed him the tea. Sean set the book on the nearby bookcase shelf and looked at me. His green eyes were serious.

"Leah, why don't you let me get close to you?"

I almost tripped. Where the hell had that come from? I gingerly took my seat on the edge of the bed. I could feel a headache beginning to start in the middle of my forehead. The last thing I needed was for Sean to start asking questions I didn't want to answer.

I gave him a sideways glance. "Sean, we're best friends. We couldn't be any closer without being joined at the hip."

"That's not what I meant," he said.

I stood up to place the glass on the nightstand and picked up Sean's toy.

"New cell phone? Does this one let you access the Internet?"

Sean's last cell had been an all-black flip. This one was shiny silver. Sean had spent almost an hour trying to convince me to let him buy me one of the things. I didn't want a leash. Pretty soon I would be required to carry one because of my job. But until they tied me down and strapped me with the damn thing, I'd be free.

I turned to see him standing two feet from me and I automatically backed up a step.

"See," he said.

"What?"

"You just moved away."

"Are you having some kind of male PMS you need to tell me about?"

"No, just proving a point." He ran his fingers through his hair. "It's like there's a line in the sand between us and when I step forward, you pull back and draw another."

"Not true." I picked up the glass of iced tea and took a sip to moisten my suddenly dry throat.

"The only time that you come close is when I need you," he said.

"You've been spending too much time watching *Tom and Jerry*. I'm not drawing any lines in the sand." To prove it I took a step forward while looking him dead in the eyes.

"Then why are you so nervous?"

"Nervous?" I licked my lips.

"Your glass is shaking."

I looked down at my right hand. Damned if the glass wasn't trembling. I put it on the table and wiped a cold wet palm against my pants leg.

"I'm sorry, Sean. It's not you. Rena's going through some things and I'm worried about her."

It was a half-truth. Her voice had sounded tired and weary in the message on the answering machine. The trip to the Bahamas wasn't going well and I didn't have a clue as to why. Then there was Lance. I kept seeing baby Michael asleep in his arms.

Still, that was only a tiny fraction of my real issues. The full truth was that the bond I had with Sean, the one created a year ago while sitting on a lonely cliff overlooking the ocean, had grown strong. The deep friend-ship had become something that I depended on, couldn't see myself living without. That I felt more for Sean than anything I ever imagined with Lance scared me to death.

The touch of Sean's fingers on my shoulders brought me out of my reverie.

"Hey." He spoke softly as he cradled my chin. "Rena'll be fine. She's a fighter, remember? Now why don't you lie down before you collapse?"

"Sean you're my guest . . ." I protested.

"Leah, don't you think it's time that you let me help you? That's what friends are for, remember?" His voice held a hint of annoyance. "Do you want to talk about it?" he asked.

I shook my head and watched as he bent down and unstrapped my sandals. As I sat on the bed, the little devil in my head started pounding harder. Thoughts of Rena, Lance, and Nine's unexpected visit swirled through my mind like a tornado.

"Lie down on your stomach and close your eyes," he ordered.

I looked into his green eyes and saw concern staring back at me.

The pounding in my head allowed for no quick comeback. I just did as he asked. I felt the bed move and then the hard warmth of his hands as they eased under my shirt and settled over my shoulders.

"Take deep breaths." Sean's voice had softened to a mere whisper.

I felt his fingers moving slowly over my muscles. They pushed gently inward, upward, and outward in fluid motions. So much for the Strong Black Woman, I thought sleepily, feeling the tension in my neck dissipate.

As I lay with my face cushioned in the pillows, I felt like a lost child. Everything seemed to be spinning out of control and I couldn't handle it. I buried my face deeper into the pillow as Sean's hands worked their brand of magic.

The sound of the ocean echoed in my ears as Sean sang a soft lullaby. His fingers, like waves, crested and rose, back and forth on my back. As I felt Simba's furry bulk settle at my feet, I let go of everything, following Sean's voice as it drew me gently into sleep.

I dreamed I was hearing one of Pop's old LP records skipping in my ear. I moved in my dream, intending to find the player and turn it off. Instead, I woke up to a heartbeat that wasn't mine and thought I was dreaming. The chest moved up and down slowly and the warmth of the arm around my waist felt solid, but I knew Sean wasn't really there. Instead, I took a deep breath and told myself it was just a dream. Then I looked up into those green eyes and watched mesmerized as his lips lowered to kiss mine. I couldn't move.

Sean kissed like a man drowning. Thirsty, smooth, long, and sweet. His fingers brushed against my neck and settled upon my cheek as my hands rested on his chest.

As he caressed me, I got lost in his kiss. Until the ringing of a phone banished the cloud of sleep from my mind. I pulled back and closed my eyes in embarrassment, but the chirping of the phone continued.

"You should answer that," I pointed out.

I watched as Sean turned and grabbed the phone off the nightstand. I had scooted over, intending to leave the room when his fingers curled around my arm.

"Stay, darling." His voice was still husky with sleep and something I wouldn't allow myself to recognize.

"What's up, Marc?" he said into the phone.

"Yeah, it's five-thirty? What's the problem?"

I sat cross-legged on the bed looking everywhere but at the man at my side.

"All right. Stop yelling. I'll be downstairs in a minute. Yeah, call them and tell them I'll be late."

The sound of the phone snapping closed drew my attention away from the sight of the curtains fluttering in a light draft.

"Leah," he said.

"Interview?" I asked and watched Sean nod. "You're going to be late."

"We need to talk."

"Later." I faked a yawn. "I'm going back to sleep and you're going to go make some people very happy."

I smiled at him, making a show of lying down and closing my eyes.

"You have to see me out."

"You are too old to be getting lost from my bedroom to the front door."

"You have to lock the door, Leah. This is New York, you know."

I rolled my eyes and got out of bed, all the while watching Sean as he bent over to put on his shoes. Even in the twilight of the room, I could clearly see his tousled hair and shadowed jaw. It should be against the law for a man to look good at that time of the morning.

I followed him to the front and stood back as he unlocked the door and opened it.

"I'll call you later," Sean said.

I nodded my head and plastered a smile on my face. "Good luck." I looked up in time to see a strange look cross his face as he looked at me. I could just imagine what he saw. I was not a morning person and I'd never be one of those people who could roll out the bed looking fabulous.

"Take care." Sean reached out and held my cheek gently before turning away.

I shut the door behind him and leaned against it with my eyes closed. I took a deep breath and looked up to see Rena standing in the hallway wearing a robe and a wicked grin on her face.

"Well, well. Looks like somebody had a man in their bed last night . . ."

I took another deep breath and prepared to explain. Then I caught sight of the shadows under my cousin's eyes.

"What happened, Rena?"

She shook her head and sighed, but I was determined. We'd never had secrets between us. If I was covering her tracks with white lies, I wanted a real good reason.

"Nina was assaulted."

The breath left my lungs in a whoosh. "When, who, what happened?"

"You might want to sit down."

We sat down together on the sofa. I sat leaning forward and Rena curled up in a little ball with one hand holding a pillow and the other absentmindedly stroking Simba.

"Nina went with a group of girls to a jazz club early last Saturday evening."

"The night of Sean's concert?" I questioned.

"Right. Someone slipped something into her drink and she almost died."

"What?"

Rena nodded. "At first she just felt a little tired and dizzy. It could have been blamed on her drinking, but Nina had a recording session the next morning, so she'd decided not to drink alcohol. All she had that night was a Sprite. Then she felt weak and couldn't think as someone began to draw her towards the exit. Lucky for her, Debra noticed that something was wrong and tried to follow. Nina passed out before he could get her out of the club."

"My God."

"It gets worse. Her heart almost stopped on the way to the hospital. The drug that was used in her drink was Rohypnol."

I rubbed my brow, trying to remember why that name sounded so familiar. Then it hit me. "The date rape drug."

"That's the one. It was too strong for Nina's system. The stuff is about ten times more powerful than Valium and her heart couldn't take it."

"Who did it?" I was angry, more angry than I'd been in a while. My fingers shook as I rubbed the back of my neck.

"Nine did it, Leah."

I just looked at Rena, the shock plain on my face.

"As Nina's friends pushed through the crowd, Nine saw them coming and got scared. He pushed her into the arms of one of his crew before bolting into the crowd and disappearing. Luckily the boy had enough sense to pull out his cell phone and call an ambulance."

"He was here. I came home and he was waiting for me." I shivered, recalling the wild, cornered look in his eyes that evening. "He seemed desperate to find out where Nina had gone."

"He should have been. Putting that drug in her drink was criminal. Nine could be facing attempted kidnapping and illegal drug abuse charges."

"Why did he do it?"

She sighed and rubbed her eyes. "He didn't want to hurt Nina. The boy has a crush on her. Somebody told him that the drug makes people relax. He wanted to talk with her and was afraid he'd get shot down in front of his crew."

"And you believe that?"

"Yes." She rubbed the bridge of her nose.

"Why?"

"Because he had his little brother in the car outside the club that night."

"His little brother?" I repeated skeptically.

"Who is apparently another big fan of Nina's. All I know is that Nine would have rather cut himself then hurt the girl. The boy was crying."

"If his intentions were so pure, why the drug?"

"Stupidity."

"Lord have mercy," I swore. "How do you know all this?"

"Nine was at the airport last night," she answered.

"What?" I exclaimed.

"So was Michael."

"Why?"

"How do you think Nine got our address?" she asked. I shook my head, not knowing where she was going with that question.

"He didn't get it out of the phone book, we're unlisted."

"I don't get it."

"Michael told Nine to come over here and find out where Nina was." She continued after pulling on the belt of her robe, "I checked my voicemail while I was in Bermuda. Michael left me messages that go from out-right threats to bribery. The man told me that he'd make sure I never worked in the business again unless I got Nina to 'forget' about the incident."

"The man can't be that stupid," I said doubtfully.

"Oh, he is, and I've got it on tape. I'm going to hand in my resignation and a complaint this morning. By afternoon it'll be all over the street."

"How do you feel?" I asked.

"I want to nail the bastard to the cross."

"Which one?" I asked softly.

"Michael. What Nine did is inexcusable and unacceptable, but he's little more than a scared boy. Michael, on the other hand, knew what he was doing by pressuring me and sending Nine over here. If I could just get him in a room." I looked down, noticing Rena's hands had curled into fists.

"I'm coming with you," I declared.

"Thanks, but this is something I need to do on my own. I have a nine o'clock meeting with the corporate executive in charge of my division and then I'm going to pick Nina up at the airport."

"What are you going to do after all this breaks?" I asked.

"Take some time and to do some soul searching. I don't think I can take this anymore. The whole game has changed, and I don't like the new rules."

"Do you want to move back to the West Coast?"

"No. That wouldn't help. It's the same no matter which coast we live on. Maybe I'll start my own label or something. I could try my hand at other things. Who knows? I've got so much going on right now that I can't even think straight."

"You know I've got your back, right?" I said.

"I know." She leaned over and we gave one another a super tight hug. "You, Ralph, Mom, and Pop are the most important people in my life."

Simba took that moment to let out a loud meow.

"You too, fur ball." She laughed, patting him on his head.

"Speaking of Mom and Pop," Rena said, standing up. "When are they due back from that cruise? Pop's going to go through the roof after hearing about what happened."

"They'll be back in two weeks."

"Now what's up with you, miss?" Rena raised an eyebrow.

"What about me?" I dropped my eyes.

"Why was I hearing Sean sneaking out your room at five-thirty this morning?"

"He had a television interview."

Rena's smile got wider and she crossed her arms.

"Oh no," I protested. "It's not what you think. We just fell asleep after talking. End of story."

"How about end of denial?" Rena shot back. "Your cheeks were flushed and you had that guilty look on your face when I came into the room."

"I felt bad for waking you up," I fibbed. I hadn't even known she was home.

Rena's eyebrow lifted. "Really?"

"We're just friends, Rena."

"For now, but it can change." Her voice filled with concern. "The line gets thinner each day. Sean's a wonderful man, but he operates in a whole other world and I don't want to see you hurt."

"Don't worry. I can take care of myself," I replied.

Rena rose off the coach and headed for the kitchen. As she neared the doorway she paused. "Cuz?"

"Yes."

Rena grinned wickedly. "You might want to check the buttons on your blouse the next time you guys just fall asleep."

CHAPTER 13

I jumped every time the phone buzzed at work that day, thinking that it was Sean. No matter how much I tried, the way we'd kissed stayed in my mind. It wasn't until around three o'clock that I got my nerves under control and started worrying about Rena. I kept looking at the clock, hoping the dial had miraculously sped up.

"Leah?"

"Yes?" I glanced up from a report I was in the process of reading to see my administrative assistant peek her head in the door.

"There's a delivery for you downstairs."

I put down my pen. "They can't bring it up?"

"The guard said something about not being able to let the guy in and that you'd have to come down and sign for it in person."

"That's odd," I muttered and pushed back from my desk. "Rachel, could you tell them I'm on my way?"

"Sure thing."

By the time I got downstairs, I was beyond curious. But the sight that greeted me as I walked to the area behind the security desk knocked me for a loop. Leaning against the wall holding a large white teddy bear, sporting a baseball cap, jeans, and a short sleeve shirt, stood Sean. I couldn't keep the look of surprise off my face.

"What—" I started.

"Package for you, miss."

"Thank you," I responded automatically as I reached out to take the teddy bear that he offered.

"Aren't you supposed to be on a plane to Arizona?" I asked.

"I'm here to take you with me," he said.

I sighed and closed my eyes, praying for patience. "I can't go with you, Sean."

"Can't or won't?" he challenged.

"You can't . . . you shouldn't . . ." I looked away and for the first time noticed the long looks that were being thrown our way by the people entering and leaving the building. This wasn't a conversation that I wanted to have in front of an audience.

He seemed to read my mind. "Marc's out front. We can talk in the car."

I nodded my head and followed Sean through the glass doors. Marc stood by the parked Town Car and opened the door to admit us inside. Once behind the tinted windows, I felt more nervous than in front of strangers' eyes. The artificial cool air sent a chill down my arms.

"You're worried about what happened this morning?" he asked.

"What?" I questioned, caught off guard by his bringing up the kiss.

"If you're upset about the kiss, I promise you'll be safe as a nun in church. You can trust that I'd never hurt you." His green eyes looked into mine.

I shook my head. Shoot, I'd probably taken advantage of him this morning and here he was thinking that I was scared of him? If only he knew. "No, Sean, it's not that I don't want to go, but I can't just get up and leave. I have responsibilities, and Rena needs me right now."

He shook his head, and I could already tell that this wasn't going to be easy. Sean liked to get his way almost as much as I did.

"What if I said I needed you?" He moved closer and took hold of my hands.

I smiled and tried to make light of the situation. "Rena needs me more."

"What about your needs? When are you going to take some time for yourself?"

"I know the story," I said and waved my hand dismissively. He'd given me the same lecture before.

"Yes, Leah, but you missed the point." He looked at me, and it was a long, almost sad look.

I shook my head and reached for the door handle, angry with Sean for pushing the issue. "No, I didn't miss the point. I got it loud and clear. When Sean Patrick Andrews, lead singer of Exile, needs me then it's okay. But when other people need me it's not. Well, I'm sorry but I can't just run off to some secluded spot in the middle of the desert and leave Rena high and dry."

By the time I finished, I couldn't breathe, could barely hear over the sound of my heart beating in my ears. I threw open the door and tore out of the Lincoln Town Car clutching the teddy bear to my chest. I practically sprinted into the office building, not even bothering to turn around as I heard Sean's voice shouting my name.

I barely made it to my office before I collapsed into my chair. It wasn't like we never fought. We'd go at it for hours over the latest ethical view or political scandal. Yet this time had been different. I hadn't wanted to fight with Sean and my victory felt hollow. As I sat there staring blankly at the report with one hand clutching a shaking pen and the other holding on to the soft white teddy bear, I wished I'd had the courage to lose.

What does anger look like? If I could paint, what color would it be? Not blood red but moonlit black shadows. It'd be the image of Rena at one o'clock in the morning, shouting at the empty wicker chair.

The sound of crying had pulled me from my restless sleep and I quietly got out of bed and walked into the living room to see her talking to the empty wicker chair. She'd found the letter. I'd buried it under a pile of mail hoping against hope that she'd just throw it away. Like the change of seasons, this was something I couldn't stop.

"I hope you rot in hell. Do you hear me?" Her voice was slightly slurred.

"Do you know what you've done to me? Of course not," she raged.

There was a brief pause and I stood in the shadows and watched her raise the half-filled glass to her lips.

"You want my forgiveness? Never. I wouldn't spit on your ass if you were on fire. If I could I'd watch you fry, hell, I'd throw the switch. Then again, that's too easy. I want you to suffer," she sniffed.

She waved her glass towards the chair. "You wanted this. Just had to go out and have another drink, huh? My parents are lying cold, so cold, under six feet of earth. They should be here," she screamed. "With me. They should be lying in bed with pillows and blankets watching the evening news and talking about having grandkids."

I crept towards her as she tossed down the contents of the glass and slammed it down on the side table.

"How do you like that price? The lives of two people for a bottle. You want my forgiveness? Bring them back to me . . . Just bring them back to me," she sobbed as I stood frozen by the child-like tone of her voice.

Always in the past I would tuck Rena into bed, curl up in her green velvet chair, and close my tear-filled eyes. I wanted it to be someone's, anyone's, fault, but it wasn't. The convicted felon whose letters begged for forgiveness couldn't be blamed for all the bad things life threw at you. Blame wouldn't lift my aunt and uncle from the grave. Nothing could take away the demons that drove Rena. The hurt stayed and that was the hardest to bear.

I went over to the table and grabbed the half empty bottle. "What'd you do that for?" Rena asked.

"Because you don't need this."

"Yes, I do." Rena tried to stand and weakly sat back down on the sofa.

I walked over and picked up the phone, thinking to call Mom and Pop.

"Damn," I muttered remembering that they were somewhere in the middle of the ocean. Instead, I looked down at the open address book on the table and started dialing.

"Who are you calling?" Rena asked, her voice slurred.

"Someone that can help."

"I don't need anyone."

"See, that's where you're wrong." I shook the phone. I knew denial like I knew the back of my hand. Rena had lived with it too damn long. I'd lived with it too long.

"I can't let you do this anymore," I muttered to myself while paging though the little phone book. My fingers shook as I pushed the buttons on the cordless phone.

"Hello?" Trey's sleepy voice came over the line.

"Can you come over?" I asked, moving towards the kitchen.

"Leah? What's wrong?"

"It's Rena." I paused. "I need your help."

"She all right?" he asked hurriedly. I could hear the sound of clothes rustling in the background.

"No, she's not," I admitted out loud for the first time. "I'm hoping that you can get through to her."

"I'm on my way, okay? Just sit tight."

"Thank you," I replied before hitting the off button on the phone. Turning, I gazed into the living room to see Rena staring out the window. The tears running down her face mimicked my own.

Later, after Trey had come and promised to take Rena home to Texas the next day, I lay in bed trying to sleep in spite of the sounds of Simba purring on the pillow next to mine. After praying to the Lord to keep her safe, I could only hope that Trey's mother could help Rena heal. And so as the clock struck three, I closed my eyes, trying to remember the low, sweet music Sean made when strumming his guitar. But the sound of Rena's pleas haunted me, following me into oblivion.

"What's up, guys?" I asked as my co-workers, Bahni and Tami, came into my office and shut the door.

"It's her, Bahni," Tami declared. I watched as she held up a newspaper picture.

"She would have said something," the young Indian woman replied.

"Look at her," Tami told Bahni. I put down my pen and looked at the both of them as if they'd lost their collective minds.

"Did you two get hold of some spiked cappuccino or something?" I asked, rubbing my eyes, trying to rid them of the itchy feeling that came with lack of sleep.

Tami walked over and laid a newspaper down on my desk. "You read this stuff?" I asked, surprised that the trendy graphics designer had a copy of the popular celebrity tabloid.

"I have to have something to look at on the train. Besides, my roommate has a subscription. She's like some kind of celebrity groupie."

"So what's got you guys so hyper this morning?" I asked.

"Tami thinks . . ." Bahni started.

"Just turn to page six," Tami interrupted.

I turned the pages and when I got to page six my stomach dropped to the floor and the office seemed to dim. I was staring down at a picture of Sean and me laughing as we walked arm and arm in the park. Against my will, I read the article.

Bahni's voice seemed to come from far away. "Tami thinks that's a picture of you, Leah."

Seems as though the media-shy lead singer of Exile has found a new muse. With Delia filming and playing with co-star Nicholas Chapman on the set of her upcoming period flick, Sean Andrews is humming a new tune. This photo, taken at Central Park by a local New York photographer, caught the happy couple at play. Sources close to Sean Andrews say the singer has purchased new Manhattan digs to be close to his new mystery lady love.

The phone buzzed and I jabbed the button on the speakerphone while gazing down at the newspaper color photo in horror. Millions of people all the world over would be looking at me.

"Yes," I said woodenly.

"Line one for you, Leah."

"Could you take a message? I can't talk right now." I couldn't even think at that moment. I couldn't do anything except breathe.

"I'm afraid he's really persistent. He's called and zeroed out your voicemail every ten minutes since nine o'clock this morning."

I felt a pain in the back of my eyes as I looked up into Tami's smiling face. The young web developer stood there staring at me as if I were Moses come down from the mount.

"I can't talk right now," I said.

"She's really busy, Trace," Bahni chimed in.

There was a pause before Tracy came back on the line. "Leah, Sean said to say 'Pick up the phone, darling.'"

My face drained of any color that I'd gained as Bahni's eyebrow arched and she gave me a curious look. Tami had no shame. "Just a friend, huh? Oh, my God, he's so dreamy. Can I get his autograph?"

I gave the auburn-haired Cal Tech graduate a look only a black woman could give. The one that sent men running, kids cowering, and told women that something was about to break loose unless one of them left. Lucky for Tami, at that moment when I really wanted to reach over my desk and wring her neck, Bahni picked up the hint and ushered her toward the door.

"You are so much cooler than that actress he was dating," Tami exclaimed. "I heard she was a real bitch. My friend Tom did her makeup for Sundance and she was like completely rude. You know she's seeing Joan Rivers's plastic surgeon."

As the door closed behind them, I sank down into the chair and picked up the phone. "You knew about the photo," I accused. The pieces began to fit together. Sean's persistence in trying to get me to leave with him yesterday took on a new meaning.

"I had an idea," he replied. "I thought you'd get upset and I hoped that it wouldn't be published," he said in a rush.

"How?" I just had to ask. Not that it mattered.

"Rick got a call on Monday morning to confirm."

"Oh, God." I dropped down into my chair and closed my eyes. "I'm in the *National Enquirer*! Sean, what am I going to do? Two of my co-workers just finished gathering in my office like star-struck teenagers."

I almost panicked. "Wait. No one really reads tabloids anymore."

"It's going to be all right," he said.

I started to calm down and scanned the article for my name. I breathed a sigh of relief at seeing that I had been labeled as the 'mystery woman.' "You're right, at least they don't have my name."

When Sean didn't say anything, I tensed back up. "Sean?"

"Other papers have picked up the photo and now it's all over the Internet. Mike started getting calls yesterday morning and the phone hasn't stopped ringing. Trey called me this morning, so I know Rena's on her way to Texas. I bought a ticket to Phoenix for you. Just show up at LaGuardia Airport for the 9:30 a.m. American Airlines flight to Phoenix connecting through O'Hare. You'll get in around 11:50 a.m."

"Sean, there are plenty of black women who look like me in New York City," I said slowly.

He sighed. "Don't question this, just be on the flight. I'll be waiting for you at the airport."

"How long do I have?"

I wanted to run home and hide under the covers and wake up in the morning to find out this was just one long, nasty nightmare.

"They'll have your name, address and life history before the eleven o'clock news."

I hung my head and rubbed my neck, feeling a migraine start in the back of my eyes.

"I can't just up and leave. What am I going to do with Simba?"

"Bring him along. It's about time I got to spend some time with him."

"It's not like I've been keeping the two of you apart," I said defensively.

"I know it's been my schedule, but that's in the past. I'm ready and willing to take care of the both of you."

"I don't know, Sean."

"Trust me, Leah. Just get on the plane tomorrow morning."

"I'll think about it."

"Whatever you decide, I'll be waiting at the airport."

I picked up my coffee cup with a shaky hand only to discover that it had turned cold and undrinkable. I closed my eyes and sighed, feeling the start of a headache. Just what I needed, a migraine. Right then it seemed like pink icing on the cake of a horrible day.

I arrived home later that evening to see a furiously blinking red light on the answering machine. I hesitated before pressing down the button: fifteen messages. Half of them were for Rena, the other half were for me.

"*Ms. Russell, Steve Hirsch from the* New York Times. *We'd like to do an exclusive on your story. We're doing an expose on the new trends in interracial dating. We think you and Sean should be our feature story.*"

<beep>

"*Ms. Taylor, Vanessa McAdams at* Newsday. *We want to tell your side of the story. Tell us about the harassment. Will there be a lawsuit? Did rapper Nine threaten your life?*"

<beep>

"*Ms. Taylor,* Entertainment News. *We'd like to interview you for our upcoming Sunday night segment.*"

<beep>

"*Ms. Russell, Karen Adder from* US *magazine. How does it feel to be Sean Andrews's newest leading lady?*"

CHAPTER 14

The next morning, I left everything behind as the plane lifted off the ground. It was an escape from thoughts of Rena, telephone calls from the press and excited friends. I was taking my life back. Lance's face could no longer cause me pain. The boy I fell in love with, the lanky go-getter on the corner, my partner in crime at church, was still alive only in my memories.

I got off the plane in Chicago and made my way to Gate G for the connecting flight to Phoenix. As I sat in O'Hare airport curled up in one of the tight black seats, I watched life pass by pulling carry-ons, holding duffle bags or pushing carts. I was the unseen voyeur watching as couples embraced and families welcomed loved ones from far away.

I turned on my iPod and put the earbuds into my ears. As the smooth sounds of jazz filled my mind the minutes ticked by and the time of my flight came closer. As Simba lay asleep in the mesh covered pet carrier on the seat next to mine, I imagined how I would greet Sean when I got off the plane. What would I say? When the gate attendant announced that they would begin boarding in fifteen minutes, I caught myself laughing at the way pretentious middle-aged business men in cookie-cutter suits herded around the ticket counter to be the first on the plane.

By the time I stepped off the plane in Phoenix, I never wanted to see anyone under the age of twenty again. Three bad kids with an exhausted mother and a stupid father had annoyed half the plane. It had gotten to the point that even the flight attendants were avoiding our section.

Holding tight to Simba's carry-all, I exited the jetway and entered the terminal. It took me a moment but I spotted Sean leaning against the windows. His sunglasses might have disguised his eyes, and the curly brown wig his hair, but nothing in the world could hide that sexy smile of his.

"Welcome to Phoenix," he said, taking Simba's carrier from me.

"Glad to be here," I replied, surprised at the happiness I felt.

"So how was your trip?" Sean asked as we made our way to the baggage claim area. "I tried to book you into first class but all the seats were taken."

"That's okay. I slept most of the way," I lied.

"That's good because we have a long ride ahead of us."

We had to wait only a few minutes for my suitcase to arrive, and by that time Simba had begun to wake up.

Sean placed my suitcase next to a bench outside and said, "Okay, you wait here and I'll run and get the Jeep."

I sat on the bench and took a deep breath of the dry air. Unzipping the top of Simba's pet case, I stuck my hand inside and rubbed his head, hoping that he'd be okay in the car. I looked up a few minutes later to see Sean jumping out of a dust-covered Jeep Wrangler.

"Ready to ride?" He smiled.

Nodding as he picked up the pet case, I followed and jumped up into the open passenger side door. Although the outside of the car was a mess, the inside was spotless.

"Sean, is it okay if I let Simba out?"

"Sure," he said, sparing me a glance before turning into traffic. "He's probably dying to get out of that bag."

I let Simba loose onto the back seat, watching as he proceeded to take up residence on the floorboard. After a few meows, he settled into cleaning himself.

"The flight wasn't bumpy?" Sean asked.

"No, actually it was pretty smooth," I answered awkwardly.

"Well, we've got a drive ahead so you might want to settle in."

"Where exactly are we going?"

"My place is about an hour south of here."

"Oh." I turned to look out the window at the passing scenery.

"I'm sorry, Leah," he said. "I didn't mean for any of this to happen."

"I know, and I don't blame you."

"You should."

"Oh, don't go all noble on me," I bit out, really looking at Sean for the first time. "We both knew this could happen. Just what my mama warned me about. When you start hanging out with the wrong crowd . . ." My voice trailed off.

Sean glanced at me. "The wrong crowd?"

"You'll get into trouble." I chuckled.

"What do your parents have to say about this?"

"Nothing yet, but I expect to get an earful when they get back from vacation." I grimaced.

"My father asked about you."

"How's he doing?"

"Nervous. He's only got one more month left as a free man."

I rolled my eyes. "It's not like he's going to jail. He's just getting married."

"Speaking of marriage," he turned towards me with a raised eyebrow, "you haven't returned your RSVP yet."

"I was going to, but I really don't think it'd be a good idea."

"Why not?"

"I don't want to make people uncomfortable," I answered vaguely.

"Try again," Sean said.

"What?"

"That was a bad excuse, Leah. What's the real reason?"

I shifted a bit in the seat. "I don't like weddings."

"It won't be so bad. They're having it outdoors in the garden."

"No, Sean," I emphasized. "I really don't like weddings."

"Because of Lance?"

I opened my mouth to deny it. Instead I sighed, "Yes."

"Did he hurt you that bad?"

"No. I hurt myself," I admitted. "I thought he'd wake up and see that I was in love with his sorry behind. I hoped that he'd be able to see behind a pretty face. Either way, I was wrong."

"You didn't commit a crime. You just got your heart bruised, that's all."

"I know. We've talked about this before," I interjected. "I still don't like weddings."

"You can not like wedding all you want. You're coming to this wedding if I have to drag you there."

"Why?"

He reached over and brushed his fingers against my cheek. "Because misery loves company and I want you with me, that's why."

Remembering the reason for my being in the middle of the desert with the man I could look at for hours just made me want to scream even more.

I woke from my nap just as the sun was going down. Soft light filtered into the bedroom through the lowered rice paper roll-up shades framed by amber-colored silk drapes. I looked around the bedroom and smiled. No denying that it was a beautiful place in which to wake. The decorator had spared no expense in creating a room that anyone would love. The room spoke of relaxation and peace.

Cool shades of white and tan came together in a soothing design. I just remembered snuggling into the fresh-smelling sheets seconds before sleep claimed me. Now awake and alert, I admired the white sheer canopy that hung from the ceiling, framing the queen-sized bed.

Pushing aside the sheets, I stood up and stretched, rubbing my hands over my arms as the cool dryness of the room sent chills over my skin. It was then that I noticed the silence. It was complete. There wasn't noise from passing cars or the ever-present sounds of life. No creaks, vibrations, ticking. It was a deep quiet that I had never experienced. It frightened me, yet at the same time filled me with wonder that the world could be so still.

"Come in," I replied at the soft knock on the door. I turned to see Sean peek in.

"Thought I heard you moving about."

I blushed. "Guess I was more tired than I thought."

"You've more than earned a long rest. Hungry?" he asked as he leaned against the doorway.

"A little."

"Good. Dinner's almost ready."

"I'm just going to hop in the shower."

"Don't rush. You've got time."

"Thank you, Sean." I looked at him and smiled. In those three words I let him know that all was forgiven and that he had been right. This was what I needed.

"Anytime." He backed out the room and shut the door behind him, leaving me alone.

I turned and walked over and opened my suitcase. Taking out a pair of slacks and a white cotton blouse as well as undies, I walked into the bathroom and wanted to pinch myself. The light peach-colored room with sand-colored inscribed tiles was a woman's dream.

A large marble sink stood by itself next to a white painted wood vanity tower. The glass framed shower stood separate from the tub. I walked over and ran my fingers over the edge of the white claw-foot tub. I'd seen bathtubs like that one only in movies or in designer magazines. Its deep polished inside spoke of long soaks with low lights and burning candles.

I smiled, seeing myself with a green oatmeal avocado facemask and hair coved by a towel sitting in the tub with my eyes closed. I moved towards what I guessed was the closet door. I pushed back the sliding door and just stood there with my mouth wide open. On one side each and every shelf was stocked with oils, soaps, gels, shampoo, conditioner, perfume, scrub, and sprays. The other side was filled with different colored towels. After digging though I pulled out a simple green tea-scented shower gel and a large, soft towel.

"So this is how the other half lives," I murmured.

Sean hadn't been kidding when he said that this house was a retreat. I shook my head in disbelief. As far as I was concerned, it could have been a resort for the rich and famous. I had spent time at Sean's place in L.A. but I'd made it a point to never wander. I didn't want to get used to the luxury. I'd never want to get caught up in the star madness. I'd clung to my simple Philly girl image like a lifeline.

By the time I'd showered and dressed, the sun had almost gone down and the clock chimed that it was eight o'clock. Taking a deep breath, I opened the door. The smell of food made my stomach rumble. As I headed downstairs, I took my time glancing around. Everything in the place seemed to fit. The paintings, the furniture, the rugs. It was as though everything had been created to be in this place, and that made it feel like a home.

The wide windows in the living room brought in the sunset and a beautiful view of the desert mesa. A white ceiling fan whirled gently, stirring the incense-scented air. Underneath the stained overhead beams, I stood by the sofa letting my eyes drift out the glass doors to the desert landscape. Brown and tan with bits of green. My eyes traced the cactus-covered ground and then I looked further out to the mountains. Sean's backyard emptied into the dry landscape. The only source of color was a barn set catty-corner to the house.

I turned away from the window and followed my nose to the kitchen. Pushing through the swinging door, I stepped into what could have doubled for a Williams Sonoma print ad. Gray commercial-sized anodized pots and pans hung from strategically placed hooks over the stove and shiny gourmet appliances sat neatly on the countertops. Sean stood by the electric grill.

I leaned against the island countertop and let out an appreciative whistle. "This is a pretty serious kitchen, my friend. I'm impressed."

Sean turned and smiled. "Believe it or not I'm a pretty serious cook."

"You cook, sing, and paint. You have the makings of the perfect man. Better watch out or you'll have every man in America trying to take you down," I teased.

"And why would they want to do that?" He turned over the salmon.

"Let me clue you in on something, my very naïve superstar. Right now it's only the single women that chase after you while the married women dream about being single and dating you. If the press got wind of your culinary skills, married women everywhere would have another skill to nag their husbands about."

Sean let out a bark of laughter before turning around and checking on the food. "You should have been a comedian, Leah. Your talents are being wasted."

"True. But I don't have the patience for show business. I'll leave that to you. So what's cooking and how can I help?"

"We're having salmon tonight with sautéed garlic spinach and baked red potatoes. For dessert, I've got spiced apple tarts warming in the oven."

"Please don't tell me you bake, too." That would be too good to be true.

"I could lie," he answered. "But I'm not a baking kind of guy. These tarts came with simple directions. Remove from box and place in oven."

I heaved a sigh of relief and walked towards Sean. I stopped next to him and noticed, not for the first time, how wonderful he smelled. "So what can I do?"

"Hmmm, how about you pick out a wine for dinner?"

"Isn't that a man's job?"

"Not tonight. The rack's over there."

"Can you at least give me some selection criteria? I'm not a wine connoisseur."

"Pick a red."

Okay, I mused, this ought to be easy. That was my thought until I opened the door he had pointed to and walked into a small wall-to-wall bottle-filled wine closet.

"You have got to be kidding," I shouted.

"You can do it."

My eyes glazed over at the sheer number of bottles. "Sean, no one needs this much wine."

I jumped when I heard his voice so close to me. "It's not for quantity, Leah. It's for selection," he said.

I turned and playfully punched him on the shoulder. "You just took a year off my life. Could you make some more noise next time?"

"I'll try."

"I can't pick a wine."

"Close your eyes and chose one."

"Why can't you do this? You're the one with the collection." I pointed my finger at him.

He leaned in closer. "I've a secret."

"What?"

"I didn't buy any of this, someone else did."

"So you don't know what to get either . . ." I smiled.

"You're wounding my pride right now."

"I won't tell a soul." I wandered towards the back wall and pulled out what I hope was a good bottle.

"Pinot Noir 1988. This has to be a good year," I proclaimed

"Why's that?" Sean asked as we returned to the kitchen.

"That was the year I got straight A's on my report card, and Rena and I got our braces taken off."

"You had braces?"

"All of us aren't born blessed with perfect teeth."

"I had to wear a retainer for three years," he replied off handedly.

My defensiveness vanished as I stared at Sean. He never ceased to amaze me. He smiled and picked up a serving plate and walked through the open doorway that led to the living room. The square hardwood table was set for two. Picking up the wine bottle and salad bowl, I followed Sean out of the kitchen. A dark-colored chandelier with candle-shaped lights hung from the ceiling, illuminating the room with a soft glow.

I took a seat across from Sean. He expertly opened the wine bottle and filled the wine glasses I held in my hand. When I handed him a goblet, our fingers touched, and I looked at him. There was a moment of staring too long, a jolt, a shiver. I shook my head to cleanse myself of the dangerous thoughts.

"If you ever decide to give up singing, you should open a restaurant," I joked after my second bite.

The salmon was delicious. It didn't just smell great, it tasted great. Butter, herbs, lemon, and the crisp flakiness of the fish filled my mouth. I knew that if Sean opened a restaurant men would come for the good food and women would come just to look at the owner. Under the soft light, Sean was a bedtime fairy tale come to life, the prince in the castle, the perfect husband, the gallant knight.

"Funny you should mention that. I've been thinking a lot about the future now that the tour's over."

"Any ideas?"

"Not yet. Jason is talking about getting into film."

"That might not be such a bad thing."

"It is when you can't act, Leah," he replied after taking a bite of the salmon.

"You could take a class," I suggested.

"I don't think that's a space I want to be in. I can't act a way I don't feel." He shook his head. "Movies are all about pretending to be someone else. I have a hard time just being me."

"Oh, well," I sighed. "Looks like Tom Cruise will be able to sleep better knowing that his career's safe."

"Tom Cruise? You're comparing me to Tom Cruise?" His tone was shocked.

I took a sip of wine and smiled. "Oh, sorry. How about Russell Crowe?"

"That's worse, not better. I was thinking Tom Hanks. I always thought of myself as being the low-key type."

I shook my head. "No, he's too much the normal guy. You're a rock star. Maybe Pierce Brosnan? He's got an edge."

"007?" He laughed heartily. "So that makes you which Bond girl?"

"Speaking of Bond girls . . . How's Dalia doing?" I asked in an off-handed manner. I'd wanted to ask that question since Sean picked me up at the airport. No woman in her right mind would be okay with another woman spending time alone with her man. Hollywood stars might live in another world, but when it comes to relationships, they are just like your average person on the street.

"She's on set in Canada, I think."

"Is she coming to visit soon?" I asked. "I hope she doesn't mind me using her stuff."

Sean looked puzzled. "Her stuff?"

"The toiletries in the bathroom," I explained.

"Leah, you're the first person I've had here besides the decorator. You can use whatever you like."

I almost dropped the heavy fork. Instead, I put it down slowly and took a long drink, savoring the warmth of the wine as it slipped down my throat. I couldn't fight the giddy sensation his announcement had caused.

"So where'd you learn how to cook like that?" I asked after we'd cleared the table and placed the last plate into the dishwasher.

"My mom was a very forward-thinking Scotswoman. She and my Dad met at the University of Edinburgh," he said.

I pulled up one of the barstools next to the island and watched as Sean operated the coffee/espresso maker. He placed two coffee-filled mugs, sugar, and cream on a wooden serving tray.

He continued, "They met at a pub late one Sunday night when all the restaurants were closed and the markets shut for the day. My dad was starving because he didn't know how to cook and didn't have any food back at his flat. Mom took pity on the poor man and took him home to her parents'."

I followed Sean through the kitchen to the back of the house. We entered a sunken den. A forest green chenille loveseat sat in the corner facing a honey maple entertainment center. Simba lay curled contentedly in the middle of a multi panel gold and maroon Persian rug. I watched as Sean placed the tray on a side bar next to a small round table that held a checkers set.

I stood next to him and reached down to lift the small wooden checker set. I picked up my cup of coffee as Sean gestured for me to take a seat in the comfortable leather chair. "Don't stop there, you've got to finish the story," I urged.

Sean took the seat opposite me. "Well, Dad always told me that he fell in love with my mom when she invited him over to dinner, but couldn't speak to her alone. So he resolved that he'd learn how to cook so he could impress her."

I leaned forward, eager to hear the rest of the story. "Want to play a game of checkers?" he asked.

"Sean, the story. You have to finish the story first."

"Where was I? Oh, Dad decided that he'd learn how to cook. So he invited my mom over for dinner one Sunday afternoon. He wanted to cook her a fancy meat pie but ended up burning it. My mom, being the smart woman she was, had come prepared. They ended up eating cold ham sandwiches."

"So how does this story relate to the wonderful gourmet dinner you just whipped up?"

"Mom didn't want some crafty upper-class girl enticing me back to her apartment with promises of home-cooked meals."

"So she taught you how to cook?" I guessed.

Sean nodded and set down his mug. "She made me peel the potatoes, chop onions, and marinate chicken."

"I'm impressed," I replied.

"Now can you play?"

"Can I play?" I tried to bluff and then looked into Sean's serious face. "To be honest, I haven't played checkers in years."

"Then I promise to take it easy on you," he laughed. "How about best two out of three? You first."

I bit the outside of my lip and placed my finger on the black checker to make the first advance. "So I take it you're really into checkers?" I asked.

"Dad loves checkers. Some fathers teach their kids baseball or basketball. He taught me checkers and football."

"Football as in American or soccer?"

"Soccer. When it rained, we'd spend time after supper playing checkers," Sean said after taking a jump. I couldn't resist the opportunity to jump one of his checkers on my next move.

"Yes," he sighed. "After my first fight at school, Dad sat me down and trounced me soundly at checkers. He taught me that the mind is a powerful thing."

"We were all about playing cards in my family." I smiled. "My mom can play a game of spades like nobody's business. Pop, my dad, taught us all how to play poker."

"Your dad taught you?"

I nodded and grimaced as he took advantage of a double jump and took two of my checkers. It was looking more and more like this wasn't going to be my night to win. "Every Saturday, my pop and his friends got together at our house to play cards in the basement. After the games were over, Pop would let the kids sit down at the table and play. We used jelly beans as a substitute for chips."

"So you're a card shark? I'll remember that."

"So what's on the schedule tomorrow?" I asked, hoping to distract him from seeing my very vulnerable positions.

"I thought we'd head out early, do a little off-road sight seeing, maybe hike a little ways."

"Sounds good. How early is early?" I wanted some serious prep time. This sista might be in the middle of nowhere but I'd be damned if I was going to look bad.

"Seven o'clock." Sean smiled as he moved his piece onto the last row. "Crown me."

"Sneak," I accused after crowning his checker and watching him take my last man.

"The woman's a sore loser."

"The competition isn't over yet."

"Spoken like a true fighter."

"That's right," I nodded. I placed my hand over my mouth and faked a yawn. "Well, I'd better turn in since I have to wake up so early in the morning."

"Come on, Leah. It's only nine-thirty."

"You know the saying: 'Early to bed . . .'"

Sean didn't look the least bit happy as I stood up and stretched. "Guess you'll have to wait until tomorrow before I beat you," I boasted.

"Leah, I won the first game."

"It's all about point of view. I'm not losing. I'm just about to make a comeback." Truthfully, I couldn't see a comeback in my future since he'd won the first game in less than ten minutes.

Sean let out a snort and stood up. "I'll see you in the morning."

"Not going to bed?" I put my hands behind my back and stretched.

"I'm going to go check on the horses before I turn in." He picked up the still-full wine glass.

"Horses?"

"I keep three here at the ranch."

"Who takes care of them when you're not here?"

"There's a private ranch about ten miles from here. They're stabled there until I come to visit."

"So the chef's a cowboy." I looked at Sean again. Each time I thought I had an idea about who he was I found out that there existed another undiscovered layer.

"Do you ride, Leah?"

I arched an eyebrow. "As in do I willingly subject myself to the possibility of death by climbing on the back of a horse?"

"I take it the answer is no."

"You are truly a brilliant man. Rena convinced me to get on a horse once."

"When was that?"

I smiled ruefully at the memory. "She wanted to show off in front of a group of musicians at a festival in Jamaica. So she challenged them to a race on the beach. Her horse got spooked and ran into mine. The next thing

I knew I was flat on my back in the sand with an aching butt and dented pride."

"I won't let that happen to you."

"That's right." I nodded. "Because there's no way I'm getting on a horse."

"Sweet dreams," he said softly.

"Good night . . . and Sean, if your mission was to make me forget about the newspaper, it worked."

I left the den and found my way back upstairs to my room. A half an hour later after changing into my pajamas and finishing my nightly ablutions, I found Simba lying curled on the chaise next to the window. He opened his eyes and let out a yawn showing his sharp teeth as I crossed the room. The quarter moon was bright that night. After getting ready for bed, I rolled up the shade, making room for Simba to jump onto the windowsill.

The pale glow of the outside lights illuminated the rock walkway from the backyard to the barn. I could just make out Sean's profile in the night. Instead of waving as he walked back towards the house, I pulled back from the window. Something in me just wanted to watch him move. He had one of those slow, distinctive walks. As he entered the house and the lights went dark, I curled up in bed thinking that some lucky woman was going to get that man. No matter how hard I tried I couldn't help wishing that woman would be me.

CHAPTER 15

"Just because my dad couldn't cook doesn't mean he didn't keep trying. Sunday morning was Dad's day in the kitchen. My mother figured out that he could make the best waffles in the world," Sean said before taking a bite.

As I cut into the large Belgian waffle topped with berries and syrup, I wanted to thank the man. I had met Sean's father only once, accidentally. As I was leaving Sean's place after an evening of pillow fights and ice cream, I met his father at the door. Mr. Andrews had just gotten back in town from shooting a documentary in Canada. I remembered the look of mild surprise on the face of the man with the silver hair and round glasses. He asked no questions, though, just accepted my presence in his only son's life.

"What do you think?" Sean asked after taking a bite.

I savored the rich, sweet taste of butter and maple syrup. "I could definitely get used to this," I said after taking a sip of coffee.

"Don't forget to eat your fruit," he pointed out.

I looked over at the bowl of strawberries, sliced cantaloupe, honeydew and kiwi. "Sean," I said dramatically, "I forgive you for waking me up at this ridiculous time in the morning. You don't have to bribe me with food."

"Just want to make sure you've got the proper nutrients."

"Hey, I eat right."

"You're getting too skinny."

I choked on a sip of orange juice. When my coughing fit ended, I looked up to see Sean's concerned face close to mine. "I'm okay," I managed to get out between breaths.

"Are you really all right?"

"Fine. Went down the wrong way."

"You probably eat bagels every day."

"Hey, I'm in New York. You have to eat bagels. Just so you know, I switch sometimes and eat a bowl of Raisin Bran," I said proudly.

He rolled his eyes and took a bite. "You need a keeper, Leah," he admonished. "A bagel for breakfast? Breakfast is the most important meal of the day."

"My vitamins are the most important meal of the day. Besides, who has time to cook in the morning?"

"You could get up a little earlier."

I remembered the three reasons that kept me from cooking breakfast and ticked them off on my fingers. "First, I already get up too early. Second, I go to the gym before work. Third, and most important, I value my sleep. Actually, I love to sleep." I smiled. Sean sighed and shook his head. I wasn't discouraged; I could see the amusement in those green eyes.

"You need a keeper," he repeated, flashing his dimple my way.

"That would imply that there's someone out there to take on that responsibility, and, at the moment, I can't see anyone volunteering for that kind of mission."

I pushed back the chair and picked up my dishes.

"You make it sound like a dangerous thing."

"That's because it is," I teased, knowing that I was one of the most laid-back sistas on the planet.

"You're harmless," he stated.

I leaned against the countertop as he placed the plates and glasses in the dishwasher. I made sure that Sean was facing me when I looked him up and down as though I were sizing up an opponent.

"Want to make a bet?" I was cocky, having won my fair share of pillow fights in the past.

"Okay. I pick the game," he answered, holding the dishtowel.

"Go for it," I responded and immediately regretted it after seeing the smug grin on his face.

"Checkers again tonight. We'll start even. Best of three games wins."

"Damn," I swore under my breath. I walked right into that one. "Not fair," I protested as Sean bent down to fill Simba's empty bowl.

"You made the challenge."

"What're the stakes?" Sean rarely played any game unless he had something to lose. Which made the game all the more interesting and winning all the sweeter.

"If I win you go horseback riding with me tomorrow morning," he stated.

"Well, you might want to pack up those waffle irons of yours because when you lose, you'll need them to cook breakfast for both Rena and me for two months."

"Those are fighting words."

"I know." I grinned before turning to go upstairs.

We managed to leave the ranch at a quarter to seven. Yawning, I buckled my seatbelt and stared out the window at the vast landscape and listened to the crunch of the tires.

"So where are we headed?"

"I've been wanting to explore this little spot about thirty minutes north of here. There's an old road I want to check out and then we can just do a little hiking."

"What's your definition of a little?'

"A mile or two."

"You have got to be kidding. I'm a city girl, remember?"

"Come on. Where's your sense of adventure?"

"I left it back at the ranch with Simba."

"You'll be fine. Just think of this as a trip to the gym."

"Sean." I pointed to the passing desert scenery as he sped down the highway. "The gym has air conditioning, first aid kits, and entertainment. This isn't even close." I yawned.

Sean reached over with his right hand and pulled my makeshift ponytail. I'd planned to wake up and make myself look at least halfway decent this morning. But I didn't hear the alarm clock. That morning I'd woken to the sensation of Sean dropping Simba on my stomach. He'd had the nerve to laugh as I let out a screech.

"Just lie back and take a nap," Sean said. "I'll wake you when we get there."

"There" turned out to be the middle of nowhere. I jumped out of the Jeep into the early sun of a desert morning. The air was just beginning to warm as we set out. Sean carried a backpack with food and water and I got to hold the camera. We followed a narrow path between the rocks. I stopped and caught my breath.

"It's beautiful, isn't it?"

I could only nod my head. A tall cactus looked beautiful in the early sunlight. Then I glanced down and screamed.

"What the hell?" Sean asked.

I had run behind him and, shivering, pointed towards the rock I'd been standing next to.

"There . . . it's over there."

I watched as he laughed and bent to pick it up.

"It's just a lizard."

He held the tiny, scaly thing comfortably in the palm of this hand. "He's just waiting for more sunlight to start his day."

"Well then, why don't you just put him back and let's move on before he wakes up."

"You're not afraid of a little lizard, are you?"

"No. I just don't believe in associating with the wildlife."

We reached a small clearing about two hours later. Thank God for the hiking boots I'd borrowed from Rena's closet. My feet were the only things that felt halfway dry. Perspiration had turned to profuse sweat about an hour earlier, and even the made-for-a-man antiperspirant I'd put on this morning wasn't strong enough.

"Break time," Sean announced, putting down his backpack.

"Thank you."

"This is supposed to be fun."

I gave Sean a tight smile before collapsing to the ground. Promptly removing my cap, I used my handkerchief to wipe at the sweat streaming down my face.

"It's hot, Sean."

"We'll head back after a break. Water?" he asked.

"Please." Lukewarm bottled water never tasted so good. I splashed a little on my face and took a deep breathe and promptly regretted it as the dust made me sneeze.

"Bless you."

"Thanks."

"How do you feel?"

I flexed my ankle and felt a spurt of pain run up the back of my leg.

"Like I'm a surprise contestant on a survival show."

"That's good, right?" he asked with a smile.

"I hate those shows." I ruined the effect by laughing. "No, really, I'm enjoying this. It's been a long time since I've been this far away from civilization."

"It humbles a person. That's one of the reasons I come out here," he said.

"It's so big, I feel dwarfed here," I commented, scanning the horizon. I saw little movement except the occasional shadow of a vulture in the distance. Phantom waves of distant, nonexistent water rippled spookily beneath a sapphire sky.

That night, after driving back and taking showers, we ate outside on the veranda. The daytime heat had quickly disappeared to be replaced with the evening coolness. We sat sipping glasses of iced tea and eating large chicken Caesar salads. I realized that the friendship Sean and I shared was no longer black and white but had subtle, curious shades of gray.

"They're beautiful, aren't they?" I murmured, tilting my head back. The darkening sky revealed clusters of bright stars in the desert sky.

"Yes, it's a beautiful sight," Sean agreed. I lowered my gaze to see that Sean was looking at me.

"You really can't see the stars well in New York," I added.

Sean pointed. "That large collection over there is Ursa Major, which is better known as Big Bear."

"And the rest?"

"Don't know. We could find out after our games of checkers."

"Come on. We're really not going to spend this wonderful evening playing checkers."

I just didn't want to lose that bet. The thought of getting on the horse Sean had shown me after we'd gotten back from hiking scared the hell out of me. Cloud might have a nice name but I could have sworn that horse was giving me a look that said, "I'm just waiting for you."

Sean laughed as he picked up the dishes.

"I've been looking forward to this all day."

"Well, I've been looking forward to kicking back with a video and some ice cream."

"You wouldn't be trying to weasel out of our bet, would you?"

"Me? Never." I tried my best to sound upset but it came out flat. "I'm just not in a hurry to damage your pride. But if you want . . ." My voice trailed off.

"What I want is you for you to feed me ice cream after I win," he said.

I placed my hands on my hips. "Hold up. Don't you mean that you'll be feeding me ice cream after you lose?"

I lost the bet, but I sure as hell didn't feed Sean ice cream as he sat there smug with victory.

"Now I remember why I swore off gambling," I muttered to myself after we'd been riding for about thirty minutes. I reached up and adjusted the wide-brimmed hat on my head.

As the dust flew into my face and my rear end went up and down, I vowed never to play anything with Sean again. Soon he drew to a stop and I reined in my horse, staring at the desert landscape.

"Okay, cowboy, what are those?" I asked, pointing to the flowers atop the cactus. I found it unbelievable that such loveliness could exist in a desert.

"Prickly pear, beaver tail, and barrel cacti. Those blooms to the left are scatterings of poppies and wild-flowers," Sean answered.

"And those?" I pointed to the objects along the trail that were shimmering pinks, golds, oranges, and reds. Larger things sported light green, bright green, orange and yellow colors.

"Rocks," he laughed while swinging down from his saddle.

"Rocks don't come in crayon colors, Sean," I said breezily.

"That's fungus *on* the rocks."

"Oh."

"Ready for lunch?"

"Yes," I answered, surprised to find my stomach growling. But as I swung my leg over the side of the horse and tried to stand up, the word pain took on a new meaning.

"Need help?"

I turned to find Sean smiling at me. I would have killed him right then and there if I could have moved. My legs felt like jelly, and I thought of just collapsing on the ground until I spotted a hairy spider making its way towards my feet.

"I'm fine," I managed to get out through gritted teeth. *Pride goeth before a fall.* I wasn't about to make a fool out of myself even if we were in the middle of nowhere with no one watching. So I straightened up and leaned a little on Cloud until I got my strength back.

After tying up the horses, Sean and I rolled out the light cotton blanket under the shadow of a tall saguaro cactus. As we sat back and ate in the silence, Sean pointed out the desert wildlife.

"Leah, turn around slowly."

I eyed the mysterious smile on his face before complying. There, just ten feet away, stood little jackrabbits.

They sniffed the air for but a second before hopping away and disappearing into the desert.

Lunch continued to be a learning session. Under Sean's direction, I learned to be still and observant. Little things suddenly didn't look so harmless. What I thought was a leaf turned out to be a horned lizard. A cute bird turned out to be a rabbit-eating hawk. I watched butterflies flit from cactus to cactus, slow-moving beetles, lizards, moths. It seemed that we'd picked the most happening spot in the desert to have lunch.

Much later after we'd eaten lunch, Sean relaxed and opened up. "Music for me has become more of an escape. It's that place I can go to get away."

I looked over at Sean and finally asked a question that had been on my mind since arriving at the ranch.

"How did you find this place?"

"Pete shipped me here after the accident," Sean replied.

"You never talk about what happened," I said.

"Right after Mom died everything took off with the group. Pete arranged for a world tour. There was always one more city or one more show before I'd allow myself to grieve. I couldn't handle it, so I turned to alcohol. I drank before going on stage and I picked up the bottle when I got off."

"The press never mentioned that you were drinking that night," I commented.

"I hadn't started. I got home that night to find that Pete and Danny had emptied the entire contents of my bar into the toilet. I went ballistic and before they could stop me I was out the door. I practically ran that family's car off the road."

Sean rubbed his temple. "Pete pulled some strings to make it look like a weather-related accident, then locked me up in a house about thirty miles from here."

"How long?"

"Four weeks."

"Cold turkey?" I asked.

He nodded and closed his eyes. "And afterward I avoided alcohol for the most part. I'd only allowed myself a glass of wine until the night we met."

"Did you drive home that morning?" I asked. My throat went dry at the thought that Sean could have put himself in harm's way.

"No way," he laughed. "I felt like absolute hell. Jerrod dumped me into one of his guest rooms until I could walk again."

"That bad, huh?" I commented before taking a sip of water.

"Worse. I learned my lesson, Leah. I'll not be doing that again."

"Good." I shivered in the heat of the sun thinking about Rena's parents. "I never told, you but Rena's parents were killed by a drunk driver."

"I'm sorry."

I shrugged as though it were something unimportant. "It's not me that needs the sympathy, it's Rena."

"But I can tell that the memory still hurts you."

"He won't let us forget. The man who did it writes Rena a letter every year asking for her forgiveness. How can he expect her to forgive and maybe get some closure when his letter reminds her of the fact that his recklessness took away her parents?"

Sean shook his head. "I can only tell you that I have to live with the guilt. It's not something that you can put in a box and hide in the closet. The parents only suffered a couple of bruises, but their three-year-old son's arm was broken. Because of me that boy's trust in the goodness of the world got ripped apart."

I could see that this was tearing him up inside. His face was haunted. "Trust me, Leah. That man can't suffer any more than he's been suffering since the accident."

"You're probably right, Sean. But there's a small place in my heart that fills with anger when his letter arrives in the mail." I looked towards the ground and followed the slow progress of a brown bug.

"Does it help you?" he asked after a moment of silence.

"What?"

"The anger. I suspect it's weighted you down for years. Let it go."

"But Rena . . ." I protested.

" . . . has her own anger and grief," he finished. "You can't live her life, her pain. Only your own."

"Have you let go of your anger?" I turned the question back at him. Sean was great at solving other people's problems, dealing with other people's emotions, just not his own.

"What?"

"The anger you have towards your mother."

He looked out over the horizon before turning those stormy eyes back to me. Too close to home, I guess. I had seen it in Rena. The anger at the unfairness of his mother's death still ate at him. Sean turned to look out into the horizon and the silence lay heavy between us.

"No."

"Why?" I pushed.

"Because I'm afraid. If I let it go what do I do? How will I sing when there's nothing inside me but emptiness?"

I looked towards the desert that I had thought so empty and desolate as the airplane prepared to land the other day. At this moment, this place with its dry earth, green cactus and rolling tumbleweeds was far from empty.

I reached up and touched Sean's jaw, drawing his eyes to mine. "You fill it up with something else."

"God, Leah. When my mother died I didn't think I would ever stop hurting. It ate at me from the time I opened my eyes in the morning until I slept at night. Only the music kept me together, but gradually the hurt burnt itself out and I was left with nothing but rage. No sadness, just anger. Placing flowers on her grave did nothing to take it away."

"You have to let go. I'm not saying forget. You have wonderful happy memories of your mother. Those are the ones you keep with you always."

"You make it sound so easy."

It wasn't. I'd filled my life with fantasies and dreams. I'd poured Rena's grief and pain into my world to fill up its emptiness. I filled myself with everything and everyone except self.

"It's not," I admitted. "It's not easy to work on dealing with your own emotions, living your life and discovering who you are."

"How?" His whispered request was an eternity of questioning boxed into one word. I looked towards the two horses standing nearby and the idea came to me.

"How easy was learning how to ride?"

He laughed. "He threw me twice."

"But you got back on?"

He nodded, understanding the direction my questions were taking.

"Yeah, I did."

"Same thing. You have to take it one step, one day at a time. I have to do the same," I admitted.

"You're remarkable."

My breath caught at his compliment. His eyes twinkled.

"Glad you think so." I shifted to ease the pressure on my sore rear end.

"I mean it, Leah Russell. I've never met a woman like you before."

"That's because you've been looking in the wrong places."

His thumb lightly caressed my bottom lip before pinching my cheek.

"I'm not looking anymore."

Sean's reply took my breath away and my stomach clenched. I moved to stand up, but he was already there holding out his hand.

"Ready to go back?" he asked, helping me to stand. Every muscle in my thighs screamed bloody murder. The pain put spin class to shame.

I tilted my head and looked up at him from the shadow of his arms. "Now I get it. Butter me up and then make me get back on that damn horse."

"We could ride double on Storm."

"No, thanks." I eyed the big evil-looking tan gelding. "Do we have to go back so soon? I'm really feeling this place."

"Ten minutes," he smiled.

"Thirty."

"Fifteen," he shot back.

"Done." I'd turned away to walk towards the food bag for a bottle of water when Sean touched my arm.

"Do you hear that?" he asked.

"What?" I strained to listen for something other than the sound of the horses.

Then I heard it, an unnatural sound in the stillness of the desert. The horses began to snort and paw at the ground. Sean froze and pulled his arms from around my shoulders. He handed me Cloud's reins and stared out towards the west.

"We've got to go." His face was closed.

"What is it?"

"Visitors."

"Visitors?" I asked. "Why in the world should we have to leave because someone wants to see the desert from the sky?"

"They're not here to see the desert, Leah. None of the local tour operators come out this way, only the photographers, so unless you want to see more pictures of yourself in the news, we need to get out of here."

"Good point."

He quickly placed his hands around my waist and lifted me up on the horse's back. My thighs protested but I held the reins tight, trying to keep Cloud from bolting. The sound was coming closer and when I lifted my hand to cover my eyes, I saw it.

At first all I saw was a storm of dust that seemed to be bearing down on us. Its swirling violence was mesmerizing. Then the sound broke the spell. There was a helicopter flying straight towards us. I turned Cloud towards Sean's mount, gave a gentle kick to her sides, and let her go. All I could do was concentrate on not falling off. Fear beat at my heart. My concentration on not flying off that horse was the only thing that kept me from screaming.

I prayed hard as the mare's hooves pounded the dirt. The wind whipped off my hat and the sound of the helicopter beat in my ears. My hands held on tight to the pommel as my legs gripped Cloud's sides. My last thought was, This is what I get for being adventurous. If black folks were meant to ride horses, the Lord wouldn't have given us two good feet and a brain.

CHAPTER 16

I filled the tub with the hottest water I could stand, then stripped and eased in. As I sat there numbly watching steam rise, I realized two things at once. First, I had never tried to find a man to love. Like Cinderella, I'd waited for the right man, the right time, perfect moment to come to me. I'd never looked because I was afraid. Lance's choosing Sherrie over me wasn't about me. I had never put myself out there as an option. I'd always expected, hoped, dreamed, and wanted but never acted.

As Sean's face swam before my eyes, I realized I didn't want to wait anymore. I wanted Sean's arms around me. I wanted the man who had witnessed all my strengths and faults, weaknesses and vulnerabilities. I stepped out of the tub when the water became lukewarm and wrapped myself in the plush towel.

I stared into the mirror, realizing that I wasn't twenty-one and in love with the wrong man. My world didn't revolve around could-have, I-wish-I-had. I could choose, and tonight I chose to put aside the past and uncertainty. As I rubbed shea butter into my skin and then pulled on my black satin nightgown, I decided it was time to change.

Sean was sitting in the den when I came downstairs, long legs stretched out so that his head rested on the back of the overstuffed chair. His tousled hair lay over his brow and his eyes were closed as I quietly entered the room. The fading sun highlighted his tan cheek. His lips were slightly parted in sleep and his face showed the lingering weariness of the hard ride back to the house.

I couldn't help studying him. He had showered and changed clothes, replacing the faded jeans for a pair of khakis, a shirt and leather moccasins. My chest tightened, my breath caught in my throat.

Staring down at Sean, I realized that this was a man who fulfilled all my desires. This was a man who would always love me more, just like my grandmother had told me years ago. But I didn't know if I could continue to walk in his world or he in mine. I closed my mind to the thought of living my life in the media spotlight, always in the glare of the public eye.

I looked down at the brownness of my hand and I shuddered to think of what I would see in the newspapers. Everything would change. It had already begun. Within twenty-four hours, our pictures would be splattered on the front of every entertainment magazine and gossip sheet in the country and I wondered if that difference would kill the bond that had grown uninvited and strong between us.

Sean opened his eyes, blinking twice to clear them of lingering sleepiness, and then he smiled. It made my knees weak, because I knew that special unpracticed smile was real. Just for me. The warmth in his emerald-colored eyes was something I'd never tire of seeing. No matter what happened this night, I would never forget the sight that greeted me when he woke. Sean looked at me as though I were a precious treasure, to be protected, loved, adored, and that alone made me want to weep.

The silence continued as the room grew dim. I could neither move nor speak. I didn't know what to say as I fought to quiet the butterflies gathered in my stomach. The smile vanished from his lips as those green eyes of his searched my face.

"Are you okay, Leah?" he asked.

"I'm a little nervous," I answered honestly.

Sean stood slowly and brushed a few strands of hair from his face. My fingers dug into the back of the chair I was standing beside. I'd been so sure that I was ready to take this last step. Positive that I would banish my ghosts and give reality a chance to wipe away the half-remembered dreams and longing.

"I thought you'd need a little time alone," Sean stated.

He had come to stand opposite me. Unspoken words seemed to hang in the air between us.

I nodded. "I did a lot of thinking."

The image of the photographer's lens flashed before my eyes. The sound of the helicopter's rotors sounded in my ears and the gallop of the horse resonated in my bones.

"Come to any conclusions?" Sean asked. There was a guarded vulnerability in his voice now.

This man who sang in front of millions, collected awards like baseball cards and was voted one of the most handsome men in America felt uncertain because of me. The way he half turned away gave me more of an insight into his inner self, the boy who knew all about rejection. Sean had been the school outcast and the class rebel. Music had become his escape, until he discovered that it could get him what he thought he wanted: money and friends.

I looked at him. "Not really. I still have a lot of things in my head."

"I didn't mean for this to happen." He tried to turn towards the window.

I moved around the chair, reached out and grabbed his hand. "But I'm here with you now because I'm listening to my heart," I continued.

I reached up to caress his cheek and whispered, "I walked up to a stranger who now means more to me than I know how to put into words."

He opened his mouth and I placed my fingers over his lips.

"You always said that you belong to me because I saved your life. Right now mine seems to be spinning out of control, Sean. The sight of the helicopter won't leave my mind. Help me take it away."

I moved my fingers from his lips and ran them over his cheek. The feel of the slightly prickly stubble coupled with the sight of my mocha-colored hand sliding over his jaw sent shivers over the back of my neck. I cradled his face in my hands and I looked into his eyes.

How could I turn from him? Some part of me was still the baby of the family, selfish. I didn't want to share him with the world; I wanted him all to myself. But as my head struggled to gain control, my heart led the way. Not even the voice in the back of my mind warning me that this would change things could stop me because I didn't care. There'd be no going back. I wouldn't go to my grave with regrets lying in the pit of my stomach.

My heart pounded as I placed my fingertips over his lips once more to silence the words I saw pouring out his eyes. As his arms encircled my waist, I leaned in close, enjoying the spice of his cologne.

Standing next to the window as the sunset bathed us in coppery highlights, I moved my hand and placed my lips upon his, catching his breath in my mouth. I wanted to seduce him with sweet loving words that would show him how much he meant to me, but I didn't have the courage.

Instead of speaking, I curled my arms around his neck and fell into his long, tender kiss, losing myself in the sensual whirlpool of desire. When his tongue caressed mine, the electric shock of my arousal could have lit up the desert sky.

"Make love to me, Sean," I whispered after pulling back.

"Are you sure?"

I looked into his eyes and the breath left my chest. He wasn't Sean Andrews, the famous rock star, or dear friend. He was a man, a man fully aroused, a man who wanted me.

"Oh, yes," I said softly. I took his hand and let him lead me upstairs to his bedroom. And in the silence, I realized that I wanted no declarations of love from Sean. I just wanted him and the magic that which always seemed to flow at the touch of his hands.

I woke up, opened my eyes and looked at the naked man lying next to me.

I'm in love with this man.

I waited for the wonder. I waited for the feeling that all is perfect in the world. Instead, I felt like a Monday morning. That Monday morning when you get out of bed and look at the bathroom mirror and lie to yourself by saying, "Damn, girl, you look good today."

Sean lay still in sleep. One arm hugged the pillow while the other lay crooked across my stomach. Lord, the man was gorgeous. His broad shoulders were relaxed in sleep and his dark blond hair lay tousled on the pillow.

Last night, he'd caressed and kissed almost every inch of my body. He'd loved me in that curl-a-girl's-toes-come-back-for-more way. I'd had the cake and drunk the Kool-Aid. It was no wonder women lost their minds. I'd left every bit of my common sense on the floor with my nightgown. I looked at him and tears burned in the back of my throat. He was so damn handsome. Not the Hollywood stuff, but the blue-gold of a summer sunrise over the Pacific, the intense warmth that turned cold sand into shimmering gold.

I wanted to bury my face in the nape of his neck and inhale, but his eyes remained closed and his parted lips emitted a sigh. Just like a man: clueless. I wanted him to wake up, look at me and curl his arms around me as if I were the love of his life. I wanted soft words and warm reassurances.

Instead, I slipped quietly out his bed and gathered my scattered clothes. Fear had me telling lies in order to protect myself because last night was too good to be true.

I'm a grown woman with needs. Uh-huh, this was just good sex. By the time I got into the shower, I'd managed to define my relationship with Sean as a loving friendship. As the warm water spilled down my back and ran over the soft, sensitive places Sean's fingers and lips had touched, I'd worked out that we were just two people who cared about one another.

When I got out of the shower and stepped into the steam-filled bathroom, I reached for the towel and stopped. Sean stood leaning against the wall, staring at me with a hungry look and a half frown. He stepped forward and reached for my towel, not for a second breaking eye contact. He took the towel from my nerveless fingers and proceeded to wrap me in the thick cotton.

As I looked down at his hands, the truth hit me between the eyes. What I felt for the man was deep and strong. Not the turn out the lights, hold me tight, and love me through the night feeling. It was a slow warmth that started in the middle of my stomach and had every other body part tingling.

I shivered at Sean's touch, loving the surprising coolness of his fingers on my skin. He leaned into me and I met him in his kiss.

It was not like the first tender meeting of our mouths. He pressed his mouth down hard on mine, as if he had better do it fast, before I could pull away. But it awakened in me a hunger to match.

"Sean," I murmured. As he wrapped his arms around me, I knew that sometime in the hours, weeks, and months that I'd known him, Sean had taken over prime real estate in my heart. Lies and truth; love and grief. As he carried me towards the bedroom, the things Sean did with his mouth and hands turned me inside out and upside down.

I had never known that feeling until then. I had never known the way it could fill you up and carry you away. That morning, he treated my body like a temple.

Every touch, delicate kiss, and warm breath was a loving prayer. As with the night before Sean stopped and placed on the condom without being asked, and his concern touched me. As he whispered questions soft and hard, fast and slow, I got lost in the pleasure of his touch.

Sean asked. His softly lilting voice asked if he had pleased me. The unselfishness of his loving touched my soul deeply, and, when we both drifted down from that high plateau, I turned my face into the pillow and closed my eyes, trapping the tears I promised I'd never shed.

Loving Sean was irresistible. It was something warm and perfect. A feeling you got to have all the time. I wondered how I would get through this, having let my fool self fall in love again.

For the second time, I woke slowly in Sean's bed. I opened my eyes to see him staring down at me with a look of tenderness. This was where I wanted to be always. Safe and loved under cool cotton patterned sheets with my body next to his. But the thought of what I looked like as the muted sun lit the room made me want to pull the sheet up over my head and hide. Mornings were not for me.

"Good morning, darling," he whispered.

"Good afternoon," I automatically corrected. Morning had to have come and gone a long time ago from the way the shadowed sunbeams were cutting across the bedroom.

"Don't . . ." I protested.

Too late. Even before I could finish my protest, Sean was kissing me. I opened my eyes to see his smile just before I felt a weight settle on my chest. I watched as Simba stepped over me and then curled up into the warm space between us. Sean started stroking his fur and I swore that cat was grinning as his loud purr reverberated through the room.

"In my head, I imagined us waking up like this a thousand times after we first met. But I just never included Simba in the scene."

"I never saw you as being a cat person," I said, changing the subject. I wouldn't allow myself to read more into his words.

"I like cats. They're like women. You never know what they're thinking." He watched me closely.

"Leah," he continued after a pause.

"Hmmm."

"Don't do that again."

"What?" I shifted under the sheet, trying to use it as a shield.

"Disappear before I wake up. You did it the first time we met."

"It wasn't intentional."

"I had a hell of a time tracking you down."

I smiled at the irritation in his voice. "You never did tell me how you found me."

"Luck. There were few beautiful women at the party," he said, reaching out and twirling his finger around a lock of my hair.

"Liar." I smiled.

Sean continued, "I bribed Hughes to get a copy of the guest list. Lucky for me you were the only Leah at the party that night."

"So what did you bribe Hughes with?"

"I have to sing at his anniversary party."

"He's married?" The gorgeous movie producer always made *People* magazine's most beautiful list.

Sean laughed at my shocked expression. "He's also got two boys and a girl."

"I didn't know."

"Famous people are human, too, Leah."

"I know that."

"Do you, now?" He raised a doubting eyebrow.

"Yes."

"Then why are you afraid?"

"I'm not afraid. I just don't understand the world you live in."

"It's the same as yours, just a little more exposed."

"Exposed." The word sounded strange to me. "There was a helicopter combing the desert to find you. I think that qualifies as a little more than exposed."

"It's all part of the game."

"I don't play games, Sean."

"Neither do I. This," he reached out and placed a kiss on my neck, "this is real. I like waking up beside you. I like the soft warmth of your skin touching mine."

I shivered.

"The emptiness of our stomachs is also real. Now why don't we take a shower and talk about this over a nice gourmet meal that I'm going to cook for you." He laughed as he pushed Simba off the bed and stood up with nothing on. I reached down and wrapped the light blanket around myself and headed towards the door.

"My shower's big enough for four," he encouraged.

I looked at Sean standing buck naked with a wicked grin on his face.

"Then it should be plenty big enough for you, your ego, and those cute hairy legs of yours."

"Ouch. That hurt." Sean grabbed his chest, pretending to be in pain.

I smiled in triumph and then ruined the moment by darting out of the room.

CHAPTER 17

By the time we finished eating lunch, the Arizona sunlight filled the house.

"Hey." Sean's voice woke me from my daydream.

"Hmmm." I turned towards him as he leaned down and kissed me.

"I've got to jump into a conference call. Do you need anything?"

"I'm fine." I yawned and reached down to stoke a softly snoring Simba.

I stood up, stretched, and watched Sean as he walked out of the room. A smile came to my lips as I eyed his backside. At least the media had gotten that right. The man had a nice one. Walking over to the entertainment center, I began to browse his extensive CD collection. I ran my fingers over titles in Italian, Japanese, French, and Arabic until I hit pay dirt. Nestled in its own compartment I found the blues sitting pretty with jazz, R&B, reggae, hip-hop, and rap.

I grabbed some old school and new school and stood in front of the stereo placing CD after CD into the player. Turning around I fiddled with the remote control until I found the right button. I stood in the middle of the sun-filled room and swayed to the sweet sound of jazz as it poured into the room from invisible speakers.

Opening my eyes after the third song had finished, I didn't skip a beat at seeing Sean leaning against the wall, staring. I lifted my hand and slowly curved a finger.

"Come on," I coaxed.

I watched as Sean sauntered over and I wrapped my arms around his hips and settled snug against his body, controlling the movement with my hands. I laid my head against his chest and we swayed back and forth as the soft tinkle of the piano and the smoky voice of Etta James filled the room.

We danced through heartbreak and pain, love and loss.

"I should have guessed," he started.

I looked up to see his quick grin. "Guessed what?"

"That you were a blues girl."

"Not true. I'm a jazz girl first," I proclaimed.

"Hmmm, I'll have to remember that." He smiled. "I always thought of you as the play-it-straight type. You know those jazz lovers get a little wild sometimes," he hinted.

"I've had my fair share of walking on the wild side," I ruefully admitted. "I've already broken rule number one of the friendship commandments. You're not supposed to sleep with your best friend."

"I'm shocked." Sean's eyes widened in mock surprise. "Could this be Leah Russell admitting to breaking the rules?"

"It's your bad influence," I charged.

"Me?" he echoed, trying to pull off a wide-eyed look of innocence.

I pointed a finger at his chest. "Yes, you. Mr. U-Turn on a one-way street."

"That was an accident."

"Really?" I raised an eyebrow.

"No," he admitted sheepishly.

"Let's not forget the time you . . ."

"Okay, woman." Sean pinched me lightly on the rear. "No need to recount all my sins. Just keep trying to reform this jaded man."

"That would take a lifetime," I grinned.

"I've got plenty of time, darling," he declared before leaning close for a kiss.

"Sean, you don't have to make any promises to me."

"Why'd you say that?"

"I wasn't kidding about breaking the friend rule," I said, looking up at him. "But I have to say that I have no regrets. I'm not sorry if this causes problems between you and Delia," I confessed. The up-and-coming actress was the last person in the world I was thinking about.

"Believe me, Leah, the relationship I have with Delia is strictly platonic."

I raised an eyebrow. "Like our friendship?"

"She is and has always been in love with Nicholas Chapman."

I drew back startled. "But the magazine said . . ."

"And we know how credible those things are, don't we?"

I shook my head, embarrassed.

Sean continued, "Now while we're on the subject, I have to admit that I'm not sorry that the press published that photo of us together."

"You're not?" I parroted, confused.

"I still dream about the first time I met you. That night on the cliffs, you were so beautiful in the moonlight. Like no one I'd ever met before."

He pulled me closer and the way he nibbled my ear sent pricks of pleasure running down my skin. "I tried to get you completely alone for months and, just when I thought I had a chance, you moved to New York."

"I didn't know," I stammered, my stomach churning with butterflies.

"That's because you're such a blind little goose," he said before kissing me. In Sean's arms I melted like a schoolgirl and we moved to the bedroom to begin a new dance. The man made it easy for me to forget Etta James's sorrow-filled warnings of morning heartache.

Much later as we relaxed together, I noticed that Sean had a faraway look on his face. His lips were parted and his eyes seemed to close slightly as he stared towards some unknown vision or listened to some silent song.

"I almost can't believe you're here. It's seems as though I've waited forever to hold you."

I smiled. "Sean, you never struck me as the patient type."

"I'm not." He reached over and tucked a stray lock of hair behind my ear. "You were skittish as a newborn filly when we first met. I didn't want to frighten you off."

"You could never scare me." I snuggled deeper into his arms. "But that hideous curly wig of yours was awful."

"You didn't like it?"

"No. It made you look like a Beatles reject."

"I'm hurt."

"Pleeze," I chuckled.

"The only other thing I've always wanted was a home of my own," Sean stated.

"Another one? You've got what?" I counted on my fingers, "Four?"

"Not like that. I want to pull into the garage and know I'm not just coming back to an empty place and cold, lonely bed. I want to have the life my parents had. Something simple and good."

"What about your singing? I thought that was all you ever wanted," I questioned, puzzled.

"I've enjoyed my career, don't get me wrong. There was a point where the only thing that I ever thought could make me happy was standing on stage and putting my all into the music and getting all that energy from the crowd because they were feeling me: my words, my tune. But I've realized that once I leave the stage I'm empty. I want a future that doesn't just have me. I want a family."

My gaze locked with his serious green eyes and I nodded in understanding. Once upon a time, I'd wanted that dream. White picket fence and all that.

"So what are your plans?" I asked, tightening the belt of my robe.

"I've thought about writing."

"Sounds right up your alley. Have you talked to the band about that?"

"No, not yet. The idea's still a little new. We're going back into the studio in a couple of months. Hopefully, I'll have figured something out by then."

"You can still have a family even if you're with Exile. I've read plenty of success stories in which celebrities balance work and family."

"And you've read about plenty of divorces. Dad never put his career above us. He tried to be home as much as possible. Mom never said anything, but he turned down a lot of offers to direct just because it would take him away from home for too long."

I stood still with my face towards the window, watching as the sun began to set and evening shadows began creeping across the desert.

"What about you?" he asked, gently massaging my back.

"This sounds crazy, but I want to adopt two children."

"Tell me more."

I shrugged and tried to sound casual as I admitted one of my lifelong goals. "When I was a little girl, two days before Christmas Mom and Dad would gather all of us kids into the car and we would go to this tall red building just outside of the city. We'd wait in the car as they went in and came out with a little boy or girl that would spend Christmas at our home." I closed my eyes seeing a little boy named Hughes as he held on tight to my father's hand.

"Mom and Dad bought presents for the kids and placed them under the tree. Every Christmas I would watch that little girl or little boy with tears in their eyes opening those packages. As I grew older and could understand why the kids enjoyed the presents so much, it tore my heart out." I could feel the wetness growing behind my eyes.

"I'm driven to help those kids. I want to give them a family, a childhood as great as mine was. So I've been building a nest egg. My plan is to buy an old house near my parents' and move back to Philly."

"And your own children?"

I turned my head to look at him and my lips curved into a half-bitter whimsical smile. "Thought about that. Who knows if I'll get married? Being single isn't the worst thing that could happen to me. Maybe that future soul mate will support my dream, maybe not. All I know is that I'm going to find that house and fill it with love."

Sean hugged me tighter to his chest and I was happy that I couldn't see his face in that instant. The conversation was hitting too close to home. I didn't want him making promises he couldn't keep and I didn't want to talk about a future in a world outside of the here and now of him and me.

I'd had dreams of Lance and they had been stolen. I learned the hard way that I had to dream alone. Somewhere along the way I quit dreaming of white picket fences, kids, and a family. That didn't mean the hope was gone, just buried. I didn't want to open my eyes to discover that all this was but another dream.

We stood looking out French doors in Sean's bedroom. I leaned back in his arms and sighed. The lingering light bathed the hills in glorious shades of soft copper and gold. I felt my heart catch at its quiet beauty. That night as I lay in Sean's arms, I vowed to take this time and lock away in my heart a treasure to be taken out and remembered when being a Strong Black Woman got to be too much.

"Get my hair wet and you're a dead man, Sean Andrews," I threatened, standing next to the whirlpool tub clutching my towel. After a nice French dinner at a restaurant in Phoenix, we'd decided to have dessert back at the ranch. Shaking my head, I wondered how I'd let him talk me into this.

"Now why'd you think I'd do something like that?" Sean asked.

I watched as his lips curled into the devilish smile that had graced the covers of albums and magazines. The sight of him leaning back in the bubble-filled Jacuzzi set off warning bells in my head while igniting a fire in my stomach.

"Come on and get in," he coaxed. "I promise not to splash you."

"I'm trusting you, Scottish," I said before dropping the towel and carefully stepping into the warm water.

"Yeah, yeah. Come over here." Sean reached over to pull me closer.

I slid back into Sean's lap and nestled comfortably between his legs. Just as I leaned back and closed my eyes, his arms wrapped around me and I felt the tickly sensation of his fingers on my stomach.

"Hey stop that . . ." I called out, almost jumping out of the water.

"Someone's ticklish," he teased.

I retaliated by pinching the sensitive inside of his thighs, ending his gloating.

"Now how was your phone call to the office earlier?" he questioned.

I fluttered my fingers in the bubbles and focused on the glow of the candles. Although I was technically on vacation, I couldn't completely get away from work. "You don't want to know."

"Come on . . . what happened?" he persisted.

I sighed. "I think every advertising exec in the office is trying to get into my good graces. After checking my voicemail, I've gotten five lunch offers, three gift certificates, and my boss generously gave me two extra weeks of vacation."

"That doesn't sound so bad. Scoot forward so I can wash your back," Sean requested.

I sighed as the warm water rolled down my back, followed by the gentle rubbing of the washcloth. "Every woman under the age of sixty wants to meet you and they've had reporters in the lunchroom trying to get the scoop on my personal life."

"I'm sorry," Sean's voice whispered. "Is there anything else I can do?" He sent chills up and down my spine by placing a kiss on the back of my neck.

"Hmmm . . ." I muttered as my eyes closed, enjoying the sensation of his warm hands gliding over my skin. "You could move a little to the left," I suggested.

"Not that. Can I help you with work?"

"Thanks, but as you said, by the time I get back to New York, this will all have blown over," I responded.

I opened my eyes and turned around slightly to look at Sean. The flickering light of the candles bathed us both in a warm, gold light.

"Your turn," I said, moving to the other side of the Jacuzzi and gesturing for him to turn around. "I'll do your back."

"But I was just getting started," he protested.

"I know," I replied, my voice a husky whisper. I smiled, letting my eyes slowly look down. "Now turn around," I repeated.

"As milady wishes." Sean grinned.

"I like the sound of that. Now come over here."

I picked up a loofah and lowered it into the Jacuzzi, then squeezed it so that the water splashed over his shoulders and ran down his back. "Bend forward a little, please," I requested and started to scrub his shoulders.

"Tell me if I'm rubbing too hard," I said after a couple of minutes.

"Did I ever tell you that from the moment you arrived at my table that first dinner we shared, I knew my life would never be the same?" Sean confessed.

"No," I whispered before the loofah slipped through my fingers. I was reaching past Sean to grab it when he turned around.

"You were so alive and beautiful," he said.

I stared into his eyes as Sean's fingers caressed the line of my neck and slowly drifted downwards to encircle my breast. I felt the tickle of his hair on my skin.

"I wondered what you'd feel like naked in my arms. Your scent, your smile, the sound of your laughter gave me a rush I hadn't felt in years," he said, his voice a seductive growl.

"Sean," I murmured as my neck fell back and I could no longer ignore the erotic sensation of his hands caressing my skin. His lips and fingers were sending my body temperature into overdrive, leaving me gasping for air.

"That," he said, his face mere inches from mine. "That sound of my name coming from your lips." He bent his head and nuzzled my neck. His teeth nibbling my skin sent waves up and down my spine.

Sean continued, "I dreamed of that sound, Leah. Night after night, lying in my empty hotel bed after hanging up the phone, I wanted you so bad I couldn't see straight."

His lips closed on mine and I wrapped my arms around him. Sean's teeth grazed my bottom lip gently before he laid claim to my body with his hands. There was no restraint in Sean's kiss. I tasted in his kiss a hunger and longing that matched mine.

My nipples flattened against his chest, aching, boiling. I pulled my mouth from his and moaned low in my throat as his lips moved downward across my skin towards my breasts.

"Sean." I could only gasp as I felt his fingers gently caressing the fold within my inner thighs. Every nerve in my body seemed to pulse in time with his fingers.

I twisted my fingers in Sean's hair, pulled his head back and kissed him. I wanted to make him burn just like me, make him hunger for my body just like I wanted his. He covered my face in tiny kisses and soft bites. It took all I had to pull away and quickly step out of the Jacuzzi.

"What?" came Sean's voice, and I bent to pick up the towel. "Why'd you leave me, Leah?" he asked as he moved to get out of the water.

The sound of my husky come-hither laughter echoed in the steam-filled room. I let my gaze drift over the sight of his body, making sure that the desire I felt showed in my eyes.

"I didn't leave you, Scottish. Why don't you come over here and let me dry you off?" I waved the towel in Sean's direction.

"You've got a naughty look in your eyes," he said, stepping out the Jacuzzi.

"Are you afraid?" I taunted, putting my hand to my waist.

"Do I need to be?" Sean asked as he reached to put his arms around me.

"No touching," I ordered, taking a step back.

"What kind of game are we playing?" He raised an eyebrow as I sneaked behind him and began to dry his back.

"It's called no touching," I answered.

"Hmmm, what are the rules to his game?" he whispered, trying to move in close.

"You can't touch me," I said slowly.

"But you can touch me?"

"Yes," I answered before placing a long slow kiss on his chest and gently raking my fingernails over his thighs.

The sound of his raspy in-drawn breath was all the gratification I needed. Moving away, I tugged on the towel Sean was holding, urging him towards the bedroom.

"Now lie down and close your eyes," I instructed. I stood by the bed and watched as Sean slid between the sheets. His eyes never left mine as I edged into the bed until I was leaning over his chest. "Remember, no touching," I warned.

"What happens if I break the rules?" Sean asked.

Instead of answering, I leaned in over his chest, letting the tips of my breasts skim across his chest as I kissed him on his lips.

"You don't want to know," I cautioned, enjoying the way Sean's pupils dilated. I loved the feel of his eyes on my body and the knowledge that I could bring him pleasure. Slowly, I let my finger trail down his body and followed each touch with a kiss and slow lick. The closer I came to his waist, the more restless his body became. And when I found him ready and I touched that place that brought me such fulfillment, his shout was all the encouragement I needed.

"You're killing me, Leah," he cried out.

"No, I'm about to take you to heaven," I announced, moving to straddle him.

Sean and I moved together as one. I felt him move upward, plunging deep, filling me as I sank down. I closed my eyes, wanting to savor the fullness, but Sean wasn't having it. Before I knew it I was pinned beneath his body with my arms around his waist.

"Sean . . ." I pleaded as he withdrew.

"Again," he groaned as my hips moved in tune with his.

I opened my eyes, staring blindly, unable to focus for the darts of pleasure rippling through my body.

"Sean, please," I called out as my legs wrapped around him, urging him closer.

"Now, sweetheart." He thrust deeply as I closed my eyes and wave after wave of sensation crashed over me. I turned to look at Sean as he rolled over, pulling me into his arms.

"Are you all right?" he asked, his hands gently stroking my back as I rested my head on his shoulder.

"If I felt any better, Scottish, it'd be against the law." I barely managed to gather enough energy to smile.

Sean's laugh was more a quiet rumble. "You never cease to amaze me."

"Surprised you, huh?" I whispered.

He raised an eyebrow and stared into my eyes. "I love you, Leah Russell."

Those words stopped my heart and left me speechless. Long after Sean had fallen into sleep I lay staring at the ceiling, wondering when I'd wake up. Wondering when the dream would end.

I woke up the next morning to an empty bed and the smell of coffee. Taking a moment to stretch, I reached over and put on the white robe laying across the chair. Just as I reached the end of the hallway, the sound of Sean's voice stopped me in my tracks.

"Damn it, John! Leave it alone! I don't give a shit about what they want. This is what I want. Do your job and get those jackals to back off."

Pause.

"That's right. It's my life, my obligations. I won't have Leah being the main course of a media feeding frenzy. Do whatever it takes, but keep them away from her."

I walked in as Sean slammed the tiny cell phone down on the table. "Good morning," I called out.

Sean's frown softened as I stood on my tiptoes and placed a kiss on his lips. I fought the urge to snuggle into the clean, crisp smell that surrounded him. The look of tenderness in his eyes melted what was left of the ice surrounding my heart.

"Good morning to you, too, love. Hungry?" he asked, giving me a hug.

"Starved," I admitted as Sean raised an eyebrow.

"Good, because I'm about to make you the best omelet you've ever had."

"That's a pretty big boast, my friend," I said before turning to pull down two coffee mugs.

"Trust me. You're going to like this omelet," he said while spraying the pan.

I smiled and gave him a pat on the rear as I passed on the way to the fridge. "I already do," I teased.

"You're wicked, Leah," he said with an easy grin.

"Hmmm." I opened the well-stocked refrigerator and pulled out the cream.

"It's such a great day outside, I thought we'd pack a picnic basket, saddle the horses, and have lunch out on the mesa."

I leaned back against the countertop and watched as he expertly folded the golden brown omelet.

"No, thanks," I said after taking a sip of coffee. I just wanted to stay right there, safe from prying eyes, helicopters, and clicking cameras.

"Come on. Don't tell me you're afraid of riding Cloud, not after the other day."

I looked at Sean over the rim of the cup. "So are you going to tell me about what's got you yelling at your best friend and publicist so early this morning?"

Sean glanced up quickly and then back down. "Do you want mushrooms in your omelet?"

"Sean," I warned. "Yes, I want mushrooms in my omelet, but don't try to change the subject."

He sighed. "The volume of calls about you has increased. Everybody wants to know about you."

"No," I corrected. "They want to know what it is that attracts you to me. What in this ordinary, everyday black woman."

Sean placed the omelets on two plates and headed towards the dining room table. "Even on your worst day, there's nothing ordinary about you."

"Thank you for the compliment, but cut the flattery and tell me what's going on."

"John wants you to take some interviews. He thinks that it'll calm the press down."

"You don't believe him, do you?" I questioned, taking a seat at the table.

He shook his head, "I don't think they're going to back off."

"I can handle it, Sean." I was lying through my teeth and we both knew it. In the space of a week, I'd jumped out of the frying pan into the fire.

"I know." He took a bite of breakfast before putting down his fork. "I just don't want you to have to deal with it."

"Thank you," I said, reaching across the table and taking his outstretched hand. "Nothing's going to change in the next couple of hours, so why don't we just enjoy this good breakfast and spend the day in bed watching TV?"

"Leah . . ." Sean started.

I interrupted by pointing at him with my fork. "Nope, don't want to hear it. Today is our day. Let's worry about tomorrow later."

His lips curled into a smile and I let out a sigh as he went back to eating. Tomorrow I'd have to wake up from the bed I'd made and all I could do was hope—hope that the sky fell, a politician slept with an aide, that some celebrity got arrested or married, anything to keep the harsh light of the media from burning me.

CHAPTER 18

I had spent the best week of my life in bed or on a horse. I sighed, looking straight ahead through the Jeep's windshield.

"You like Arizona, don't you?" Sean asked as we drove along the empty highway towards the airport.

"I do." I loved the mesas and the cacti, the sweet silence interrupted by the call of a lone coyote. There was peacefulness to the desert.

"Ever since you came here, you've been happy. Are you sure you want to go back? I can still turn the Jeep around."

"No. I can't hide forever. My parents are coming back in a few days, Sean. There's no way they're going to miss all that stuff in the news."

"You could call," he suggested.

I rolled my eyes. "There are some things you can't do over the phone." I laughed.

"I'd be more than willing to be there with you, Leah."

"Oh, no," I half shouted, then calmed down. "I know that you only want to help, but the best thing that you can do for me is to stay away until the reporters find another target."

"You shouldn't handle this alone."

"You mean my parents?"

"No, I mean everything." I could hear frustration barely checked in his voice. "I want to help you," Sean said.

My voice softened. "I appreciate that more than you know. You've become my knight in shining armor, you know that?"

He briefly glanced my way, then returned his attention to the road. "You're just saying that."

I shook my head. "You know me better than that. I only say what I mean. You've saved me from my worst enemy."

"Who's that?" he asked.

"Myself." I laughed.

"I want you to stay."

"We can't hide out here forever, Scottish," I said, using my nickname for Sean.

"We could try."

I sighed and turned to look outside at the passing scenery. "Are you deliberately trying to make this harder than it already is?"

"That depends. Is it working?" he asked.

"Would it make you feel better if I said yes?"

"Yes, Leah, it would."

"Then feel better, Sean," I replied honestly.

Several heartbeats passed before I asked, "So when will you be back in New York?"

"Pretty soon, I think, but I don't have to be back in the studio until next month," he answered.

"That's good," I said as Sean brought the Jeep to a stop next to the curb. I turned to pick up the pet carrier.

"No, let me get that." He jumped out of the Jeep and went around to the back.

I hopped out the passenger side and was immediately greeted by a curbside check-in attendant.

"Good afternoon, miss. Where are you flying to today?" he asked.

"Leah!"

I turned around to see Sean standing by the Jeep. "I'll meet you in front of the ticket counter. I'm going to park the car."

"Okay." I smiled before turning back to the airline associate. "Sorry about that that."

"No problem. Will you be checking two bags?"

"No, just one. I don't think my cat would appreciate flying in the cargo hold," I joked.

"Okay, looks like you're set. Final destination LaGuardia Airport, New York City. Your flight leaves out of Gate D4. Have a nice day."

"Thank you. You do the same," I replied, giving him a two-dollar tip before stepping through the automatic glass doors.

Stepping into the airport terminal was like stepping from an oven into a freezer. The refrigerated air sent chills up and down my arms. Looking at my watch, I saw had about an hour before the plane was scheduled to depart. With Simba in hand, I took a seat near the ticket counter and waited for Sean.

I had to wait only a few minutes before I spotted the familiar swagger coming in my direction. I noticed the way female heads turned as he walked towards me and smiled. Sean bent over and kissed me on the cheek before picking up Simba's bag.

"So, do we have to put the big guy through X-ray?" Sean asked.

I shook my head, laughing. "I don't think so."

"So are you ready to go?"

"To be honest I really don't want to go. Simba doesn't, either."

"Good, I don't want you to leave, either."

By the time I looked up we'd walked through the terminal and had reached the waiting lounge outside of the security checkpoint.

Sean gave my hand a gentle squeeze. "Hey, there's something I need to do. I'll be right back."

"Okay." I took a seat at the window and pulled out the *Essence* magazine I'd picked up at O'Hare on my way to Phoenix. I tried to read the articles but found my mind drifting.

"Leah?"

"Hmmm . . ." I looked over to find Sean lounging in the chair beside me.

"Are you okay?"

I turned, giving Sean a reassuring smile. "I'm fine. Just a little sad."

"Why?"

"I hate saying good-byes," I replied.

"This isn't good-bye, Leah."

I stood up and took a step back. "I know, but it feels like it is."

"Trust me. This is only the beginning," he boasted.

I rolled my eyes as he gave me a wink before pushing his sunglass back up. "You are something else, Sean Andrews." I laughed as we held one another's hands. Before I knew it, the announcement came over the speaker and we both stood.

"Time for you to go."

I blinked my eyes to clear away the hint of tears before meeting his gaze. "Thank you for a wonderful time."

"Can I get a kiss before you leave me?" he said, giving me a devastating grin.

I took a step towards Sean and, uncaring of the prying eyes, kissed him full on the lips.

"Good-bye, Scottish," I whispered, feeling regret twist in my stomach.

"Good afternoon, ladies and gentlemen. We would like to begin boarding American Airlines Flight 1168 to O'Hare International Airport. We will be boarding by row number. Anyone in rows one to ten, please beginning boarding."

It took me less than ten minutes to pass through security. As I boarded the DC-9, I carried Simba's carry-on in my left hand and sorrow in the other. All I wanted was the strong, sensitive, sexy man who gave me butterflies in my stomach and dreams of happily ever after.

CHAPTER 19

Resist Mars's plans to run away. Looking? Follow your Mom's love advice, courtesy of romance-friendly Venus. Found him? Lean on his strong shoulders around the twentieth, when Mercury rocks your world. Work. Save the windfall from Juno. You'll feel more confident with a nest egg than without.

Too little too late. So much for horoscopes, I thought. I put the magazine back in the seat pocket and bent down to check on Simba. The cat was snoozing away in the dark green nylon bag. Sean had bought the deluxe bag with mesh windows just before my move to New York. Releasing a sigh, I leaned back against the headrest, not bothering to look out the window.

Unbidden, the image of my grandmother rose in my mind. Her words seemed to haunt me as the murmuring of my fellow passengers and the sound of the classical music faded away. I could hear grandmother's tear-stained voice as she gazed up at her black and white wedding portrait.

"Only give your heart to a man who loves you more than you love him. You hear me, girls? Make sure he loves you more than the last piece of food on his plate, more than the last nickel in his pocket, and more than the shirt on his back. Only marry the man who loves you most, and he won't leave you blue. That's what I did," she stated. My grandmother's eyes had glistened with unshed tears as she stared at my grandfather's smiling face.

It wasn't the movement of the plane that pulled me from memories, but the feeling of hands at my hips. I opened my eyes and turned just in time to see Sean's face as he inserted the buckle on my seatbelt.

"You . . ." I couldn't get the words out.

"Yes?" he smiled.

"How . . . why?" I stuttered.

"I bought the last ticket and bribed the woman who would have been sitting next to you," he explained.

"Why, Sean?"

"Do I really need to tell you?"

"Yes. I need to hear your words."

"Because I love you, darling, and I realized that letting you go back alone could jeopardize our relationship."

I caught the glance of the older woman across the aisle and looked away. Unfolding the thin airline blanket, I leaned against the pillow I'd placed against the window. I turned away and closed my eyes, determined not to burst into tears. The last week of my life had been too good to be true. But Sean's presence in the seat beside me changed all of that.

"It's a long flight."

My heart began to thump as he whispered in my ear. I squeezed my eyes a little tighter.

"And I'm afraid of flying," he continued. I suppressed the urge to smile at the child-like tone of his voice.

"I need someone to hold my hand."

As soon as he finished the sentence, the thin blanket moved as his hand slipped underneath to rest on mine. His shoulder settled next to mine and I felt the scratchy feel of his five o'clock shadow on my neck.

"Much better," he murmured.

"I'm seeing a new side of you, Sean," I said, barely hearing my voice over the sound of the flight video.

"Oh, and what side didn't you see last night, darling?"

I felt the blood rush to my cheeks, but ignored the way my body reacted to the memory of our lovemaking the night before.

"The pain-in-my-ass side," I responded sweetly, needing to inject a little levity into the situation. "If you weren't such a good friend I'd cheerfully slap you."

"That's because you care so much," he paused. "And Leah?"

"What?" I bit out.

"We are so much more than friends."

"I'm not an obsessed groupie, Sean," I said. The words flew out of my mouth.

"I know you're not, but I am," he whispered in my ear before placing light kisses on my neck.

I turned towards him and tried to read his face, but couldn't. It was like learning a new language and I didn't know the words, couldn't form the letters.

"Did I ever tell you that the week before my mother died Exile's second album went platinum?"

I nodded my head, remembering that he had spoken briefly of the event that night on the cliffs.

"I listened to Mom throwing up after every meal, watched her lose the sparkle in her eyes, watched her lose her hair and lose so much weight that she was nothing but skin and bones. The person who was so much a part of my life was transformed into someone shriveled and wasted. As the press surrounded my parents' home and hounded me, I sat by her bedside with my father, both of us powerless to stop the cancer from destroying her." His voice came soft, almost as if he were talking to himself instead of me. That handsome face grew tight with grief.

A lump formed in my throat. Sean's grief was so deep and so real I could drown in it.

"I've learned the hard way that life isn't something you take for granted, Leah. Time is precious. If you find someone that makes you happy—completes you—you've got to grab on tight and never let go."

I felt his fingers wrap around mine and I relaxed into the seat and gave Sean a gentle kiss on his lips. There was nothing I could say, so I let that gesture speak for me. He closed his eyes and with his fingers entwined with mine we both drifted into sleep as the plane pulled away from the earth and climbed towards the clouds.

Taking off didn't turn out to be a problem, but landing and getting out of the airport turned into a nightmare. Simba's sedative had worn off and the cat was less than pleased. Even though it was against regulations to let the cat out of the bag, the flight attendants couldn't keep from falling over themselves to pet Simba while he lay in Sean's lap.

"Should have upgraded to first class," Sean complained.

"And you didn't why?"

"All sold out, and everyone I might have bribed was on the plane."

I just glared at him. Screaming on an airplane was a bad idea, but I wanted to so bad. The flight attendants wouldn't leave us alone, and even the co-pilot came all the way to the back of the plane to get Sean's autograph for his wife and daughter.

Sean just took it in stride and even tried to pull me into the madness, but I wasn't having it. I wanted to get as far away as I could from people with awestruck eyes and from Sean with his charming, butter-couldn't-melt-in-my-mouth speeches. And when the time came for us to head out of LaGuardia's doors, I would have hopped into the nearest cab, but Sean, damn the man, wouldn't give me my suitcase and cat.

"I'll take you home."

"I don't want you to take me home," I replied.

"You're not taking a taxi," he said.

"Well, I'll take a car or hop on a bus." I moved to grab my suitcase from his hand, but a series of camera flashes caught me off guard.

"Sean, look over here," a voice yelled out as a photographer rapidly took our picture.

"Come on, darling," Sean urged.

We made it through the airport's glass doors and as a black Lincoln Town Car rolled up and stopped. Sean continued to walk towards the car, carrying both my bag and Simba. I just stood there on the sidewalk blinking my eyes to get rid of the floating dots from the camera.

"Come on, Leah," he yelled out. I could see the heads turning in our direction from other people waiting for rides or taxis.

My face burned and I just wanted to stamp my feet and bawl. I didn't want to ride with him. Hell, I didn't even want to talk to Sean. From the minute I had awoken on the plane with his hand wrapped around mine, I had wanted to get as far away from Sean as possible. Arizona was a dream, a nice fantasy, and the long plane ride with all the fans plus the photographers in the airport had brought reality back to my doorstep.

I watched him as he stood with his hand on the door beckoning me towards him as Nick stowed my suitcase in the trunk and placed the pet carrier in the front seat. I gritted my teeth and walked towards Sean, just imagining the many different ways I could wipe that smirk off his face.

"Now don't be mad, darling," he said once the car was moving and I was buckled into the backseat.

Annoyed that he'd manipulated me so easily, I snapped, "Don't talk to me."

"But we need to talk," he coaxed. "I want you and I want to be a significant part of your life."

I swallowed. While my heart just wanted to start singing, my head intervened. "I don't think so."

"Why?"

"Because I can't deal with everything around you."

"It's hard at first, but you get used to it after a while."

I crossed my arms and glanced out of the window. Bad traffic conditions had brought the car to a standstill.

"That may be the case for you, but I don't think I can handle the media. I like being just one more sista walking down the street or sitting on the train. The thought of losing that anonymity scares the hell out of me."

"I understand, but you can't let your fears keep you from this." He leaned over and kissed me. Not that nice kiss you see on TV as the woman turns to leave, but a hard kiss, the kind that says you don't have an option, that this stuff is so good there's no chance in hell you can walk, crawl or run away. He kissed me like he meant it and neither of us came up for air until the car inched forward.

I opened my eyes and looked into his smiling ones. "Don't do that," I ordered.

"Why not?"

I couldn't come up with a good enough reason to save my life. "Because . . . ."

"Yes?" The jerk was almost at the point of laughing out loud.

"Never mind. Look, Sean, I . . ." *I'm in love with you,* I wanted to say, but the words stuck in the back of my throat.

"I'm sorry, but this still doesn't feel real to me."

"So are you telling me you don't feel this bond between us?" he asked. A look of hurt flashed across Sean's face. It seemed to be my night for making street corner confessions.

"No." I shook my head. That was the last thing I meant for him to think.

He continued, "That the days and nights we spent together in Arizona, not to mention this past year, mean nothing?"

"No, Scottish. That's not what I'm saying at all. They matter more than I can ever say and you know that. I just need some space. Things have changed, we've changed. Before it was just you and me. Now it's changed to *us* and I'm having a really, really hard time making that adjustment."

"I'm trying to understand, Leah."

"I know, and I'm not making this any easier." I sighed and leaned on his shoulder.

"I know you don't like the media spotlight."

"True, but that's only a small part of it. The big thing is me. I still think that this is just some fantasy and I'm going to wake up and you'll be gone. I keep telling myself that so when the day comes that you call me on the phone and say that you're in love with some gorgeous model, or famous actress, I won't fall apart."

"I wouldn't do that to you. You know me. There's nothing that I haven't told you, no secrets and I'm not the type person to betray you like that."

"My head knows that but my heart can't seem to see the light. I see you as two different people." I raised one hand. "There's Sean that I met on a cliff over a year ago, the one that I know loves cartoons and Mexican burritos." I raised the other hand. "Then there's the Sean I read about, the one that's a rock star."

"You can't get more real than this." He ran his fingers through his hair and sighed. "I'm bleeding here. I want to help you. Just tell me what to do."

I wanted to tell him to just hold my hand as he was doing now, but I didn't. I had to do this on my own. There was a part of me that wanted to run as far and as fast as I could from Sean, from the relationship, and that was the part I needed to deal with.

Placing my fingers to his cheek, I fought to hold back tears. "That's the thing, Sean. You can't help me with this. I just need to get myself together. If we're going to do this 'build a relationship' thing, I want to be no less than 100 percent committed. I need time, okay?"

He shook his head and still held onto my wrist gently. "Not okay. I'm not a modern man and I won't be a brief fling. I know you better than you think. You're scared of this and if I let you, you'll run. I'm sorry, but I can't let you go."

"I'm not asking you to let me go. I'm asking you for time. I need you to wait for me, Sean."

He released a heavy sigh. "How long?"

"Two months."

"I'll give you one," he replied.

"I'll take it."

"That's a long time to not see you, hold you, talk to you."

"I know. It's not going to be easy for me, either."

"Good." He said that word with such vehemence I had to smile. "I'm holding you to this, Leah. Good or bad."

I nodded. "Good or bad."

Then he bent his head down and kissed me. It only took two seconds for that familiar warmth to slide up and down my spine as Sean's fingers stroked the back of my neck. When he broke off the kiss, all I wanted to do was grab the man and just lock him up in a room somewhere. His kisses were that good and that addictive. Forget work, and who needed sleep? I just wanted him.

He pulled back after the car came to a stop. "Just so you know what you're going to be missing."

"Don't worry. You're an impossible man to forget."

"Are you sure?"

"No," I replied honestly. "But it's something I have to do, and you might want to do the same as well."

"What's that?"

I playfully hit him on that shoulder "Think, man . . . think. I love this confidence you have, but I'd feel better if you thought about this as well. I don't enter into things lightly, Sean, and right now you are very important to me."

"You've been an important part of my life since I met you. One month isn't going to change my feelings, and I can only hope they won't change yours," he said.

"My feelings about you won't change. I've just got to do some work on the other stuff. I need to unpack some of the emotional baggage I'm still carrying around."

"Work fast, okay?" He tilted his head to the side and flashed a dimple my way.

"Okay."

Before Sean could say another word, I was out the door. Nick had conveniently taken my bag, along with Simba, upstairs. Unlocking the door, I carried everything inside the empty apartment, shut the door, and sighed.

A few mornings later, I sat at the kitchen table with a pen, pad and a cup of coffee. I looked up at my cousin's relaxed posture and breathed a sigh of relief. We'd both talked about how nice our mini-vacations had been, but neither of us had given out the details. All I knew was that Trey had taken an emotionally exhausted Rena home to his parents and returned her to me a changed woman.

Rena read out loud, "Extremely laid back, needy, dog-like five-and-a-half-year-old gray and fluffy neutered Persian cat seeking playmate. Likes seafood-flavored cat food, tuna treats, Spanish music and the Discovery Channel. New friend must be de-clawed, litter trained with energetic personality. Strays need not reply. simba@petmatch.com."

Rena placed the paper back in my hand. "What is this?"

"One of our major accounts is a pet food manufacturer. I thought it'd be a great marketing idea for them to have pet classifieds on their website."

"Personals for pets?" Rena's forehead wrinkled with doubt.

"Yeah. Simba's in the house by himself every day. I'm sure he wouldn't mind having another cat to chill out with."

"The cat's neutered, Leah."

"Girl, get your mind out of the gutter. I'm not talking about that kind of company."

When we both stopped laughing I asked, "So what do you think?"

"Honestly?" Rena questioned. "I'm thinking you're a little too attached to that cat, but I kinda like the idea."

I took that moment to bend down and pick up Simba. "Good, because I'm emailing the mock ad to the advertising exec tomorrow."

"Enough about work. Your butt's been back from Phoenix for three days and I've yet to get the scoop about the trip. How was it?"

"What can I say?" My lips curled into a soft smile. "I really enjoyed it. Sean and I went hiking and horseback riding in the desert. Arizona's a beautiful place. You should go visit."

Rena leaned closer and rested her face in her hands. "Uh huh. So now that you've told me what I could have gotten from *People Magazine*, tell me what I really want to know. Like what the boy did to put that smile on your face."

I looked down at Simba to hide the flush I knew was rising to my cheeks. "Hey, I don't get into your business with Trey," I countered.

"And? I've already told you the man turned me out. I'm not going to front about that. Trey even makes mornings look good."

"Okay, let's say that not only does the man cook in the kitchen, he's got rhythm on and off the stage," I hinted.

Rena laughed, "You've been bitten, girl. You're in love."

"Yeah, I ain't the only one," I said, pinching Rena's arm playfully.

How wonderful love was, I thought, shaking my head and placing the cat on the floor.

Later on that morning, as I looked down at the website designs on my desk, I realized how much Sean's absence was both a blessing and a curse. Instead of missing the man, I concentrated on my job. Flipping the mock-pages and making comments on the ad placement consistency, I was reaching for my coffee when the intercom buzzed.

"Leah."

"Yes?"

"John Liscinsky is on the line for you."

I sat up in my chair as my heart skipped a couple of beats. The advertising executive could make or break my career.

"I'll take it."

I took a deep breath before picking up the phone. "Good morning, John. What can I do for you?"

"Get me the person who came up with the pet classified. The client loved it so much they're willing to make a small donation to the local pet centers for each classified ad placed on the website."

"That would be me," I said, slumping back in the chair in disbelief.

"Good . . . good. Then I'll see you tomorrow for lunch. I'll have my assistant make the reservations for the executive dining room. Say twelve-thirty?"

"Fine."

A smile lit my lips as I put down the phone. Life just didn't get better than this.

CHAPTER 20

"Really, Leah, I don't want you to.think that your personal life has any kind of effect on your position."

"Of course, Tom." I smiled and watched as my manager sat back in the chair and crossed his legs.

"I've got to tell you that I haven't seen anything like this happen in all my years in the business. I mean we're getting calls from all the companies we couldn't even touch. Everybody wants us to come in and help them with their strategy."

"I'm glad for the extra work." I nodded. "With the second class of summer interns starting next week, we should be able to meet the increased demand."

"Right, of course. Speaking of demand," Tom cleared his throat, "I've gotten a lot of questions about whether or not you might be in a position to get Exile or Sean Andrews to meet with us, maybe do some business. Rick mentioned this morning that our top automotive client would pay through the nose to get the band to sign an endorsement contract. Hell, they'd be just as happy with a commercial or a voiceover."

I felt like beating my head against the wall. Tom wasn't the first and he wouldn't be the last. "Look, Tom . . ." I started.

"If you could just mention this to Mr. Andrews or his manager . . ." he interrupted.

I watched as he jumped up out of his seat when his cell phone rang. "Just think about it, okay? You've got my home and cell number, feel free to call me anytime."

After lunch, I leaned back in my chair and closed my eyes, feeling the beginning of fatigue.

"How could you have just sat there while I poured my heart out?" came a woman's voice.

"What?" I opened my eyes to see Fran in the doorway. I hadn't had a chance to talk with her since the afternoon she had broken down in my office.

I turned from the computer screen and stood up slowly. "Why don't you close the door and tell me what's up?" I asked.

Fran strode over to my desk and contemptuously tossed a copy of a national tabloid down.

"It must have been funny for you to listen to me talk about my man while you're shacking up with Mr. Rock Star."

"Wait a minute. What do I have to do with this?" I asked, confused.

"You're such a hypocrite, telling me that I should just let him go," she waved her hand. "I should have known you were a sell-out. Got your nice title, corner office, so you have to go out and get a white man."

I felt as though I had been slapped by the venom in her voice.

Fran continued, "Yeah, my man wasn't perfect, but he was a black man trying to make it in a white world and I should have helped him in the struggle."

"Fran." I said her name in a low, stern voice. Inhaling deeply, I released my breath slowly. "My personal life and who I date or do not date is, first of all, none of your business. Second, I didn't tell you that you should give up on the man. Hell, I didn't give you any advice at all because I didn't know what to say."

"With good reason," she shot back, taking a seat in the chair. "Here you are having a secret affair with a man that doesn't even acknowledge you. Are you that far gone?"

"Far gone?" I demanded. "What are you talking about?"

"The man kept you in the closet, honey. He's fronting in public with his blue-eyed, blonde-haired girlfriend and keeping you on the side."

"Wrong." I shook my head. "That was my choice. My relationship with Sean Andrews is nobody's business."

"Not anymore," she said, looking pointedly at the front-page picture of Sean and me on horseback.

"Look, Fran," I sighed, trying not to go on the defensive. "I have never been, and will never be, a sell-out. To be honest, I'm offended that you even put that out there. I love my job and I'm respectful and friendly with all my teammates. Now I'm very comfortable with my blackness and with myself."

I saw the anger drain from her eyes as I continued. "If I remember correctly, what I told you when you were crying in that very chair was that you should take some time to discover who you are and what you want before making hasty decisions."

"And I took that advice. I went home and I let him leave."

"You want to blame me for his leaving you?" I asked.

"No," she admitted reluctantly.

"Then what is it? We've been cool since day one and I'm hurt that you would come in here and drop this stuff at my feet."

"I thought . . ." she started and stopped.

"Come on with the truth. I've about had it with people looking at me like I just stepped off the moon." I wanted to hear it. Ever since Bahni and the others rocked my world with the photo of Sean and me together, every person of color in the office had stopped speaking when I walked into a room or went to get water.

"Let me break this down for you, Leah. We don't like it."

"We don't like what?" I repeated.

"Ever since it came out that you're dating that singer, every senior manager in this place has planted their lips on your rear end."

"So this is about office politics?"

"No. It's about you dating a white man. There are plenty of single black men out there and you went out of the house and got yourself a white man."

"And that bothers you?"

"Yes, it does." She crossed her legs and looked straight at me.

I sat down in my chair and picked up a pen. For a moment there was only the hiss of the air conditioner.

"I think I expected this from black men, but I didn't think I'd hear it coming from you."

"Because I'm black?" Fran answered.

"No, because you're a woman and you've seen the good and the bad of a relationship," I stated.

"With Black men," she said pointedly.

I shook my head. "I really don't have to justify my relationship."

"No, you don't," she agreed. "But I just thought I'd clear the air."

"I appreciate that, and I know where you're coming from. When I was in college seeing a black man with a white woman twisted my stomach. But no matter how I felt, I respected his decision. Life in California was different, good and bad. I care more for me now."

"And the fact that he kept your relationship on the D.L. doesn't bother you?"

"Sean has never kept me on the down low. I made that decision. I like to keep my personal life private, and he went along with it." My voice softened at the mention of Sean's name.

"How can you take it? The competition. All those women. White women," she emphasized.

I shook my head. "If I had a nickel for every time I compared myself to white woman I'd be richer than Oprah."

"Oh, Lord yes!" She laughed and then sobered up. "You're in love with him, aren't you?"

"Yes, I am," I admitted out loud for the first time.

She sighed, "I'm sorry, Leah. I shouldn't have come at you like that."

"Just don't make a habit of it," I answered back.

"Thank you."

"No problem."

"I'll talk to the other guys, but they're pretty pissed."

I stood up and we gave each other hugs. "That's okay. I seem to have a natural tendency to piss off people with small minds." I laughed. When Fran joined in I knew that everything between us would be okay, but the rest? I didn't have a clue.

After she left, I looked down at the collection of hastily shot pictures of Sean and me leaving the airport. My hair was a mess and he was smiling even as I glared at him. I sat down and sighed. It wasn't as though I was in the paper for committing a gruesome crime or doing some heroic deed. My life was under public scrutiny because I was dating a superstar, and that, more than the attention paid to our interracial relationship, was what bothered me the most.

The incessant sound of tapping roused me from my light doze. Lines of sunlight formed random designs on the walls and floor. I glanced at the clock and then rolled out of bed at the sound of knocking. Running a hand through my hair I walked to the front door, unlocked and opened it, not bothering to first take a look thru the peek hole.

"About time you opened the door! I was about to call your landlady."

My eyes widened and my mouth dropped open. "Mom . . . Pop. What are you doing here?" My parents stood in the hallway glaring at me.

"I don't know why your father's here," Mom answered, walking through the doorway. "But after listening to dozens of messages from your brother, church members, and friends, letting me know that my girls have been in every newspaper from here to China, I'm here to straighten this mess out."

"Mom . . . Pop," came Rena's sleep-laden voice from the back. Mom rushed past me and enveloped Rena in a big hug while Pop walked in and shut the door, then pulled me into his arms. I shook my head and felt tears well up behind my eyes. The light scent of sweet tobacco filled my nose. "What's wrong, baby?" he asked.

Feeling like a dam had burst, I started pouring everything out. "I don't know, Pop. I'm a mess. Lance's got a baby, Rena fell apart, I was in the *National Enquirer*, and I'm not sure what's happening anymore."

Pop pulled away and I looked up as he stared down at me. "You listening to me?"

I nodded my head.

"It's gonna be all right, you hear?" Pop said reassuringly.

I hugged him closer. "I'm so happy you're back. You and Mom can't go on vacation again."

"I heard that. How did the two of you survive by yourselves in California?" Mom asked in an exasperated voice. "We leave you for three weeks and all hell breaks loose. Look at the two of you. Clothes all wrinkled like you been sleeping in them. Both of you look like you haven't had a good meal in months. I want the two of you to pack your bags. You're coming back home with us until this mess blows over."

"Mom," I started, and stopped as her eyes narrowed. I looked over at Pop in desperation.

"Leah, it's real nice outside. Why don't you and your mom go for a walk?" Pop suggested.

"That sounds like a good idea," Mom agreed and started for the door. I followed dutifully behind.

"But . . ." I protested.

"Leah, I want you to take your behind into the bathroom, get cleaned up, and go outside with your mother," Pop said in no uncertain terms.

Knowing that I would never be too old for my father to spank, I grabbed some clothes out of my bedroom, took a quick shower, brushed my teeth, tamed my hair, and got dressed.

Less than an hour later after my parents had settled their bags in Rena's bedroom, Mom and I went outside. As soon as we got to the sidewalk, Mom started asking questions, "Now why didn't you tell me that you were involved with that rock star?"

"We were just friends." I shrugged.

"From what I saw on the cover of those gossip magazines, it looked like more than friendship to me. But that's beside the point. Now . . ."

I interrupted and got straight to the heart of what was bothering me. "Mom, you've seen the pictures. Does it bother you, Sean being . . ."

"What?" she interrupted. "Handsome, rich, famous?"

"Non-African American."

"White," she corrected.

"Yes."

She gave me a hard stare. "You know I raised you to be open-minded."

"You also raised me with the idea that Prince Charming looked exactly like Billy Dee Williams."

She shook her head. "I won't lie to you, baby. I'd prefer that you date some nice young professional black man, but I can't live your life or tell you who to date or who to love. I just pray for your safety and hope for your happiness. If this Sean Andrews is the one that makes you happy, then I'm happy."

I sighed and stared up at the sky, "Mom, isn't love supposed to conquer all?"

"I wish," she snorted. "You've been watching too many movies, Leah. Love's a powerful thing but you can't keep a marriage going with love alone. Love is a small thing when your father's snoring wakes me up in the middle of the night."

I laughed as Mom continued. "Sweetheart, I've always told you that relationships take a lot of work. You gotta be patient and accepting. You have to love and accept the person you're with: snoring, pipe smoking, and all. Don't mean you have to like everything about him, but you have to respect him and you have to love him despite the things he's gonna do that drive you up the wall."

"Is that why Pop's always complaining about having to sleep on his side?"

"That's right," she said smugly.

"I'm not sure I can do it."

"It's a little harder for you young folks today. You have so many issues you gotta deal with, and I don't want you hurt." Her voice trailed off and I looked into my mother's dark brown eyes as she smoothed my hair.

"But . . ." I added.

"Nothing worth having comes easy. I always told you children that."

I sighed, knowing she spoke the truth. "I still don't know what to do."

"Then tell him, Leah. Let him know how you feel and if he can't think of a way to make it better, then you gotta do some searching. Love is wonderful, but you still have to be at peace with yourself. I don't want to be nosey here," she continued.

"Yes, you do."

"I'm your mother so I get that privilege. Haven't you known him for a while?"

"Strictly as friends."

"And it's changed?"

"Yes, and I don't know how to handle it. I love him, Mom, and he says he loves me," I admitted. "But a part of me still doesn't believe this is the real thing. Maybe I just need some time to get my head together. I asked Sean for space."

"That's a good idea. Why don't you take some time off work and come back with your Pop and me?"

"Nice try, but I just got back from vacation and somebody's got to look after Rena."

"Leah, Rena is a grown woman. It's time you started looking after yourself."

"But . . ." I protested.

"But nothing," she gently scolded. "You've got more than enough to worry about. You let Rena and Trey worry about each other and you work on getting your house in order."

"Speaking of Traxx, I mean Trey," she said, "we'd probably better head back before Rena has your Pop all tied up in knots."

"You don't think she's giving him any trouble, do you?"

I gave Mom a look and, arm and arm, we both turned back, laughing.

"Thanks, Mom."

Mom was wrong, but not by much. Pop was only talking, but not just to Rena. Sean was sitting next to him.

"Yes, just come on over about one o'clock. I won't have my girls to provide the usual excellent meal service, but we play a mean game of poker."

"Mr. Russell, I'm honored at the invitation. Your daughter showed me a trick or two."

I almost tripped on the rug at the wink Sean gave me. The reminder of the game of strip poker we played the night before our trip back to New York sent blood rushing to my cheeks. Luckily no one caught the exchange between the two of us.

"Welcome back." His face lit up as he stood and walked towards me. "Your dad has invited me to Philadelphia next Sunday for a poker game."

I ushered him into the kitchen for a little privacy. "I thought you would be out of the country?"

"Change of plans. We're going to be playing a benefit concert in Philly that Saturday."

"Oh."

"I know that I'm not supposed to be here, but I had to see you one last time before I left."

I swallowed hard before responding. "I miss you, Scottish."

He placed his fingertips underneath my chin and lifted my face toward his. "Come with me, Leah."

"I can't. Not yet."

"All right. I still plan on playing poker with your dad next week."

"Watch out or he'll take you to the cleaners."

"Don't worry about me, darling. I've got a few tricks up my sleeve."

"I know." My smile grew bigger at his little boast.

"I think your dad likes me."

I suppressed the urge to laugh. Pop was friendly to everyone. It was that friendliness that had lulled all my ex-boyfriends into a false sense of safety. Then, before they knew it, Pop had them sweating as he asked them questions about every aspect of their lives.

"Beat my dad at poker and he'll definitely like you."

"Care to give me some pointers back at my place?"

"Sean," I warned.

"Just a thought," he responded.

"So what are your plans for the next month?" I asked and inwardly cursed. "Sorry. I don't have the right to ask that question."

"Yes, you do. I'm going to do some writing, play a few shows, and spend some time with my dad." He continued, "I mean what I say. I love you. When you're ready, let me know."

I nodded my head as words of love and declarations of affection sat on the tip of my tongue. This was so much harder than I had thought. "Take care, Sean."

He didn't say good-bye or good luck. He just kissed me tenderly before leaving. I didn't see him to the door. Instead I touched my lips with my fingers, trying to fight the sinking feeling that I'd made one of the biggest mistakes of my life.

CHAPTER 21

"What's wrong?" Rena asked.

"Nothing. Why would you say something's wrong?" I replied with my finger hitting the left arrow key. I could hear her moving around in the bed but couldn't turn to answer. I just watched as the second multi-colored row disappeared.

"You're playing Tetris."

"And . . . I like to play the game now and then."

"You've been playing it non-stop since Mom and Pop went to bed."

"So . . ."

"When you got that 386 PC in college, you'd play Tetris whenever exams came around. Then when you broke off with what's his name . . ."

"Chris."

"Yep. When you turned down his proposal, you played Tetris all weekend. Then there was . . ."

"Okay," I replied. "Is there a point to this trip down memory lane?"

"Sitting there playing that game isn't going to solve your problem."

"I'm not trying to solve any problems. I'm just trying not to think about them," I shot back.

"It's three in the morning." She yawned louder. "What happened between you and Sean?"

"Nothing," I quickly denied.

"You only play Tetris when you're upset. Did he say something to you?"

"Besides 'I love you and I'll wait'?" I hit the start button for a new game.

"Oh, hell. What did you say?"

"I told him I needed space."

"How much space?"

"One month and at least two time zones."

I looked up as Rena's hand reached down and hit the off button on the laptop.

"Please don't tell me this has something to do with Lance, because if it does I will beat your stupid behind."

"No, this time it's all about me." I stood up and stretched. "I'm terrified, intimidated, and confused. I love Sean but there's this self doubt problem I'm having."

"Why?" Rena asked.

"Sean's surrounded by some of the most beautiful women in the world."

"So?"

"Every time I look in a magazine and see some actress Sean's dated, I think of everything I'm not."

"Think about this: The man is interested in you for everything you are, and I don't just mean the physical thing. He's seen you when you wake up, cuz, and I know what a scary sight that is."

"Shut up."

"Just kidding. For real, when you walked into the apartment tonight if looks could speak the one Sean gave you said, 'What the hell have I been doing with my life without you?' And this is not the first time I've caught him looking at you with his heart in his eyes."

"Lord, Rena, I hope you're right."

"Have you ever known me to be wrong?"

"Yes." I shook my head. "I just need time to think, that's all."

"While you're doing your thinking just remember what Pop always told us. If you're going to have to pay for it, get what you want and what you need. Otherwise you're going to be miserable as hell paying that monthly note."

"He was talking about buying a car," I reminded her.

"Anyway," she said, fluffing the pillow, "it's almost four in the morning and you know Mom and Pop aren't going to let us sleep late."

"I love you, Rena." My voice came out small and tiny.

"I love you, too. Now turn out that lamp so I can get some sleep."

It had been four weeks since the last time I saw Sean, and every day I missed him. I missed the phone calls, emails, and text messages. He hadn't even called to check on Simba. I'd asked for a month and when I looked at the calendar yesterday the month had officially ended. Since the night I told him I needed time, each morning I got out of bed with Billie Holiday's sweet, solemn voice singing 'Good Morning Heartache' in my head. I felt the blues deep in my stomach, like a weight that wouldn't leave. The worst was that I had brought it on myself. But today is going to be different, I vowed.

"I want Tina Turner's legs," I shouted over the music blaring in the background. The stair climber underneath my feet was moving at full speed and sweat dripped in my eyes.

"Girl, the way you're stomping on that machine, you'll have a better set of legs," Carol declared.

I tried to smile and just gritted my teeth as the speed on the Stairmaster inched up another notch. This was my penance. I couldn't stop thinking about Sean. I missed my sensitive, sweet, fun-loving, and sexy best friend. The damn man haunted me. It had gotten to the point that I couldn't even get in the shower without thinking about him and wanting to cry. I'd lost my appetite and I couldn't even enjoy my rum raisin ice cream.

As Tina sang out *'What's Love Got to Do with It?'* over the gym speakers, I could only answer, "Everything." I was miserable without Sean, and living with my cousin wasn't helping. Rena was on cloud nine with Trey just about living at our apartment. I was the one who'd said I needed time and Sean was the one who'd said he'd wait. After looking at the *Star* that I'd found sitting in the middle of my desk yesterday morning, I'd concluded that he didn't look too miserable. Just the memory of the red-head I'd seen in the picture made my blood boil.

"Leah!" Carol shouted.

"What?" I panted.

"Don't you think you might want to slow down a little?"

Think. That's about all I'd been able to do. There had been no phone calls, letters, or surprise gifts. Nothing.

"I'm fine," I answered.

"Yeah, and I'm Whitney Houston," Carol answered sarcastically.

I turned to look at her.

"Girl, call the man," she urged.

"Who?" I managed to ask through gritted teeth as pain started running up and down my legs.

"Sean. Who else, fool?"

"No," I answered shortly. "I mean really, what's the point? Sean doesn't seem to be missing me. The phone hasn't rung once."

"What's wrong with your stubborn behind? You've been irritable and moody ever since you got back from Arizona. Why don't you just call the man? Talk to him instead of spending time either playing Tetris or working out at the gym," she advised.

The pain left my legs and went to my head. As I opened my mouth, the world began to spin and my legs stopped moving as I swayed with dizziness. Blinking rapidly, I found myself holding on to the side rails of the machine.

"Are you okay?" Carol asked. I opened my eyes to see Carol standing next to the machine with a gym trainer next to her.

I waved my hand. "Don't y'all worry about me. I'm gonna be all right." My voice was slurred, and before I could take another breath the gym dropped away and all I saw was black.

"Congratulations, Ms. Russell. You're not sick," the doctor announced.

"Then what's wrong with me?" I asked anxiously.

"You're pregnant."

I stared at the petite curly haired woman as if she'd grown two heads.

Pregnant. Blinking, I inhaled deeply, trying to push down the scream that threatened to erupt from my throat. Terror brought on by the thought of raising a child suffocated me. When I opened my eyes nothing had changed. The doctor was still standing there with a big goofy smile on her face as if this was an EPT home pregnancy kit commercial and I was going to start jumping up and down with joy.

"Pregnant?" Somehow I made the word sound like a fatal disease. The woman finally picked up a clue.

"Your blood sugar level is pretty low and you need more iron in your diet. I'm going to write you a prescription for some prenatal vitamins."

I shook my head, trying to clear my thoughts as the doctor continued.

"Now you can still work out, but as you get closer to your due date only moderate and low intensity exercise is allowed. You should also decrease the stress in your life and get more rest," she advised.

"Pregnant," I repeated. How? Then my mind slid back to my last night with Sean in Arizona.

"Don't worry, dear, everything's going to be all right."

"No, it won't," I contradicted. I had just become one of the fastest growing segments of the U.S. population: black single mother. Lance. I lay back and buried my face in my hands. I'd said so many nasty things. My own hypocrisy made me want to weep.

"Here's a great pamphlet that you can start reading."

I looked up at the brochure in her hand. "What to Expect When You're Expecting." I almost lost it. I looked around the small room and got up to gather my things.

"Here's a list of obstetricians that I highly recommend. You can't be more than five or six weeks, but I suggest you go ahead and book an appointment."

"Thank you, Dr. Cassidy." I grabbed the paper and the book. I wanted to get as far away from that smiling woman as possible.

"Cheer up. It's not the end of the world." She patted my shoulder.

At that moment I wanted my mother more than anything else in the world. I wanted her arms around me so I could weep. I wanted the smell of home and the sound of my father opening the freezer to pull out my favorite ice cream to make me feel better. I just wanted everything to be okay.

I walked out into the waiting room and saw Carol typing away on her laptop with a pen in her mouth and a cup of coffee by her side. She looked up and took one look and me and the pen dropped out of her mouth. She hurriedly put the laptop to the side and stood up.

"Talk to me, Leah," Carol demanded.

I couldn't seem to get the words out. I thought about the little person that was living inside me. I pictured Sean's smile. I wanted my baby to have his smile and that dimple in his left cheek and all of a sudden the doctor's words became more real.

"I'm pregnant, Cece."

"Say what?" she yelled.

"I'm gonna have a baby." My voice was a mere whisper.

"Sit down, girlfriend, before you fall out."

"What am I going to do?" My response was more of a sob than a sentence.

"Breathe, Leah. Just breathe." She held onto my hand.

She whipped out her cell phone and started dialing. Her finger almost touched the talk key before I stopped her.

"Who are you calling?"

"Rena."

"No!"

"What's the matter with you?"

"I don't want anyone to know yet, Cece."

"It's not like I'm calling the *National Enquirer*. They already got your business in the street. I'm calling your cousin Rena."

"I need some time to deal with this. Please don't tell anybody." Mom and Pop. How the hell am I going to tell my parents that I'm pregnant? Not to mention work. The liberal management at the advertising agency wouldn't blink an eye at me having a child out of wedlock, but it still bothered me.

Carol broke into my runaway thoughts. "I know what you're thinking. Your family ain't gonna so much as blink when you tell them the news. Shoot, you been telling me your Pop's been after you for grandkids."

I smiled at her attempt to cheer me up. "Pop wanted me to be married when I made him a grandfather."

"And you think you won't be? Leah, you and I both know that actions speak louder than words. And Sean's Andrews's past actions practically shout that the man has been in love with you for months. No man who sent you half the flowers in Holland, rang your phone almost every night before you went to bed and put up with your crazy behind is going to do anything but put a ring on your finger."

"Am I really crazy, Cece?" my voice wobbled a bit.

"No, honey you're not." Her voice softened. "You just like to give. You give and give and give and you never ask for anything in return. That's one of the things I love about you, girl, but I think it's time you start getting."

"I'm not that selfless."

"Don't give me that. Every time someone tries to do something nice for you, you just freeze up because you don't know what to do. You're just so used to taking care of everybody else you don't leave time for anyone to take care of you."

"Sean did, and now he doesn't even call me anymore." I sniffed, feeling tears fill the corners of my eyes.

"And look how long it took you to wake up and smell the roses. That man has been trying to get into your mix for as long as you've known him."

"No . . ." I stopped at her raised hand and serious look.

"Listen to me. I'm your friend and I've never told you wrong. Sean is a man. Men need to be needed. Look at that crazy husband of mine. You were with me when he finally got up the nerve to propose. He didn't think he had anything to offer me, thought I didn't need him. It took me breaking down with a panic attack after losing my first big case for him to see that he needed him more than anything in the world."

I sniffed and wiped at my eyes, feeling a little better. "I love you, Cece."

"I know." She hugged me tight. "Now get your butt together and let's get out this office because I'm hungry and the diner on the corner is calling my name."

I stowed the pregnancy book in my duffle bag and followed Carol out the door.

"Hi." I managed a weak smile as Lance opened the door with little Michael cradled in his arms. The answering smile I saw on his face wrapped me in memories of kindergarten and chocolate milk.

"Come on in," he welcomed.

I held out the large shopping bag like a peace offering. "This is for you."

"Can you take him?" he asked.

"Sure." I held out my hands and Lance handed the baby over to me. I took a seat on the couch and began to play peek-a-boo with little Michael.

"You know you're famous, right?" Lance said over the noise of shuffling paper.

I ignored him and concentrated on the beautiful sight of Michael's toothless grin.

Lance continued, "The radio personalities can't seem to stop talking about you and that rock star."

"Can we not talk about this, please?" I made an effort not to look at Lance. A shudder wracked my body at the thought of being the subject of a talk show host's sick fantasies.

"These are cute. Where'd you pick up the clothes?" he asked, referring to the pants and shirts I'd picked up for Michael.

"Old Navy."

"Old Navy?" he repeated.

"It's just like Gap, but the clothes are a little more casual."

"Thank you," he said after laying the clothing back in the box.

"Welcome."

"So how long have you been holding out?" I noticed Lance's voice had turned cooler by at least ten degrees.

"Holding out?" I repeated.

"About the white boy."

"He's not a boy, Lance."

"Okay, what's with the white man?" His question was anything but casual as he leaned over to wipe a little bit of dribble from little Michael's mouth.

I looked up from Michael and met Lance's guarded face. "We've been friends for over a year."

"So that's what they call it on the West Coast, huh?"

Refusing to go on the defensive, I barely kept the anger out of my voice. His whole attitude was beginning to piss me off.

"Look, if you have something to say, say it," I challenged.

He drew back and crossed his legs. "Why?"

"Why what?"

"Don't give me that, Lee. We grew up together. You expecting me to be cool with you and whitey?"

"I've learned to stop expecting anything from you, Lance. What I hoped was that you would be more open-minded."

"About as open-minded as you were when you found out about my son, right?" he replied sarcastically.

"Look. Don't make me regret pulling your scrawny behind out of the pool back when we were kids," I warned, reminding him of the time a dare almost got him drowned. "I'll admit I was disappointed in you, but as you can see from my being here, I support you one hundred percent."

He sighed and sat back, "You're right. I owe you more than this."

"Damn straight."

"It's just of all the sistas I know, you were the last person I thought would cross that line."

"And what line have I crossed, Lance?" I asked, frustrated.

"Don't give me that."

"Is it that imaginary color line you're thinking about?" I shifted to look him full in the face. "Is that what's got you so uptight? So Sean's not a black man. Big deal."

"It is a big deal, Lee. It burns me up to hear some guy talk like this rock star you're dating has won some competition and scored one for the white guys." Lance's voice was filled with indignation.

"What do you think this does to me?" I asked, shaking my head. "Do you think I like being in the news? Do you think I get a kick out of being the topic of people's conversations?"

"Then cut him loose. Let the man go before he pulls you down."

I collapsed back into the couch and let out a loud sigh. "It's not that easy. For starters, I'm in love with him." I opened my eyes and looked into Lance's fawn-like eyes. As they searched mine I leaned in closer to tickle the baby with my nose.

"What am I missing here?" Lance asked.

"I don't know, you tell me." I turned the question around, surprised by his perceptiveness.

"Something else is up, Lee. I'm not as blind as I was back in college. Something's got under your skin, I can feel it."

"It's nothing," I lied quickly, looking away from Lance. I didn't want him to see the glimmer of tears that had come unexpectedly to my eyes.

"Yes, it is," he declared. "Come on with the truth, supergirl," he urged gently, taking the baby from my arms.

"I'm pregnant," I said softly.

"Did I just hear you say you're pregnant?"

"Yes, you did."

"Damn," he cursed.

I looked over to see him staring at me as if I'd just grown another head. "What are you going to do?" Lance leaned in closer.

I shrugged. "I haven't figured that out yet."

"Does Mr. Rock Star know?"

"I haven't told Sean yet."

"Your parents?"

"No!" I exclaimed, standing up and wringing my hands.

"You have to tell them."

"When I'm ready," I shot back, following him into the bedroom and watching as he laid little Michael on the bed and began to change his diaper.

"Man, you're stressed about this, aren't you? I've never seen you lose your cool like this," Lance said while patting baby powder on Michael's little bottom.

"Please excuse me for not being as excited about parenthood as you when you found Michael outside your door," I replied sarcastically.

"Whoa . . ." He raised his hands in surrender. "No issues here. I was a mess. But look at me now." Lance smiled, pointing to his handiwork.

I looked down at the happy infant and my mouth softened into a smile. "Thank you," I said softly.

"For what?" he asked.

"For putting me in check," I replied.

"No, the only person here that deserves some thanks is you," Lance said as we walked into the living room.

"Now," he turned to pick up the phone. "Why don't you take a seat? We can kick back and I'll order in some food."

I shook my head. "I'd better start for home. They're working on the subway this weekend, and I'm trying not to get stuck."

"No sweat, I'll drive you back to your place. Little Mike loves to ride," Lance said, dialing. "You want Singapore noodles or Pad Thai?" he asked.

"Nothing spicy. I'll take the Singapore noodles," I said, taking a seat on the sofa. "And a spring roll," I added.

"You got it," Lance grinned. I leaned back on the cushion and picked up the remote control to turn on the TV.

"Just like old times, huh, Lee?" Lance commented after pulling me into his arms.

I took a deep breath and focused on the opening title of the movie. Just like old times.

CHAPTER 22

"Hey, Leah," came Lance's voice.

I turned my attention from the sight of the Brooklyn skyline.

"Yeah?"

"I've got another option for you," Lance said.

"Come again?"

"How about you move in with me and little Michael?"

"Have you lost your mind?" I asked. His question seemed to come out of nowhere.

"Hold up. Hear me out first. I told you that I was going to move back to Philadelphia, right?"

I frowned slightly. "You're relocating to work in the Philly office?"

Lance nodded. "I can't raise Michael on my own, and I think that he needs to grow up around family."

"That sounds good."

"Well, if everything goes okay I'll be closing on the Baileys' house in three weeks and selling the condo in two," he stated.

"That's fast."

"They're moving down to South Carolina to be with Mary."

"That's their oldest daughter, right? The one who went to Howard?"

"Yep, got a nice house and wants them to live with her. Anyway, their place was just renovated about a year ago. Central air conditioning, new windows, remodeled kitchen and bathrooms and a lot of other things."

Lance continued, "The house has four bedrooms, a huge attic and a finished basement that I'm going to turn into a home office. There's a backyard big enough for a garden and a nice-sized garage."

Lance pulled into an empty parking space and cut the motor. "It's the perfect place to raise kids, Lee."

"Lance," I began, then paused, not knowing what to say.

"You don't have to give me an answer now. Just think about it, okay?"

I nodded my head before getting out of the car. Too many things were going through my mind at the moment to focus. I paused before shutting the car door.

"Take care, Lance."

"You, too."

I had put my keys down on the side table when I spotted someone out of the corner of my eye. I told myself it was a dream. Sean wasn't sitting comfortably on my couch. No, he was on the West Coast hugged up with the newest actress of the month. I'd seen it all in my head as I stared at my ceiling at three o'clock in the morning. I'd cursed that man as I saw myself going through labor while he danced cheek-to-cheek with some famous actress.

"Leah, I love you," he said as I stood frozen with Simba rubbing against my ankle.

I stared at Sean, noting the shadows under his eyes. The evil imp in me wanted to smile at his suffering. It made me feel good that I hadn't been the only one losing sleep.

He continued as he moved towards me. "I love the things you do, the way you move, the sound of your voice, the way you look at me with utter trust and warmth in your eyes. I like talking with you, holding you, making love to you, waking up next to you. I've never felt this way before. You make me whole and I can't stomach the thought of not having you in my life."

I shook my head as my stomach rolled. He was saying everything I wanted to hear. All the words a man who loved me more would say. And as he pulled me into his arms, just like some spineless weak heroine in a trashy romance novel you never want your mother to find out you read, I closed my eyes and pushed him away as my stomach heaved. Right in the middle of the most important moment in my life, I rushed to the bathroom and promptly lost my Thai dinner in the toilet bowl.

I came back to reality lying on my bed with Rena glaring at me.

"What's wrong with you?" she asked. My cousin sat down on the side of the bed and shook her finger at me. "Nothing that sleep and vitamins won't cure," Rena mimicked my response. "You lied to me, Leah."

I opened my mouth to protest, but before I could say a word Sean entered the room. "And when were you going to tell me?" Sean's angry voice contradicted the look of worry on his face.

I wanted to close my eyes and pretend that this was just a nightmare.

"Oh, no, you don't try that sleep mess with me. We want some answers. Carol called, asking how you were, and I told her you'd passed out in the bathroom."

"All right," I interrupted Rena. "I'm not sick. I'm pregnant. Big deal. I found out two weeks ago."

"We're going to have a baby," Sean whispered shakily before catching himself and standing up.

"Rena, could you pack her some clothes?" Sean asked.

"Gladly," she responded.

I watched as Rena stood up with a smile on her face. "Why?" I sat up looking at the both of them.

"We're going to Las Vegas."

"Las Vegas?" I echoed.

"We're getting married."

"Oh, no!" I shook my head. This girl wasn't getting hitched at a twenty-four-hour drive-through.

"Whether you like it or not," Sean continued as though he hadn't heard my protest.

I tried to sit up and paled as my head swam. Sean was at my side in a second. "Calm down, darling. Think of the baby."

I took a deep calming breath and forced myself to relax "I am not getting married . . ."

"Yes, you are."

" . . . in Las Vegas," I continued.

"I know you're just upset, but you're carrying our child. We've got to make some decisions."

"Look, Sean," I said, my voice gaining strength. "Being pregnant may have changed my perspective, but I haven't lost my mind. I've got a twenty-five-year commitment on top of nine months of pregnancy. Technically, you are not responsible." The thought of raising a child alone scared me to death. I felt tears start behind my eyes.

"Have your feelings for me changed, then?" His voice softened.

"No." I shook my head. "But I'm not marrying you because I'm pregnant."

"Then would you marry me for your dreams?"

"What?"

"The big old house filled with love. That's why you and I are going to get married. It's not just your dream, it's ours. That's why I'm asking you to be my wife. Because of love, honor, trust, and happiness. I can't let you take that away from me. Leah Russell, will you marry me?"

I let out a broken sob at his question. Those words were worth more than all the gold in Fort Knox, but only if I allowed myself to believe them.

"Don't cry." Sean wiped my tears away with his thumb. "This is real. I love you and I'm not going to go away when you open your eyes. I'm not going to pretend this isn't as wonderful as it is just because we started out as friends and became lovers. I don't plan on making Lance's mistake. You are a treasure and I'm not a stupid man. I plan to keep you and love you for the rest of my days."

I thought that it might have disappeared, but as Sean took my hand and we sat facing one another on the bed, I felt it swirling heavy between us, that potential unknown wonder, the connection filled with hope and affection. It was the lifeline that had pulled him back from the cliff, the bond that held us together. I wanted to reach out and touch his face and forget everything that had gone so wrong. The urge to just ignore all the negatives that came along with being with Sean was strong, but I drew away.

"No matter what you want, it's not going to change the fact that you're a celebrity and people want into your life." I pressed my nail into his chest. "They want to know everything, and I can't deal with that, Sean. I won't have my personal life, not to mention this pregnancy, on full blast in the media."

"It'll change, Leah. We'll be old news soon."

I shook my head. "You don't know that."

"Trust me. I've been in this arena for a while. This will all blow over."

"I do trust you." I smiled at his optimistic expression. "But I can't take the risk of you being wrong. I can't."

"What do you mean? What have you done?"

"I've decided to go home to Philly, Sean," I lied, saying the first words that came to mind. "I'm going to buy a house down the block from my parents. The family's moving down to North Carolina. I want my child to be surrounded with family and have a normal life."

As soon as the words left my mouth I wanted to take them back. No matter how he grew up, my baby would be different. Sean Andrew's child. I rubbed my temples; it was something I didn't want to think about.

"And you think that I don't want that?" Sean questioned.

"No, I'm sure you do. But this whole dream you have of you and me getting married can't happen. This isn't a Disney fairy tale and I'm not Cinderella. We're not gonna have one of those happy endings."

"Wait a minute. I plan on being a big part of our daughter's life."

"Son," I corrected. I wanted to have a boy. "And I'm cool with that. We'll just work out some arrangements in terms of visitation."

"Visitation?" he repeated.

I rushed, "I can support the baby on my own. You don't have to worry about getting some wild lawsuit."

"I don't care about the money. I've never cared about money." Sean shook his head. "And I don't want to 'work out' some kind of arrangement. I want to marry you. I want to be a family."

I steeled my heart against the soft look I saw in his eyes. "Well, people in hell want ice water," I said sarcastically. "I want my private life back. I don't want to see pictures of myself in the *New York Post* or to be the main topic of some television gossip show."

"You're scared, Leah."

"Damn right I am."

"It doesn't have to be that way. You don't have anything to be scared of. Let me help."

"No."

"Darling . . ."

"Oh, no," I waved my hand. "Don't try it, Sean. Just go back to your life. Go on tour, go back to the studio, go back to the desert. Hell, date a model. Just forget about me."

"Not gonna happen."

"Do it for me, Sean. I've got this figured out and there's nothing you can do to change my mind."

"Do you really believe I'm going to walk away from this? I love you. Not to mention, you're carrying my child."

"My child. And yes, I expect you to let me go." My voice rose an octave. "You owe me, Sean, for saving your life, for our friendship. This is how you're going to pay up." I was pulling out all the stops. I knew that man better than I knew anyone and I knew he wouldn't make this easy.

"Stop it, Leah." He grabbed my flailing hands and held them to his chest. "I know you love me and I know you're scared, but this is us, darling. You and me. There are no photographers or reporters here. Together there's nothing that we can't face. We can move to Europe if that'll make you happy. Hell, how about an island in the middle of nowhere? Just don't let this go," he said before kissing me.

Then the world just fell away and there was nothing but the sensation of Sean's hands on my back and his lips on mine. When he pulled away, I wanted to pull him back. I wanted this to last not for a minute or an hour, but the 'til death do you part' kind of forever. I knew he'd fight for me come hell or high water, and that was all I needed.

"Sean." I put my finger to his lips to silence his next words. "Thank you," I said simply. "Thank you for being such a wonderful man. I know that I'm not really making any sense. But ever since I left Philly and moved to L.A., I've been reacting to events in my life: Lance's wedding, Rena's troubles, the press . . . you and me. I don't want to do that anymore. I need to regain control of my life and my emotions."

I took his hands within mine. "That's one of the reasons I didn't tell you about the pregnancy right away. I love you so much it hurts. Not seeing you gave me the time I needed to see how much you mean to me."

I continued, "I love you, but I can't just stroll blindly down the aisle just because I'm pregnant."

"No, you and I will be getting married because we're meant to be together. This ring belongs to you and only you."

The way he bent down on one knee and pulled his hand out of his pocket revealing a beautiful ring stopped my heart. I couldn't hold back the tears at his words and his gesture.

"Oh, Lord," I whispered in disbelief.

"I've been thinking about putting my mother's ring on your finger since the time we spent Arizona."

"But . . ." I started looking into his green eyes.

"No buts. You and I are going to be getting married, Leah Russell, and it can't happen soon enough for me," he said, pulling me close.

"I love you, Scottish," I whispered, feeling the warmth of his arms wrapped around me. I closed my eyes and smiled. Who would have guessed? I, the little girl who grew up dreaming of the boy next door, had found that in helping out a stranger I'd gained the love of a lifetime.

ABOUT THE AUTHOR

Angela Weaver is a Southern girl by way of Tennessee. She has lived in Pennsylvania, Texas, Washington, D.C., New York, and Japan. An avid reader and occasional romantic optimist, she began writing her first novel on a dare and hasn't stopped since. On weekends she can be found working in the yard, reading or working on her next book. Visit her online at *www.angelaweaver.net*.

Coming in November from Genesis Press:

Keith Walker's sensational Fixin' Tyrone

CHAPTER 1
THE ERIC INCIDENT

This went against so many of Mia's rules.

She'd been dating Eric for only two months. It wasn't necessarily too soon to have sex with him; her rules for sex were based on the quality of dates rather than calendar time, but this particular position was generally taboo for newbies. This was more of a fifth or sixth episode type of thing. Yet on only their *first* sexual encounter, Eric had her bent, exposed and vulnerable.

Yes, *vulnerable.*

A case could be made that all intimate maneuvers put women in positions of inferiority, but Mia knew better. At least with missionary you could *look* at him. You could see his eyes, his expressions, and if you worked it just right, you could see that he wasn't in very much control at all. Mia has seen eyes cross, tears of joy, inarticulate babbling, and even *drool.* But doggy style is different.

Some women view it as just another facet of their sexual repertoire. Some even *prefer* it to regular sex, but for Mia, this was something special; something almost *sacred*. With missionary you can fool yourself into believing a meshing of souls is occurring as the sweat on your bellies mingles, but with doggy style, there's no holding, no kissing. When you're on your knees, there's only raw sex. You're reminded that men are dogs and you might start to wonder if this makes you his bitch.

Any man who thought he was going to simply fold Mia into whatever position he pleased during their first episode of intimacy had another think coming.

Yet there they were.

And this wasn't something you could just *roll* into; it took conscious body placement; willingness on both sides. And Mia had no idea what was going on back there. Eric could be smiling. He could be laughing. He could be rolling his eyes in boredom or he could have one hand in the air like he was at the rodeo. He could be texting his friends or throwing up gang signs.

Westsiiide!

Even if your man is serious about the encounter, doggy style is not the position for new, gentle lovers who want to develop a spiritual bond. But it felt good. Mia gripped the mattress and lowered her head and moaned into the sheets. Eric wasn't just back there pounding senselessly. As implausible as it was, Mia felt he was actually *making love* to her. He was like an erotic masseur. Hands were here. There. He rubbed her shoulders. Traced a finger down her spine. He caressed her back, and then her sides. His hands slid across her ribs and settled on her hips. He fondled her ass and then was back to her neck again.

Giving herself to a new partner normally made Mia awkward and unsure of her movements, but there was no hesitance with Eric. She didn't even feel like she was with a new lover. He touched every spot she wanted touched. He knew when she wanted more or slower or faster. He was as smooth as a ride in a limousine. He was good.

Too good?

Experienced?

A ho?

Mia forced the thoughts from her head.

Why do you always go there? Does there always have to be something wrong? Why not just enjoy the here and now?

So she did.

Mia wasn't always an audible love-maker, but since they were already so far past her normal pace of things, what did it matter? She moaned, and this seemed to invigorate Eric. He moaned, too, and their noise together was almost enough to drown out Jagged Edge, but no one drowns out Jagged Edge. On a CD player near the bed, the lead singer crooned about how he felt like he'd walked right out of heaven after losing his girl.

Mia felt like she was walking right *into* heaven. It was much too soon to entertain such thoughts, but sometimes—sometimes it felt so good, and the music was just right, and the motions were so pleasing—sometimes it's okay to let your heart wander just a little.

Pipe layers like Eric are few and far between.

He slammed in deep, reaching depths unexplored in *years*, and Mia cried out in pleasure. *This* is what she had been waiting for. This made up for Richard's pygmy penis, Roland's stanky drawers, and Colin's premature ejaculations. Mia didn't care anymore about this going against her normal pace, and she didn't care what faces Eric might be making—or *whatever else* he might be doing back there.

If he *did* scream *Westsiiide!* Mia would twist her fingers, cock her head, and holler out with him—it was *that* good. And the girls at the beauty shop would definitely hear about him tomorrow. Mia would get her unkempt sex-hair fixed with a smile, and she might even get a pedicure if she could straighten out her toes by then.

They climaxed together.

Mia's legs trembled and she sank slowly until she lay prostrate. Eric followed her down, still inside, and he lay on top of her. His body was warm, and it felt good to feel him all over. He breathed against the back of her head. He lifted her hair and kissed her on the neck. He kissed behind her ear and she hummed. Eric knew where all of her buttons were. He sucked her earlobe and told her she was beautiful. He told her he didn't think he'd ever felt as good as he did right then. He seemed poised to tell her he loved her, and Mia was almost ready to believe him if he did.

It was that good.

After a few minutes of snuggling and spooning, he asked her if she wanted to take a shower.

"Do you have to work tomorrow?"

"No. I try not to work on Saturdays," she said.

"But last week—"

"I know. I had to catch up on a few things. That's not the norm."

"So, do you have to leave, or can you stay tonight?"

"My sister's watching the kids," Mia said, looking forward to spending the twilight hours with him for the first time. "What about you?" It was after ten, but Eric worked at the post office and kept odd hours. In the two months they'd been dating, Eric had shifts that started as early as 2:00 A.M. and as late as 11:00 P.M.

"No, I'm off tonight," he said.

Mia smiled.

Eric ran water for their shower. Mia stood next to the sink and studied the floral design on the shower curtain rather than her own reflection. As with many women, Mia was not one hundred percent pleased with her figure, and she felt exposed in those bright lights. She stood five feet, nine inches tall and was thin in the waist with shapely hips. She was dark-skinned, the color of cherry wood, with large eyes and full lips. At only 129 pounds, she knew she was *fine*. She needed only to wear tight jeans to the market to be reminded of this, but her breasts were only an A cup.

Some men considered this a failing. Having never stood nude before him, Mia wasn't sure which end of the spectrum Eric was on, but he cleared up any confusion with an unrestrained ogle.

He eyed her with a smile like a child on Christmas.

"You look *real* good, Miss Clemmons."

"You're making me nervous."

"Why?"

"The way you're looking at me," she said, but smiled; her hands unconsciously meeting between her legs.

He held his hands to his sides. "You're not the only one naked."

"Yeah," she said, taking in his full physique unabashedly. Eric wasn't necessarily the most handsome man she'd been with, but she couldn't find any blatant flaws. He was completely bald. That wasn't Mia's thing, but he was also clean shaven and she did like that. The only hair on his head was his thin eyebrows. He reminded her of Tyson Beckford before he went scruffy.

Eric had almost a hundred pounds on her, but he was six feet, two inches tall. He had broad shoulders and a nice chest. His pecs actually had definition. So many men his size had those downward pointing nipples that gave the impression of man boobs, but Eric's upper body was nice.

He didn't have a rippling six-pack, but his stomach was flat, and the further down she gazed, the more impressed Mia was. Small men are quick to remind you the length and width come second to the way you work it—Mia has been with a few who actually proved that adage right—but with Eric she would have the best of both worlds. And as fine as he was, Mia didn't feel she was extremely lucky to have a stud like Eric naked in his bathroom. On the contrary, she felt she *deserved* a man like this.

Mia was thirty-two years old, professional, and college-educated. She had two children with two different fathers, but any man who considered her babies a hindrance was welcome to lose her number. Mia knew she was attractive; she never needed makeup to enhance her beauty. Finding a man was never a problem for her. Finding one who wasn't married, unemployed, uneducated, an ex con, a pimp, a gigolo, a hustler or a player was the hard part. That had proved more difficult than finding the Holy Grail.

But Eric had a government job, drove a Beamer, had his own home, and (this is going to blow your freaking mind) he had *no* children. Not a one. He had never been married and, unless Mia totally misread the previous hour's activities, he was not gay. Eric watched the *news*! That may be no big deal to some, but Mia had dated guys who didn't know the difference between *Enron* and *Exxon*. They could rattle on and on about how Kobe shot the lights out last night but couldn't find China on a globe if their life depended on it.

"The water's hot," Eric said.

"I know this is going to sound cliché," Mia said, "but I don't usually do this."

"What? Take showers? I couldn't tell. You smell like an autumn breeze."

She rolled her eyes. "Yeah, *okay*, but I'm talking about you, and me, in the shower *together*."

"Why?"

"Cause we're still new. I mean, we made love. That was good—"

"That *was* good."

"Yes, that was good, but I'm still not totally comfortable around you." She smiled and blushed, but he didn't notice.

"So . . . you don't want to take a shower?"

"Yes, I'm going to take a shower. I just want you to know that I don't usually do this with a guy I've only–"

"You've got a great body," he said.

"Thanks, but—"

"Come here."

They showered together. Eric's two-bedroom flat wasn't the most spacious, but his bathroom was larger than most, and the tub easily accommodated them without any awkward squeezes. All squeezes were soft and sensual.

He lathered up a mesh sponge and washed her back. From behind he soaped up her breasts and belly, but when he went down further, it was almost too much for Mia to bear. She turned to face him and found the space between them compromised.

"Wow," she said, looking down. She felt like a kid at the candy shop. *Is that for me?* She took the sponge from him and rubbed his chest and stomach.

"You're beautiful," he said.

Mia looked up at him and he kissed her, slowly. She dropped the sponge and caressed his throbbing member. Any doubts about Eric's strength were vanquished when he grabbed her buttocks and hoisted her into the air. Mia wrapped her legs around his waist and he smoothly entered her again.

You're moving too fast. This is not good.

The warnings were blaring, but Mia was finding it harder and harder to listen to her inner voice. The bathroom filled with steam, and she imagined they were making love in a hot spring. Eric was more vocal this time, which allowed her to be more vocal. His thrusts were slow, but hard; rough, yet passionate.

He turned and leaned her against the back tiles and they stared into each others' eyes. He sucked her neck and she nibbled his ear. Her breaths became heavy and pained, and, when he climaxed this time, they were very wet and very close; breast to breast, belly to belly, cheek to cheek, soul to soul.

2009 Reprint Mass Market Titles

January

I'm Gonna Make You Love Me
Gwyneth Bolton
ISBN-13: 978-1-58571-294-6
$6.99

Shades of Desire
Monica White
ISBN-13: 978-1-58571-292-2
$6.99

February

A Love of Her Own
Cheris Hodges
ISBN-13: 978-1-58571-293-9
$6.99

Color of Trouble
Dyanne Davis
ISBN-13: 978-1-58571-294-6
$6.99

March

Twist of Fate
Beverly Clark
ISBN-13: 978-1-58571-295-3
$6.99

Chances
Pamela Leigh Starr
ISBN-13: 978-1-58571-296-0
$6.99

April

Sinful Intentions
Crystal Rhodes
ISBN-13: 978-1-585712-297-7
$6.99

Rock Star
Roslyn Hardy Holcomb
ISBN-13: 978-1-58571-298-4
$6.99

May

Paths of Fire
T.T. Henderson
ISBN-13: 978-1-58571-343-1
$6.99

Caught Up in the Rapture
Lisa Riley
ISBN-13: 978-1-58571-344-8
$6.99

June

Reckless Surrender
Rochelle Alers
ISBN-13: 978-1-58571-345-5
$6.99

No Ordinary Love
Angela Weaver
ISBN-13: 978-1-58571-346-2
$6.99

2009 Reprint Mass Market Titles (continued)

July

Intentional Mistakes
Michele Sudler
ISBN-13: 978-1-58571-347-9
$6.99

It's In His Kiss
Reon Carter
ISBN-13: 978-1-58571-348-6
$6.99

August

Unfinished Love Affair
Barbara Keaton
ISBN-13: 978-1-58571-349-3
$6.99

A Perfect Place to Pray
I.L Goodwin
ISBN-13: 978-1-58571-299-1
$6.99

September

Love in High Gear
Charlotte Roy
ISBN-13: 978-1-58571-355-4
$6.99

Ebony Eyes
Kei Swanson
ISBN-13: 978-1-58571-356-1
$6.99

October

Midnight Clear, Part I
Leslie Esdale/Carmen Green
ISBN-13: 978-1-58571-357-8
$6.99

Midnight Clear, Part II
Gwynne Forster/Monica
  Jackson
ISBN-13: 978-1-58571-358-5
$6.99

November

Midnight Peril
Vicki Andrews
ISBN-13: 978-1-58571-359-2
$6.99

One Day At A Time
Bella McFarland
ISBN-13: 978-1-58571-360-8
$6.99

December

Just An Affair
Eugenia O'Neal
ISBN-13: 978-1-58571-361-5
$6.99

Shades of Brown
Denise Becker
ISBN-13: 978-1-58571-362-2
$6.99

2009 New Mass Market Titles

January

Singing A Song…
Crystal Rhodes
ISBN-13: 978-1-58571-283-0
$6.99

Look Both Ways
Joan Early
ISBN-13: 978-1-58571-284-7
$6.99

February

Six O'Clock
Katrina Spencer
ISBN-13: 978-1-58571-285-4
$6.99

Red Sky
Renee Alexis
ISBN-13: 978-1-58571-286-1
$6.99

March

Anything But Love
Celya Bowers
ISBN-13: 978-1-58571-287-8
$6.99

Tempting Faith
Crystal Hubbard
ISBN-13: 978-1-58571-288-5
$6.99

April

If I Were Your Woman
La Connie Taylor-Jones
ISBN-13: 978-1-58571-289-2
$6.99

Best Of Luck Elsewhere
Trisha Haddad
ISBN-13: 978-1-58571-290-8
$6.99

May

All I'll Ever Need
Mildred Riley
ISBN-13: 978-1-58571-335-6
$6.99

A Place Like Home
Alicia Wiggins
ISBN-13: 978-1-58571-336-3
$6.99

June

Best Foot Forward
Michele Sudler
ISBN-13: 978-1-58571-337-0
$6.99

It's In the Rhythm
Sammie Ward
ISBN-13: 978-1-58571-338-7
$6.99

2009 New Mass Market Titles (continued)

July

Checks and Balances
Elaine Sims
ISBN-13: 978-1-58571-339-4
$6.99

Save Me
Africa Fine
ISBN-13: 978-1-58571-340-0
$6.99

August

When Lightening Strikes
Michele Cameron
ISBN-13: 978-1-58571-369-1
$6.99

Blindsided
Tammy Williams
ISBN-13: 978-1-58571-342-4
$6.99

September

2 Good
Celya Bowers
ISBN-13: 978-1-58571-350-9
$6.99

Waiting for Mr. Darcy
Chamein Canton
ISBN-13: 978-1-58571-351-6
$6.99

October

Fireflies
Joan Early
ISBN-13: 978-1-58571-352-3
$6.99

Frost On My Window
Angela Weaver
ISBN-13: 978-1-58571-353-0
$6.99

November

Waiting in the Shadows
Michele Sudler
ISBN-13: 978-1-58571-364-6
$6.99

Fixin' Tyrone
Keith Walker
ISBN-13: 978-1-58571-365-3
$6.99

December

Dream Keeper
Gail McFarland
ISBN-13: 978-1-58571-366-0
$6.99

Another Memory
Pamela Ridley
ISBN-13: 978-1-58571-367-7
$6.99

Other Genesis Press, Inc. Titles

A Dangerous Deception	J.M. Jeffries	$8.95
A Dangerous Love	J.M. Jeffries	$8.95
A Dangerous Obsession	J.M. Jeffries	$8.95
A Drummer's Beat to Mend	Kei Swanson	$9.95
A Happy Life	Charlotte Harris	$9.95
A Heart's Awakening	Veronica Parker	$9.95
A Lark on the Wing	Phyliss Hamilton	$9.95
A Love of Her Own	Cheris F. Hodges	$9.95
A Love to Cherish	Beverly Clark	$8.95
A Risk of Rain	Dar Tomlinson	$8.95
A Taste of Temptation	Reneé Alexis	$9.95
A Twist of Fate	Beverly Clark	$8.95
A Voice Behind Thunder	Carrie Elizabeth Greene	$6.99
A Will to Love	Angie Daniels	$9.95
Acquisitions	Kimberley White	$8.95
Across	Carol Payne	$12.95
After the Vows	Leslie Esdaile	$10.95
(Summer Anthology)	T.T. Henderson	
	Jacqueline Thomas	
Again My Love	Kayla Perrin	$10.95
Against the Wind	Gwynne Forster	$8.95
All I Ask	Barbara Keaton	$8.95
Always You	Crystal Hubbard	$6.99
Ambrosia	T.T. Henderson	$8.95
An Unfinished Love Affair	Barbara Keaton	$8.95
And Then Came You	Dorothy Elizabeth Love	$8.95
Angel's Paradise	Janice Angelique	$9.95
At Last	Lisa G. Riley	$8.95
Best of Friends	Natalie Dunbar	$8.95
Beyond the Rapture	Beverly Clark	$9.95
Blame It On Paradise	Crystal Hubbard	$6.99
Blaze	Barbara Keaton	$9.95
Bliss, Inc.	Chamein Canton	$6.99
Blood Lust	J. M. Jeffries	$9.95
Blood Seduction	J.M. Jeffries	$9.95

Other Genesis Press, Inc. Titles (continued)

Other Genesis Press, Inc. Titles (continued)

Ebony Angel	Deatri King-Bey	$9.95
Ebony Butterfly II	Delilah Dawson	$14.95
Echoes of Yesterday	Beverly Clark	$9.95
Eden's Garden	Elizabeth Rose	$8.95
Eve's Prescription	Edwina Martin Arnold	$8.95
Everlastin' Love	Gay G. Gunn	$8.95
Everlasting Moments	Dorothy Elizabeth Love	$8.95
Everything and More	Sinclair Lebeau	$8.95
Everything but Love	Natalie Dunbar	$8.95
Falling	Natalie Dunbar	$9.95
Fate	Pamela Leigh Starr	$8.95
Finding Isabella	A.J. Garrotto	$8.95
Forbidden Quest	Dar Tomlinson	$10.95
Forever Love	Wanda Y. Thomas	$8.95
From the Ashes	Kathleen Suzanne	$8.95
	Jeanne Sumerix	
Gentle Yearning	Rochelle Alers	$10.95
Glory of Love	Sinclair LeBeau	$10.95
Go Gentle into that Good Night	Malcom Boyd	$12.95
Goldengroove	Mary Beth Craft	$16.95
Groove, Bang, and Jive	Steve Cannon	$8.99
Hand in Glove	Andrea Jackson	$9.95
Hard to Love	Kimberley White	$9.95
Hart & Soul	Angie Daniels	$8.95
Heart of the Phoenix	A.C. Arthur	$9.95
Heartbeat	Stephanie Bedwell-Grime	$8.95
Hearts Remember	M. Loui Quezada	$8.95
Hidden Memories	Robin Allen	$10.95
Higher Ground	Leah Latimer	$19.95
Hitler, the War, and the Pope	Ronald Rychiak	$26.95
How to Write a Romance	Kathryn Falk	$18.95
I Married a Reclining Chair	Lisa M. Fuhs	$8.95
I'll Be Your Shelter	Giselle Carmichael	$8.95
I'll Paint a Sun	A.J. Garrotto	$9.95

Other Genesis Press, Inc. Titles (continued)

Other Genesis Press, Inc. Titles (continued)

Meant to Be	Jeanne Sumerix	$8.95
Midnight Clear	Leslie Esdaile	$10.95
(Anthology)	Gwynne Forster	
	Carmen Green	
	Monica Jackson	
Midnight Magic	Gwynne Forster	$8.95
Midnight Peril	Vicki Andrews	$10.95
Misconceptions	Pamela Leigh Starr	$9.95
Moments of Clarity	Michele Cameron	$6.99
Montgomery's Children	Richard Perry	$14.95
Mr Fix-It	Crystal Hubbard	$6.99
My Buffalo Soldier	Barbara B. K. Reeves	$8.95
Naked Soul	Gwynne Forster	$8.95
Never Say Never	Michele Cameron	$6.99
Next to Last Chance	Louisa Dixon	$24.95
No Apologies	Seressia Glass	$8.95
No Commitment Required	Seressia Glass	$8.95
No Regrets	Mildred E. Riley	$8.95
Not His Type	Chamein Canton	$6.99
Nowhere to Run	Gay G. Gunn	$10.95
O Bed! O Breakfast!	Rob Kuehnle	$14.95
Object of His Desire	A. C. Arthur	$8.95
Office Policy	A. C. Arthur	$9.95
Once in a Blue Moon	Dorianne Cole	$9.95
One Day at a Time	Bella McFarland	$8.95
One in A Million	Barbara Keaton	$6.99
One of These Days	Michele Sudler	$9.95
Outside Chance	Louisa Dixon	$24.95
Passion	T.T. Henderson	$10.95
Passion's Blood	Cherif Fortin	$22.95
Passion's Furies	AlTonya Washington	$6.99
Passion's Journey	Wanda Y. Thomas	$8.95
Past Promises	Jahmel West	$8.95
Path of Fire	T.T. Henderson	$8.95
Path of Thorns	Annetta P. Lee	$9.95

Other Genesis Press, Inc. Titles (continued)

Other Genesis Press, Inc. Titles (continued)

Other Genesis Press, Inc. Titles (continued)

Order Form

Mail to: Genesis Press, Inc.
P.O. Box 101
Columbus, MS 39703

Name _____
Address _____
City/State _____ Zip _____
Telephone _____

Ship to (if different from above)
Name _____
Address _____
City/State _____ Zip _____
Telephone _____

Credit Card Information
Credit Card # _____ ☐ Visa ☐ Mastercard
Expiration Date (mm/yy) _____ ☐ AmEx ☐ Discover

Qty.	Author	Title	Price	Total

Use this order
form, or call
1-888-INDIGO-1

Total for books _____
Shipping and handling:
  $5 first two books,
  $1 each additional book _____
Total S & H _____
Total amount enclosed _____
Mississippi residents add 7% sales tax

Visit www.genesis-press.com for latest releases and excerpts.

WIN A
FREE
GENESIS PRESS BOOK
Please fill out this form with your email address and send it to us at:
Genesis Press,
Post Office Box 101,
Columbus, MS 39703
or email it to
customerservice@genesis-press.com
and we will put your name into a drawing for a free Genesis Press Book.
WRITE EMAIL ADDRESS HERE
Winners will be chosen on the first of each month. ONE ENTRY PER CUSTOMER